THE BOOKS BY ROSEMARY NESS-BITNER

PASSION
(THE FIRST VOLUME)

1 THE BUTTERFLY YOU LOVE
2 A WOMAN'S VOICES
3 PROMISCUOUS DREAMS
4 BUTTERFLY CONFIDES
5 FLUTTER BRAND
6 BUTTERFLY TRADECRAFT
7 MOTHER'S LOVERS
8 RUBY BUTTERFLY
9 BUTTERFLY MORALS
10 TROPHY BUTTERFLY
11 LOVE AND LOVERS

INSANITY
(THE SECOND VOLUME)

12 MURDER PROPERLY DONE
13 LOVE AND MADNESS
14 BUTTERFLY LOVE

REINCARNATION
(THE THIRD VOLUME)

15 CRIMSON MARIPOSA
16 CRIMSON AND PINK
17 LUST WHEELS
18 YES FOR LOVE

APPENDIX (MARTY'S CHARACTER COMMENTS, AFTER BOOK 18)

JOSH

SEAN

CRAWFORD

VANCE

TRAVIS

PHILLIP, MARSHAWN, STEPHON, MELVIN, ALVIN

WANG LI

BETH

KATHY

GERALDINE

TRUDY

CONSUELO

TAMMY

ABOUT THE AUTHOR

Sometime in my childhood, around the age of eleven or twelve, I witnessed a man do something terrible to a helpless kitten. Seeing what he did made me feel wretched; but he seemed pleased with himself. That's when I began thinking about people. Before that afternoon, I more or less assumed all adults behaved the same. Neither my mother or my father would ever be cruel to an animal the way that man was. I thought all people were gentle and sweet, like my parents were. Suddenly, I realized I didn't know much about people at all. That's when I started thinking about how each person is different from every other. I made mental notes about what this or that neighbor did; how they reacted to different things; what they said about different things; and how they behaved around different people. As life went on, I became less and less of a participant in things like art and drama clubs or sports. I became less of a participant in life and more of an observer. I love to read. My interests range widely. I especially like history and historical fiction where character and personality traits provide insights into fascinating human behaviors. Observation of others has become my main interest. Human interactions intrigue and entertain me. It's like having my own, personalized, spectator sport, like some people enjoy watching baseball and football.

As a teenager, I began feeling felt pretty smug about my understanding of people. I thought I understood people pretty well. But in my twenties, I experienced another realization. A girl friend, whom I thought I knew, shocked me. She told me how she really felt about boys, dating, relationships, romance, sex, children, and abortion. Her pleasant veneer masked her duality; revealed her whole different character. I had no idea her mind was so complex or that her character could be so manipulative, deceitful, and fluid. That's when I began studying deviant sociopathic and psychopathic personalities; especially when they became involved in romantic and sexual relationships. I now appreciate that an element of their conduct resides in many of us. People fascinate me, especially in the different ways they relate to romance and sex. I believe I've just begun to learn about them; knowing it will never be possible to know all there is to know.

I love writing. Packaging hidden personality traits in fictional characters and weaving these characters into a cohesive fictional story is my joy. I began writing as a hobby. It challenged my English grammar skills and traveled my mind along many uncharted, whimsical paths. Writing relaxes me and I enjoy doing it. A friend suggested I write a book; and I did. But when I finished it, I felt incomplete. So, I tore that book apart and created an eighteen-book series that packaged many fictional characters into a cohesive saga.

I looked at this effort as an opportunity to make the characters 'fit' into my beliefs about the reincarnation of human souls. I believe spirits exercise influences over our thoughts and lives. Their spirit sense, guidance and wishes orchestrated the behaviors of *'THE SECRET BUTTERFLY SERIES™'* characters. My old ways of thinking and relating changed into something new and far more fascinating; the butterflies' thoughts, feelings, and perspectives. My eyes are open. My soul flutters high. My hopes are boundless. I now see many things I could not see before. And I had fun writing about them.

INTRODUCTION FROM THE AUTHOR

I did something for you. I murdered the Devil. It was hard work, but worth it. He was a devious character. Killing him took planning and persistence, but I did it. I'm not talking about the way I murdered him. You can read about that. That was the easy part. It spices the story. I'm talking about the challenging part; getting him out of my mind, and helping you getting him out of yours, by understanding the ways he did things; his image projections; his deceits, controls, manipulations, ambushes, and double dealings; recognizing his Grand Master, button pusher, lever puller superiority complex; learning how he planned ahead to move goal posts, before revealing where the original goal posts were; seeing how he got the other characters to believe everything was for their benefit, not his; those kinds of things. I finally understood that I wasn't imagining these things. I wasn't paranoid. You're not paranoid, either. It's him; his character; the way he's wired. There are mean, nasty people in the world. Their consciences don't stop them or give them pause. They lie, cheat, steal, and kill. This saga will help you recognize them. The devil in this story was among the very worst of them.

His murder was my contribution to humanity. I wrote the Secret Butterfly Series™. There's where I exposed him and murdered him. I chose Series characters who helped explain the environment that produced him. You'll see how his persuasions spawned all sorts of evils; how his psychic cancer entered thought; ate love, family, and integrity. He wore different masks. Look behind them. You'll understand how his evil destroyed people's lives. Recognize it. Don't let it possess you. Heal yourself if it already has.

I'm relieved to be rid of him. Writing revealed him; killed him; and healed me. That son of a bitch tried to kill me. Not joking. He tried hard. He tried often. And he almost succeeded. But I couldn't let that happen. I had to toughen up. I had to fight back. People needed me. I chose the hardest choice I ever chose. I fought the toughest fight I ever fought. I won that fight because there is love in me; love for life; and people. Lots of love; tons and tons of it. I couldn't let him get me like I was just one of my Series characters; couldn't let him take away my love; just couldn't let that happen. My fight is finished now; finally, over. I survived.

Rosemary

THE BUTTERFLY YOU LOVE©

BOOK ONE
of the
SECRET BUTTERFLY SERIES™

A NOVELLA

By

Rosemary Lightfoot Ness-Bitner

DEDICATION

THE SECRET BUTTERFLY SERIES™
is dedicated to those who stand up for their beliefs.

THE BUTTERFLY YOU LOVE© novella
is dedicated to children who need love.

"Understanding your oppressor is the first step to freedom."

Rosemary Lightfoot Ness-Bitner

The print version layout of THE BUTTERFLY YOU LOVE© was done by Andrea Reider. I'm Melanie Monarch, your audio book narrator.

The cover was done by Cheeky Covers.

Each character seeks love. Their behaviors weave threads into a tapestry. The tapestry reveals us.

SECRET BUTTERFLY SERIES™ CHARACTERS INRODUCED IN "THE BUTTERFLY YOU LOVE" (MAJOR CHARACTERS ARE BOLDFACED)

Readers reference guide to where a character is introduced.

(CHARACTER, DESCRIPTION OF CHARACTER, AND CHAPTER WHERE CHARACTER IS MENTIONED)

THE BUTTERFLY YOU LOVE© (BOOK ONE)

MISS INIQUITY, MARTY'S SERIOUS VOICE, CHAPTER(CH)1

MISS SHAMELESS, MARTY'S CAREFREE VOICE; CH1

MISS PROMISCUITY, MARTY'S OBSESSIVE-COMPULSIVE SEDUCTION VOICE; CH14

MARTY, DAUGHTER OF TWO BIOLOGICAL FATHERS, GORGEOUS NYMPHOMANIAC SEDUCTRESS, LOVER OF BOB AND MANY OTHERS, MURDERESS; CH1

DAVID, SOCIOPATHIC CEO, CRIMINAL GENIUS, MURDERER; CH1

BOB, MARTY'S FIANCE AND SOULMATE; BARBARA'S LOVER; CH1

MRS. O'DELL, THEORIZER, FOURTH OF MARTY'S FOUR
PSYCHOLOGISTS; CH1

MRS. MARTINSON, THE FIRST OF MARTY'S FOUR
PSYCHOLOGISTS; CH1

SUSAN, MARTY'S MOTHER; JOSEPH'S WIFE; MARVIN'S
LOVER; NARCISSIST; CH1

MISS CARBOY, SECOND OF MARTY'S FOUR
PSYCHOLOGISTS; CH1

MR. SORBER, MARTY'S GEOMETRY TEACHER AND
LOVER; CH1

WEX, THE WEXLER BAXTER SCHOOL FOR GIRLS; CH1

OLD FRED, A SQUIRREL ADORED BY MARTY; CH2

BARBARA, INDIAN PRINCESS (AKA LITTLE SPARROW),
MARTY'S ANTAGONIST; BOB'S LOVER; CH2

LITTLE SPARROW, STUNNINGLY BEAUTIFUL INDIAN
PRINCESS (AKA BARBARA); OFFICE WHIZ KID

MRS. SCHNELL, THIRD OF MARTY'S FOUR
PSYCHOLOGISTS; CH2

PICASSO; DALI; TONY CURTIS; ARTISTS ADORED BY
MARTY; CH2

ABBA; OLDFIELD; CAMILLE ST. SEANS; MUSIC ARTISTS
LIKED BY MARTY; CH2

TRUDY, MARTY'S ROOMMATE AT WEX; CH3

MRS. HIGGINBOTTOM, ASST. HEADMISTRESS AND DO GOODER OF WEX; CH3

ED BLANTON, TRUDY'S FATHER, CRAFTY, BRASH, POWERFUL EXECUTIVE, SWINDLER, SUSAN'S LOVER; CH3

MARGE BLANTON, TRUDY'S MOTHER, SOCIALITE, RACIST AND RELIGIOUS BIGOT, MURDERESS; CH3

MRS. MALONEY, AKA, SUSAN MALLORY, CORP. VP, MARTY'S MOM, MARVIN'S LOVER, MURDERESS; CH3

MR. JOSEPH MALONEY, MARTY'S FATHER (DADDY), SUSAN'S HUSBAND; AUDITOR; CH5

BARRON, MARTY'S LOVABLE BOXER DOG; CH5

MARVIN, BUSINESS GENIUS, FOUNDER OF SUSTACK INVESTMENTS, INTERNATIONAL RAT LINE OPERATOR FOR JEWS ESCAPING NAZIISM AND, LATER, FOR NAZIS ESCAPING TO THE AMERICAS, MONEY LAUNDERER, JEWEL TRADER, HUSBAND OF ELOWEISS, SUSAN'S LOVER, DAVID'S FATHER; CH5

BETHANY MALLORY, SUSAN'S MOTHER, MARTY'S GRANDMOTHER, RELIGIOUS CHRISTIAN ZEALOT; CH5

MARIA, MARTY' S BEST FRIEND AND LESBIAN LOVER, ASPIRING, SUICIDAL OLYMPIC SWIMMER; CH5

EVELYN, COURTNEY, AND TRUDY, SNOBS, WEX CLASSMATES OF MARTY; CH5

MRS. RAYBENALD, BULLY, RELENTLESS PERFECTIONIST, OLYMPIC SWIMMING COACH AT WEX; CH6

HARRY, DEMENTED WEX FACULTY MEMBER, CO-CONSPIRATOR IN SWINDLE; CH7

TOMMY HORN, MAN'S MAN, NO NONSENSE MINE MANAGER OF THE BIG JENNY (WORLD'S BIGGEST COAL MINE); CH8

DONNY AND BILLY, TWINS, MARTY'S LOVERS FOR SEX EXPERIMENTS; CH10

TATTOO ARTIST, MARTY'S LOVER; CH13

SLIM, OILMAN, CATTLEMAN AND RANCHER, MARIA'S HUSBAND, MARTY'S LOVER; CH14

RUSTY, ZEB, BEAUTY, STARLIGHT, HORSES OF SLIM AND MARIA; CH14

JOHN, BRAWNY, POWERFUL UNION BOSS, LOVER OF SUSAN; CH15

DARREN, FOOTBALL PLAYER, BOYFRIEND OF CAROL, LOVER, SOULMATE OF MARTY; CH15

CAROL, DARREN'S GIRLFRIEND, PSYCHIATRIC PATIENT; CH15

CARL, TOP SALESMAN, MOST EXCEPTIONAL LOVER OF MARTY'S MANY LOVERS; CH15

BIG DOG, CARL'S, AND MARTY'S NAME FOR CARL'S PENIS; CH15

CARL'S WIFE (NAMELESS), CLOSET LESBIAN, NEUROTIC PSYCHOTIC; CH15

MARSHAWN, MARTY'S LIBERATION LOVER, PORN PARTNER; CH15

AALIYAH, MARSHAWN'S GENITALLY INFIBULATED, FRUSTRATED WIFE

CONSUELO LOVELY, EDITOR OF 'WONDERFUL WORLD OF PORN' MAGAZINE; CH15

SHEILA, MATH GENIUS; LOVER OF CC, HUD, PASQUAL, PROFESSOR VICKERS, DEAN WILSON AND LOTUS FLOWER LULABELLE WONG (PROSTITUTE); DANNY'S HUSBAND; BUTTERFLY FRIEND OF MARTY; MARTY'S REINCARNATED PERSONA; CH15

CECILIA OR CC, SEX WORKER, LOVER OF HUD AND SHEILA; AS BUTTERFLY FRIEND OF MARTY; CH15

CONNIE, NYMPHO HEIRESS, LOVER OF GEORGE, MOLE AND PAUL, DAUGHTER OF HOWARD ROCKMAN; BANK TRAINEE; CH15

MOLE, GENIUS BOND TRADER, INTEREST RATE FORCASTER, LOVER OF CONNIE; CH15

JOANNE, WAITRESS, PROSTITUTE, GIBBY'S LOVER; CH15

GIBBY, VETERAN MARINE CORPS SNIPER, ASSASIN, PTSD AFFLICTED SERIAL KILLER, JOANNE'S LOVER; CH15

LINDA, BANK LOAN OFFICER, FINANCER OF
REVOLUTIONS, LOVER OF CARLOS (AKA SEBASTIAN);
CH15

SANDRA, BUXOM BLONDE, IRRESISTABLE FUCK BUNNY,
WALTER GRAY'S (BANK CEO) PRIVATE SEX TOY; CH15

PATTY, MEAN SPIRITED PRISON WARDEN, SADO
MASICIST NYMPHO; CH15

MONARCH, HIGHEST ORDER OF BUTTERFLIES,
ATTAINED BY REINCARNATED NYMPHOS; CH15

PIERIDEA, LESSER SUPPORTING BUTTERFLIES; CH15

"MY EYES ARE WINDOWS TO MY SOUL
FREEDOM FLUTTERS WITHIN MY WINGS;
BLOOD DRIPS FROM THE HEARTS I STOLE
AND JEWELS AND FURS ARE SPECIAL THINGS;
THAT I LOVE, AND LOVE AND LOVE"

Marty's soul

Hello dear readers and listeners. I'm Melanie Monarch, a Monarch butterfly. About nine billion years ago the Butterfly Galaxy was populated by butterflies and humans, like you. It uniquely had the most beautiful butterflies in the universe, us gorgeous Monarch butterflies. Over millions of years the spirits of Monarchs and humans developed a symbiotic ability to communicate with each other. We learned to read each other's thoughts.

Four billion years ago, a big bad black hole came along. It began eating the Butterfly Galaxy. In order to save the humans and lovely Monarchs from the big bad black hole, the Universal Spirit of all Living Things, or U, loaded some humans and Monarchs into a special spaceship. It traveled faster than light to the Milky Way Galaxy. There, it discovered Planet Earth.

Spaceship commander, Tiffany Ann, studied Earth and decided it was the perfect planet to begin populating of the Milky Way Galaxy with humans and Monarchs. She sent a small contingent of one hundred men, one hundred women, and ten Monarch mating pairs down to Earth with orders to go forth and multiply. Two women in this landing party carried a special, highly experimental, nympho DNA strand in their bodies.

Butterfly Galaxy's Monarch butterflies and humans successfully populated Earth. As years passed, humans who carried the novel nympho DNA strand propagated more rapidly than humans who did not carry the strand. According to Mrs. O'Dell, world renown psychologist who specializes in understanding the nympho DNA strand, humans who carry the nympho strand are now ten percent of Earth's human population. She calculates that ten percent is critical. It's the percentage population portion where the strand mutates magically, through limbic alteration. Humanity has reached the milestone where the highly sexualized, emotive limbic zone causes human DNA to mutate into nympho DNA strands. From this point forward, humanity's nympho population will experience explosive, exponential growth. Mrs. O'Dell theorizes that humanity lives on the cusp of becoming a nymphomaniac population.

Mrs. O'Dell explains that a strange thing happens after women possess the nympho DNA strand. The mutation process causes women to no longer feel social pressures to reproduce or have families. The mutant DNA strand assures their sexualized limbic zone that reproduction is strictly optional; a matter of individual choice. But this same DNA strand instructs them, for their psychological wellbeing, to make love often, with multiple partners; and experience sexual pleasures in varied forms. Mrs. O'Dell assures her patients that shamelessly fornicating, for pleasure's sake, is a mentally healthy, liberating necessity; a normal response that releases natural desires and relaxes tensions. She tells them they cannot help having the mutant DNA strand, nor should they attempt to resist the natural impulses it causes.

Her patients are often chastised and labeled promiscuous and immoral by those who do not possess the mutant strand; but she encourages them regardless. She observes that perceptions are rapidly changing. Butterflies whole-heartedly agree with Mrs. O'Dell. We understand humans. We've read your thoughts and heard the voices in your minds for millions of years. Like Mrs. O'Dell, we also notice changes in trends. We see that promiscuous behaviors of nympho humans are becoming widely accepted. Shameless nympho immorality is encouraged and highly honored in esteemed social circles. Enlightened humans understand and accept this important behavioral change. We butterflies applaud this enlightenment.

I, Melanie, had a recent chat with my lovely Monarch friend, Goody. She told me a story that was passed down to her by her famous, matriarchal mother, Poon. It's about humans who experienced profound relationship changing events; and a particular woman who confided with her voices about her lovers and dilemmas. I'll relate Goody's story to you, exactly as she told it to me.

THE BUTTERFLY
YOU LOVE

CHAPTER ONE

I'll speak in a monstrous little voice. (Shakespeare: A Midsummer's Night's Dream)

Your mind is your greatest deceiver. It's easy to believe you are invincible. It's harder to imagine that someone plots to murder you. (Rosemary Lightfoot Ness-Bitner, author)

Is morality good? Are you sure? (Rosemary Lightfoot Ness-Bitner, author)

All women need love; some need every form of it. (Rosemary Lightfoot Ness-Bitner, author)

VOICES OF DILEMNA

"Do not let him know that he upset you. Don't let him have one little hint that you were scared, or that you believed he was serious. If he gets a small glimpse of that, he'll want to use you in even nastier ways. Tell him that you are fine with ending it. Be sincere; matter of fact. Remember, even though you need his financial institution to give you legitimacy, he needs you just as much as you need him. Who else would help him commit the murders? Make him believe you'll be okay after leaving him. Make him think you're willing to walk away and never look back. Convince him that your life is moving on, without him. If he doesn't try to stop you, leave him for real. Either way, your life will go on. Remember: He needs you more than you need him."

Marty leaned on her porch railing, and looked over her back yard. She was hearing the advice from Miss Iniquity, her most cautious voice. Iniquity was her serious, well-grounded, anchored to reality voice. Iniquity always talked sense to her. *'Is David playing one of his games with you?'* Iniquity kept repeating that same question. It echoed in Marty's mind, challenging her. She thought hard, but kept coming up with the same answer.

'I don't know. What if he isn't?' Marty was frustrated. She tried reasoning with the persistent voice that echoed in her head. *'Perhaps I really am going to get a twenty percent raise and a diamond neckless; and a floppy-eared rabbit; and perhaps I just went through another episode of David playing his game of "Gotcha." He knows how much I love animals. He's seen my dream picture of a floppy-eared rabbit. He knows I want one. He knows how much I'd love him. Yeah, I could see that he's just playing me. He'd get a real yuck out of toying with me. He treats me like I'm his human Yo-Yo. First, he throws me away from where I was, close to him; you know, where he's calling me partner and holding my trusting heart in his hand. And the next thing I know, he's tossed me way far out, away from him and his world, like he's sending Yo-Yo Me to an outer orbit; and now, clever David, is using a rabbit to lure me back; soften me up; reel me back. That would make me close to him; and tight with him, again like nothing happened. Why? So, he can do it all over again? What should I think about this?*

'He's done this before. This time, he set everything up, so I could take Bob away from Barbara. It was perfect for me and for him. He didn't like them being together, doing their own deals. He told me to split them up. He sent her to administration, on the eighth floor; and he moved Bob to investment sales; working side-by-side, with me, on seventh floor. I did exactly as David instructed. I seduced Bob. I was thrilled to follow orders. Bob is remarkably handsome; well-muscled; well-endowed; and incredibly strong. We went on road trips for an entire year. I had the time of my life! He is a fantastic lover. We made love all over the country. And, David paid our expenses. It was a corporate sponsored honeymoon; except we didn't get married. I stole Bob

from Barbara, just like David ordered me. He had to know Bob and I would fall in love; but then he fired me for falling in love with Bob! He pretended the whole romance was my fault! What did he expect? Did he think I can just turn love off, like I have a mechanical on-off switch? Can you explain this?

'Help me, Miss Iniquity. Is this angst just another one of David's manipulation games within some bigger, more serious, game? We both know he's a manipulator.'

'Well, reach back in your memory, as far back as you can go,' replied Miss Iniquity. 'What can you remember about David and the ways he's treated you before?'

'Okay, there's not that much to remember. There was that time when we were children. I was six years old. That was the only time in my twelve years away that my mother, Susan, brought me home from boarding school. I had that two month visit during that terribly hot summer. Dad had only been dead for one year. Mother and I were at the company's summer party at David's parents,' home. Servants catered it. They walked around offering food and drinks to everyone. I remember lots of white linens and people talking in small groups. It was unbearably hot. I felt clammy and faint. I wanted to drink water and sit down. I remember there were lots of dandelions on their huge lawn; and the grass was wilted grayish and brown-edged. I also remember lots of grasshoppers. They kept hopping onto the patio deck where people were talking.

'David was there, too. I think his parents expected him to play with me; but he didn't want to. He walked around with a magnifying glass, looking for ants. He burned them by focusing sunlight on them. Marvin, his father, told him to stop. David didn't listen. He kept burning ants. Then, Marvin took the magnifying glass away from David. David ran down the yard screaming; then he walked onto the driveway, looking for ants. Whenever he saw an ant, he stomped on it and yelled "Die, ant, die!" He was cursing at the ants. Marvin told him to stop that, too.

Then, David went somewhere. He was gone for a short while; but when he came back, he had some firecrackers. He returned to the driveway. He found some little ant hills beside the driveway, where the little red ants lived. He set off his firecrackers in those little ant hills. He laughed like a crazy person while he blew up those ants. He screamed "Die ants, die!" again. I remember, even at my young age, thinking there was something wrong with David. He kept going after those innocent, defenseless ants, like he was obsessively compelled to murder every ant in the world. It didn't seem normal.

'Eloweiss, David's mother, screamed at Marvin and told him to "do something" about David. Marvin went into the house. After a while he came out with a soccer ball and gave it to me. He told David that he wanted David to play with me. He said he wanted to see us playing together with the soccer ball. I remember foot-dribbling the ball, because I'd learned how to play soccer at WEX school. I kicked the ball nicely over the grass to David, the way you pass the soccer ball to a teammate in a game. David didn't kick the ball back. He picked up the ball and threw it at me as hard as he could. I put out my little hands to catch it, but it hit my fingers and jammed them. I still remember the pain. I thought David broke my fingers. I screamed and cried. I couldn't understand why David did that. I never did anything to him. But it seemed like he intended to hurt me, like he hated me. Then, David came and held my hands in his hands. He kind of felt my fingers. Then he told me I'd be all right. He was right about that. None of my fingers were broken.

'Marvin yelled at David for behaving badly. David yelled back at Marvin. He told his father that he didn't want to play stupid games with a stupid girl. He behaved like an impossible jerk. Marvin and Eloweiss ordered him to leave the party and go to his room. As David left the lawn party, when he was behind Marvin's back, he flipped Marvin the bird. I saw that. Then, David went inside. I knew then, that David behaved like an imp with anger issues. He has not changed much in

twenty years. He just disguises his imp tendency better now; but some-times it leaks out, like a couple days ago when he fired me for doing what he told me to do.

'He's always had issues with his parents. Marvin and Eloweiss are dead now, but David still has not made peace with his parental issues. I think that explains why his behaviors are so quirky. Now he wants me to forget that he fired me. He wants me to meet him in his barnyard and explain my feelings about men. He said he needs to hear how a woman feels about men, to understand his mother. I think it's a little late for him to understand Eloweiss. She's dead. But maybe explaining my feelings will help him understand why he never got along with her. I don't know. I'm not a shrink. It's confusing.

'After Marvin sent David to his room, I remember being tired. I could barely stay awake. I laid down on the grass. Mother picked me up and carried me to Marvin. He was tall and thin and had silvery black hair. He was sitting on a large lawn chair. Mother laid me on Marvin's lap and asked him to please hold me and rock me to sleep. Mother kissed Marvin's cheek. I remember feeling weird when she did that. Something wasn't right about the way Mother was with Marvin. I wondered how Dad would have felt about seeing her tenderly kiss another man that way. I remember wishing Dad was holding me, instead of Marvin. I missed him terribly. I remember Marvin hugging me for a short while; then he bounced me on his knee. That didn't feel right. I didn't like it. I didn't think Marvin had any right to bounce me up and down while holding me around my waist like that. I was so tired, I just wished he would stop. I was only a little girl. But I sensed there was something dysfunctional about the interactions between Mother and Marvin.

'Then, Eloweiss told Marvin to put a lawn chair under one of their huge Elm trees; and lay me on the chair, so I could sleep in the shade. Eloweiss brought me a glass of cool water and a big, soft pillow to lay my head on. Then she took my little hands in her big hands. She felt over each of my fingers with her fingers. She seemed

to be studying my fingers to satisfy herself that none of my fingers were broken. Then she smiled at me. I remember she had gold teeth in a couple places. She lifted both my hands to her lips and kissed them. Her kisses felt like she sincerely meant them; and then, through her teary eyes, she said to me: "You are Elohim's beautiful, innocent child." At that time in my life, I didn't know Elohim was the Hebrew word that means: "My God, who is my friend." I thought Eloweiss didn't know my name was Marty. I believed she had me confused with someone else's little girl. But I didn't correct her mis-name. I thought, "why bother?"

'Eloweiss was kind to me. I remember she had an honest goodness about her. She had a huge body. She wore a baggy white dress with large red flowers printed on it. She was very heavy, and her weight made her breathe with a wheeze. She also had a slight flowery scent smell about her. It was a much weaker scent than Mother's. And when she walked away from me, she didn't actually walk like normal people walked. She slowly stumbled forward in a controlled, forward fall. I know now it was an effort for her to bring me that pillow and the water. Her disease had started to show. I remember feeling sorry for her. She was very sweet and sincere. I believed she wanted to be my friend, like we were related, somehow.

'Now, thinking back on that day, I didn't notice any affection between David and either of his parents; or any affection between Marvin and Eloweiss. None. Just an unspoken tension, except when Marvin yelled at David. Then, I felt Marvin's anger break the tension. That's all I can remember about that day when I first met David. I did not see him again, until many years later; after my affair with the president of the Plaintown Bank, and when I started working at the Firm.'

'Are you remembering anything else?'

'No, Iniquity, after that day my memories are more about my times at WEX school and my best friend, Maria. That's the only memory of David that I have from before I worked at the Firm.'

'Okay, well, let's put your David thoughts to rest for a while. You need to relax. Only think pleasant thoughts. You know it's important for you to do that.'

'Yes, Miss Iniquity.'

Marty sat looking over her back yard, hearing advice from Miss Iniquity. Iniquity was Marty's 'Serious Voice,' her well-grounded inner voice that tried to talk sense to her. *"Ask yourself: Is there some linkage that possibly ties these events together? David first has you seduce Bob, his top salesman. David then sets up the executions. You did the murders the way he told you to do them; and then you almost achieved your long-sought intimacy with him. Then, only a few days later, David acts suddenly shocked and irritated that you fell in love with Bob. He's so upset that he fires you. Now, just yesterday, David knocks on your door and tells you he desperately wants you back. Has David gone crazy; or is he playing some game with you?"* Iniquity kept repeating that same question. Marty kept coming up with the same answer.

"I don't know. Perhaps he is. Perhaps he isn't," she answered the voice in her head. *"The thing that doesn't fit with your linkage theory is that the executions were the result of my slip up. I should have known better and kept my mouth shut. I can understand why he got emotional. I exposed him. Perhaps I should just take David at face value. That way I won't have all this brain damage. Perhaps he's simply being truthful. Maybe I really am going to get a twenty percent pay raise, and a diamond neckless, and a floppy eared rabbit. Maybe my firing was all a big joke. Perhaps David is just putting me through another episode of his 'Gotcha' game.*

"Yeah, I could see David doing that. He gets his yucks out of toying with me. He treats me like I'm his human Yo-Yo. First, he brings me back from where I was. He keeps me close to him, tightly holding my life and career in his hand. Then, just when I feel safe and secure, he flings me far out and away from him; like he's tossed me into his outer orbit;

like he doesn't need me anymore. Then he reels me back in again. He's done it before. It isn't new behavior. Do you think it's because he can't help himself? Maybe it's just his management style? Maybe my angst is over some minor manipulation game that David is playing inside of a bigger, real game, whatever that is? I could see David doing that; stacking one game inside another game. I've seen him do that to his secretaries. It's classic David."

"Where will we put the rabbit coup?" interrupted Miss Shameless. She was Marty's 'Devil May Care' voice, the inner voice that always told Marty there was nothing to fear. She always got Marty's mind thinking ahead of where things were. She made Marty feel it was okay to get in front of events, anticipating them. Marty couldn't think of a single time when Miss Shameless wasn't spot on. But every one of those other times had to do with men that Marty eventually seduced. Shameless was always right about what would happen those times. Most men were predictable. They always caught up to the seductions that Marty planned for them. And Shameless always made sure Marty had her way with them. Shameless was Marty's conscience freeing voice for her seductions. She continually reminded Marty that she had no moral compass. That emboldened Marty's cavalier lewdness. And Marty's temptation tactics always paid off. She seduced every man she targeted. Many of those men bonded as Marty's long-term lovers. They came back to her, time after time; addicted to her; wanting more of her.

But her situation with David was different. It wasn't about seduction tactics or romantic conquest. It was about dealing with mercurial David; or deciding to leave him and not deal with him at all. Today, Marty was undecided about whether she should even listen to Miss Shameless. Her Devil-May-Care voice seemed out of place, somehow.

"In front of the tool shed, where the bunny will get good sun and where I can watch him while looking from my kitchen window," Marty

decided she could not shut Shameless out. She decided to answered her voice. *"But why am I even talking with you, Shameless? I still haven't figured out whether David is playing a game. All you voices know that I've made enough money to walk away clean. Maybe I should. Sooner or later, there's a real chance that David will get found out. Then I'll be caught. He'd blame the murders on me. He'd be convincing too. He's a very slippery con artist. I could see everything come crashing down on me. I'd spend the rest of my life in jail. A judge would sentence me to life without parole. David would get a fine and probation with community service. He's a smooth talker. I'm not. I run the bigger risk if I we get found out. I don't want to spend the rest of my life in jail. I don't think any of you would like talking to me in jail, would you? So, please, all my voices, be quiet and let me think a minute."*

"Yeah, that's a good spot for him." Miss Shameless ignored Marty. She was good at interrupting Marty's concentration. She couldn't imagine the two of them not doing more of the naughty seductions they did. Marty and her voice, Miss Shameless, lived in an immoral, uninhibited groove together.

Shameless successfully sidetracked Marty's thoughts. Marty decided to procrastinate about her 'What to do about David?' decision and listen to Shameless instead:

"You could put his food and water bowl out in front of his hutch and watch him come out. He would give you a warm fuzzy feeling every time you saw him. You know he would. And the thing you need most is having your warm, fuzzy feel-goods. You could bring him inside the house with you, whenever you felt lonely and scared. You could squeeze him and hug him and nuzzle your face in his fur. He'd love that and you would too. You know I'm telling you the truth. Admit it."

"There you go again. You are putting the cart before the horse, Shameless," said Marty to her voice. *"I wish I could get you to stop. I need to be done with your interruptions. I am facing some serious, fork in the road decision stuff here. I need to think about the right thing to*

do for my life. I'm going inside now. I'm ordering you to stay outside. Be quiet and stay out of my head, until after I figure this out."

Marty was tormented by her conflict. David had suddenly fired her three days before. He told her that the reason for her dismissal was that she had seduced Bob, the Firm's best salesman. But she couldn't help wondering whether there was another, deeper reason. David knew her porn career was taking up more and more of her time. He also knew that demands for her time by her Premium Porn Members was exploding. Wealthy men, movie stars and sports stars were paying millions of Dollars to spend weekends and weeks away with her; and that took time away from her sales duties. But those reasons made no sense to her. She was highly successful at persuading many of her Premium Service Members to become Firm clients and invest their assets in the Firm's financial products. Her financial product sales were skyrocketing. It was a win, win for her and David. Hadn't he recently praised her stunning sales success and applauded the rapid growth in the Firm's assets under his management? Why not do more of the same?

Marty knew David needed her for the murders they did. Those murders were essential to the success of David's drug sales, prostitution, human trafficking, and money laundering criminal empire. Any of David's managers or employees who stole from him or who squealed about his operations was, without exception, executed. David depended on Marty to perform the executions. That's what stumped her about his decision to fire her. He had acted uncharacteristically emotionally and illogically. And that wasn't David.

Marty reflected long and hard about David's outburst. She concluded that he must have temporarily lost his mind. She couldn't imagine any other woman in the Firm who would be willing to risk life in prison for committing murder. Besides, no other female employee had her same brazen shamelessness and sex appeal. They'd be out of place trying to master her seductive routines. She had worked very hard on those dances. She had strained her muscles beyond imaginable limits; perfected every movement; every phase of her seductions; mastered her midair Chinese Split; pelvic lifts; undulations; back arches; sensual stimulations; exquisite fellatios; every movement and detail choreographed and performed exactly as David wished. She succeeded every time. No victim had ever escaped David's murder chamber. She concluded that David had not groomed another woman to replace her. His outburst seemed even less logical.

David had told her that she had achieved the impossible. She had attained perfection! He applauded her recent successes. He watched every seduction and execution. He deduced that every victim considered her irresistible. Everyone succumbed with no resistance. David had even upped her murder bonus payments to one hundred thousand Dollars. But, Marty surmised, David had to intuitively know that she was no longer doing the murders for money. He could see how much she enjoyed them and the orgies afterwards. He hugged her tightly after that last night in the chamber. She felt certain that they were finally going to make love. They'd talked frankly about it. He told her how much he looked forward to it. David couldn't possibly have doubts about her willingness. She had offered him sex several times before, during and after the last murders.

David emphatically said that he wanted to; that he desperately needed her. He had kissed her cheek and her neck. She was stroking his cock while they hugged. He clearly wanted her. His extreme hardness wasn't faked. His passion was right there. She felt it in his warm breath on her neck; the way he nuzzled against her. She heard it in the soft moaning that came from deep inside him. They felt each other's need. So why hadn't they? It was almost like he had forced himself to toy with her; like he knew that he was the one man she wanted more than all her others; so, he tortured her by denying her. That behavior fit David. That was his genius. It was a technique he used to gain power over others. She concluded she was in one of David's power plays. There was nothing about her, from David's perspective, that made her exceptional; let alone an equal. That had to be it! Intimacy would shatter David's equality barrier. And David was not ready for that.

That was the David she could understand. But the act of firing her, she did not understand. That put a new twist to things; something she'd never seen before or expected. She strained her mind, trying to come up with the reason. What could possibly have made him so furious? His face was anger rage. What was it about him that she, his partner in so many murders, could not understand? She couldn't think of any logical answer. She was ready to give up on David and the Firm; and move on with her life. She had told herself: *"I have money. I have fame. I have incredible skill sets. I have billionaires begging me to marry them, if I want that. I don't need to take this abuse from David. Not anymore."*

But then, yesterday, he had come to her house. He was his ultimate casual self, dressed in a green leisure suit with his cowboy boots; smelling like his barnyard, after coming straight from his barnyard. His personality was completely opposite from how he had behaved at the office. That day he sputtered spit, like an erupting, angry volcano. That beet red face! She feared he would rupture a blood vessel.

But when he came to her house, he was a different person altogether. It was like his angry temper tantrum never happened. She even noticed herself wondering if it really had happened or if she had only been dreaming. But it had happened! She had no illusions about that. Yesterday, oddly, he was all smiles and goofy chuckles, like some transformed person. He always disarmed her when he became boyishly goofy like that. He presented her with a pearl neckless as a peace offering. She didn't need it. Her Premium Members had given her several of them. Then he offered to rehire her and give her a twenty percent pay raise. She didn't need his money, either. He should have known that. He had to know what she really wanted was him. Him in bed, with her.

Him, with his cock inside her. Him, telling her he loved her. He and she as equals. Her mind spoke to her inner self: *'Yes David, the neckless and the money are nice. A girl always likes more nice things and more money; but can't you see it's you I want, David. I want your heart, David. I want your cock inside me. I want us to fuck. I want you to love me.'*

She had held back, not agreeing to return; hoping for more from him; waiting for an offer of something that signaled there was a personal interest in her; something that touched her heart; hoping to at least receive something that might lift her hopes; hope that love was not far away; perhaps seeing him reach, possibly stretch to leave his other self and come to her; and become intimate. Then, when he recognized her skepticism, he promised he'd give her a diamond choker neckless and a floppy-eared rabbit, if she'd only, please, just come visit with him at his barn tomorrow afternoon.

He told her he needed her help. He said he needed to understand why he had such a volatile temper. He revealed his deep-seated misconception about women. He said he needed to straighten it out. He said he needed her; he believed she could help him with his problem; but he stopped short of saying he loved her. He always stopped short of saying those *'I love you,'* words that meant everything to her. It seemed like he knew she desperately wanted to hear him say them; but by not saying them, he could retain some small measure of control over her.

"Come to my barnyard tomorrow afternoon. I'll give you your rabbit and the diamond neckless," David promised. It was his *'let's make up and be friends again,'* offer. That was so *'David.'* His impish boy persona always broke through his gruff facade. He could make people believe they had never seen him angry in the first place. When he stood there in her doorway, looking sheepish and apologetic, she saw the same David who brought her bone chips for her roses.

"Oh David, you're making my heart leap. I very much want that bunny. It will bring us closer together. You are melting me. You are so

sweet! How do you know me so well?" Marty sensed her resistance was melting. She knew David's offer of a floppy eared rabbit was a gift from his heart. He had to know her true heart, to offer her a bunny. She believed the bone chips were also a gift from his heart. He brought them in early Spring, when the ground softened; when her growing rose canes craved phosphate nourishment. He had admired her roses and compared them to his. Roses somehow connected his spirit to hers.

They shared a comradery of interest in roses. *"I want your roses to be as beautiful and healthy as mine,"* David told her. Roses were somehow symbolized their mysterious connection; their imaginary intimacy and shared destiny. Roses helped Marty see David as a thoughtful, nurturing, caring friend. When she was at his house, she saw and smelled his roses. When she was home, she saw and smelled her roses. Roses represented a continuum for her, a sense that David was always with her; thinking of her; daily reminding her of their friendship. She felt fortunate to know this good-natured side of him. Roses entwined their spirits.

Yesterday, he pleaded his case beautifully. He told her he had completely changed his mind. He berated himself, telling her he realized that he was totally irrational about firing her; that he badly needed her exceptional, unique talents. He also needed to understand some vexing mysteries about women. He didn't know where to turn or whom to ask. He needed to know her mind; understand how she thought about things. If he could do that, he implored, he'd be able to understand women, especially why his mother treated him like she did. He believed a new, enlightened understanding would be cathartic. He tear-eyed when he told her he needed to take this huge step forward. His contrition seemed honest. Was it? Regardless, it produced the desired effect. Marty became wistful:

'I so much hope that everything he said is true. Please, spirits, let it be true. Please let this David be the true David, like the beautiful David

he was in the underground chamber. I'll never forget that special eve-
ning, just a short while ago. There we were in my dark endless heaven,
my secret void of bottomless immoral freedoms without any distracting
stars; only the two of us, my victims and the chamber's soft mauve light-
ing. He held my naked body close to him, spooning me while we both
stood upright. He stimulated me so wonderfully while I perfected my
new method. His tender kisses on my neck and his warm breath on my
cheeks lifted my feelings above anything I'd ever felt before. I visualized
the widening chasm between us and our victims. My last cloak of moral
conscience fell away.

'I breathed freely again, knowing that my secret was safe, because
they would be gone. I could stop worrying about being betrayed. I was
leaving their control, like a butterfly leaving its cocoon. I felt free and
wonderful about my transitioning, thanks to David. My life would
go on. I'd be free! I'd keep my fame and disassociate myself from their
chapter of my life. I was awakening; totally independent in the early
dawn twilight of my glorious new life. Everything was beautiful. David
adored me. He even told me he worshipped me while I destroyed them.
I was the Sphinx, reincarnated. My deceptively lustrous face distracted
them from the merciless murders I did with my razor-sharp claw. My
inner lioness relaxed and smiled. My treachery pleased me. My feel-
ings felt no tension; only bliss and ecstasy. I felt deliciously wonderful;
released! David knew I appreciated that he set up their executions.

'I was safe in David's arms; my benefactor, trusted partner. I put the
threat of discovery behind us. I gushed. I'm certain he felt it. His arms
tightened around me. His fingers pressed me harder. I know he loved me
in that moment; loved my irredeemable evil; loved how we would be for-
ever inseparable after this! How perfect was that moment! We obliterated
the last remnant of my moral compass. I had no further need for morality
now; no need to pretend I ever did. Finally, together, we solved the nag-
ging problem that I foolishly created. I redeemed myself. I became my
freed, guiltless self; giggling and laughing while murdering; while ending

it. Only David could have made that glorious night possible; brought feelings of relief and release from deep inside me.

'I imagined his lips would soon press against mine; David wanting all of me. I was hungry for that. I imagined the warm pressure of our bodies coming together. I knew he wanted to kiss my hungry mouth; grasp my ass in his hands and enter me. I could read his mind. Like me, he was eager to interrupt the killings and make love. The spontaneity was there. I felt it every time his skin touched mine. We were incredibly close to taking that important step. I have never felt more certain of my feelings.

'Afterwards, while he sponge-bathed and massaged me, I felt certain we would finally have our intimacy. His hands were so loving while he rubbed oil into my mons and perfumed me. He even massaged and kissed my feet. I saw a David I had not believed existed. When he asked me if I had any regrets over killing them, I just put my hands behind my head and erupted in laughter. I told him no. Absolutely, not! That's when he hugged me and told me he was immensely proud of me. He even said I was his goddess and he adored me. My nipples and Miss Muffy loved his tender touchings. I remember how my body melted and quivered. Eager. I was so, so anxiously eager! And the occasion was so perfect. I wanted to celebrate what we had done. I wanted him more that night than I've ever wanted any man. He was about to become my most wonderful seduction. I felt certain that David and I were about to have our first intimate moment.

'But then he delivered the pang of our reality. Our lives were ordered and compartmentalized. Sales, pornography, and the murders were mine; the businesses, legitimate and illegitimate, were his. Like separate chambers with separate rules and authorities, we dared not open our respective doors and move freely within each other's spaces. Except for the necessary overlap of our murders, I knew that reality. And it stung; pained me. David designed our arrangement that way. It was the perfect deception. And it worked beautifully, moneywise; but I hated it. I wanted so much more. I wanted him.

'*My heart sank when it didn't happen for us. Why didn't it happen that night? Why did we have to follow our own stupid rules? Why didn't we suspend those rules; simply become lovers; let intimacy open the doors of our compartments; break our self-imposed barriers down; work out something new? Mergers are our Firm's specialty, David. Why not us? Why not a merger of our souls? No registration filings. No shareholder proxies. Just us two humans, coming together! It would all be so easy, so complete. David, please hear my thoughts, like you are here with me now, and I am speaking with you. When I see you again, will you remember that you promised me intimacy? Then, why not, David? Why didn't we? Will you tell me, honestly, so I won't go crazy? Why did you just suddenly stop and stare at me that way? Where did your mind go? What changed? I remember your sweet kiss on my forehead while you held my face in your hands; your eyes swimming in my pools; drinking me in and loving me; taking in my feelings of love for you. I know you love me, David. I can tell. Then, your softly voiced "goodnight" and your effusive praise for my beautiful murders in the chamber.*

'*You had to do that, didn't you David? You had to impress upon me that oppressive sense of our boundaries. And you would not allow yourself to cross over to me. But we almost did it that night, didn't we? We were almost there, weren't we David? You know we were. I hope your thoughts can hear mine. I hope you can feel the same desires that I'm feeling. We were on the cusp of it; about to tumble into each other, lose ourselves in our love, weren't we? I'm certain you felt it, too. I know you were ready. We should have finished what we started. You know it's true. You can't deny your feelings forever. You know you can't. If I do come to see you tomorrow, will you please be that David that you were that night; that David that I need and want? Will you please, finally, let yourself have me?*'

But with David, Marty could never be sure about his look. Did it reflect his genuine feelings? Did it ever? Did he ever, honestly, have any feelings at all, for anyone or anything? She knew David was an accomplished con artist. There was never any way for anyone to be sure of what David really felt; or whether one was just seeing another one of David's misdirects. He could change his mind in an instant; become a totally different personality. It was impossible to know where David's mind was. That's what made it so hard for Marty to believe anything he said. His behavior was beyond crazy. But Marty knew that classifying David as crazy was like trying to stick a pin in liquid mercury to fasten it to the sky. She knew better than to believe he was crazy. There was some real reason why he came to see her. It was impossible for anyone who knew him to conclude that David was crazy.

How many times had she allowed herself to believe that David was crazy, only to discover he wasn't? He was just being his evil genius form of crazy. She'd seen that uncanny unpredictability in David at least ten times. She'd seen him fake out regulators, salesmen, clients, and other employees. Hell, the entire office was David's world class con job. It was only a sanctimonious, highly regulated business front for his other, highly profitable illegal businesses; his drug sales, money laundering, prostitution, and human trafficking; and especially his ingenious murder for hire and body disposal operation. She knew all about these horrible, depraved operations and David's coldly inhuman personality. She accepted his sociopathy; actually, she admired his numbness to feelings; that void inside him which he so carefully nurtured. Sometimes she entertained the thought that he was trying to become some unfeeling, emotionless persona that he idolized but could not quite attain. She also knew it was important not to carelessly assume away her cautious thoughts. She appreciated that David was an incredibly dangerous man; that he might possibly hurt her. Miss Iniquity had often reminded her that he could. David could become the deceptive persona of the Devil himself while he was behaving like an honest businessman. Devil David could smile into your face, chuckle heartily and merrily joke along with you, while slipping his knife into you without you even feeling it.

David often played head games with Marty. He gave her the green light to romance Bob and several of her other seductions; even paying for her expenses. But for those endeavors, David always made his money back and more, from Marty's fabulous sales. Those sex and money for sales games seemed similar, to Marty, to the game she found herself playing with David now. David always won at those games; always made back more money than he advanced. And she always won, too. She noticed that. But David always got something more than money out of it. Her sense of self sank a little lower after each seduction conquest. Somehow every conquest gave David a small incremental increase in the control he had over her. She had, thus far, been okay with that. She accepted her lower self-esteem as her price for the bigger bonuses, the bigger commission percentages, and her salary hikes. She knew she needed to be true to herself, like her shrink said she should. Her lower self-esteem feeling had lifted recently. It wasn't troubling her like it had before. Her porn films and Premium Member services were doing extremely well, giving her increasing confidence and a sense of independence. Also, she had recently been forthright with David, telling him that the murders were troubling her conscience. Just speaking that truth to him lifted her self- esteem. But her newest feelings confused her.

Recently, her self-esteem feelings had skyrocketed. Amazingly, David had helped bring that change about. Uncanny David understood her need to lift her feelings about herself; and he had the presence of mind to step in like he did; when he did. That's what made him so special. Since their talk she now visualized herself as a goddess while committing the murders. David had helped get her over her troubled conscience problems. He must have intuited that the murders created awareness issues and lowered her self- esteem. He was patient and reassuring. He took his time explaining things to her until she completely understood them. He made sure she accepted the moral need for performing the murders. David had convinced her to think about murder in her new, *Goddess* way. He helped her understand that committing murder was a healthy, expressive way to help her feel good about herself. He helped her realize that murder was the relief valve she needed. Murdering relieved her sales pressures. Murdering also boosted her ego.

David understood that Marty thrived, childlike, on praise over every improvement to her seduction and dance routines. He patiently coached her through those pre-murder improvements until he saw her become the carefree, perky, sassy, bright eyed, radiant, optimistic Marty who had first joined the Firm. Watching her self-esteem grow made David happy. That's why he patiently explained that there was nothing wrong about committing murder. He explained that murdering people was merely the natural progression of her executive career development. He helped her believe that she greatly benefitting her victims by saving them from miserable lifetimes in prison.

Thanks to David's coaching, Marty's mind was at ease with committing murder. She felt an inner glow about her self-worth. She knew she was doing something important to help the Firm; and that David understood her needs. She had high confidence in herself because she knew he cared about her like he did. Her career and compensation experienced a meteoric rise thanks to his guidance. The way he thoughtfully nurtured her was the good, caring side of David. That's what she valued and loved about him. That's why, whenever she had doubts about him or about the heinous things that he required her to do, she always concluded that he was acting in her best interests. And that she should trust and obey him.

She was relieved when he came to see her yesterday. She almost cried for joy when she saw him at her front door. But she arrested her tears and put on her best puzzled-look face. It was hard to not let David know that she was thrilled to see him, because she was. She had come to depend on him for her legitimacy as a businesswoman and for a large portion of her income. His visit reassured her that he needed her. Her doubts about his mutual loyalty evaporated like fog burned away by morning sunshine. She was ready to do as he asked, before he even spoke a single word.

David was a diabolical character who possessed a rare skill set. He unfailingly knew how to make Marty feel good about herself, whatever the circumstances. He understood and forgave her screw ups. That's what stumped her about the sequence of events that led to his visit. Before he abruptly fired her, he had recently praised her and told her that her last murder was beyond wonderful. He was ecstatic about how smoothly it went. She was eagerly looking forward to performing her next murder, and hearing David pronounce that it topped her latest one. She had even mentally rehearsed several minutely changed details that would make her next routine her finest ever. During that hour before he summoned her to his office, she was focused on choreographing her music with her dance moves and knife placements. That's what made her termination such a rude shock. But that was last week.

Today was the day after David came to her house to undo all the chaos he'd caused. She sat on her back porch looking over her yard. It was an idyllic midafternoon, her favorite time of day. The sun was warm but not too hot. There was a faint breeze. It was a gentle, shoulder-season breeze that carried with it a hint of fall. She wore only her shorts, blouse, and sandals. She watched her favorite squirrel eyeing her roses; sizing up a potentially bountiful rose hips harvest. She liked the way her mind drifted away from her problems while she watched animals. Her latest shrink, Mrs. O'Dell, said that watching animals was good because seeing them living uncomplicated lives relaxed her tensions.

'Well,' she thought, "I'm finally getting a good sense of mental balance in my reasoning, like Mrs. O'Dell said I needed. I feel a slight chill. This is a good time to go inside, brew a cup of tea; and sit and think quietly about how this latest uproar with David started; how far I've progressed; and whether I really want to go further, especially now that I have Bob, who truly loves me. And now being three months pregnant, I know I must make some serious decisions. I've been told I should stop and think when I find myself in situations like this. Mrs. Martinson, my first shrink, said that. She said thinking about the consequences of what I'm considering doing helps sort things out.

'I'm going to try to think things through, even though David said my shrinks were just jealous of me; and that their psychobabble stuff held me back from making money. I wonder, sometimes, whether David is afraid I'll tell Mrs. O'Dell, my favorite shrink, about our murders, but I promised David I'd never do that; and I haven't done that. And David surely knows I'd never break a promise to him. After all, secrets between friends are really secrets.

'David knows I'm loyal. He's told me many times that he knows I'm loyal. So, I'm sure he trusts me. And he knows I'm special. He always tells me that, too. So, I'm sure I'm good with David on a personal level. Maybe he just had one of his temper tantrums that day. Maybe that day was as bad for him as it was for me? I hope not. I don't like to think about David getting upset about anything. He has a tough life; with his headaches and his big responsibilities and all the companies he needs to manage. Mrs. O'Dell says I shouldn't feel sorry for David, but I do sometimes. Considering all the problems he's got, he's a joy to work with. I guess I honestly love him on some level. It's just that it's so hard to totally love someone when there's no intimacy. I'm going to try hard, though, to think things through this time, like Mrs. Martinson said; and not let my emotions get in the way of my common sense. I'm not even going to allow myself to think about what I'll say to David at the barnyard, because I'm not even sure I want to go there.'

"That sounds like your best idea, girl," chimed in Miss Iniquity. She was Marty's most respected voice. She was the most thoughtful voice; the cold-hearted, calculating, no-nonsense bitch voice; the one that figured plusses and minuses, comparing the time involved with the dollars they'd make. Everything Marty did, Miss Iniquity translated into money. Iniquity was a predator animal; a cougar that calculated calories needed for calories gained; the requirements for a seduction to take a man's money. Marty knew she should pay attention to Iniquity:

"You are away from David now. Why is that? Ask yourself: why does he want you back? He has broadcast his heavy burden about misunderstanding women his entire life. You've known for years that his mother hated him. He told you that before. Big whoop! He tells everyone that. That doesn't mean it's true. But at least it's consistent; so, his invitation to meet him in his smelly barnyard makes some sense. Maybe at some point in life all men want to understand women, especially their mothers. But maybe David has another reason to want you back. Think hard. What might that be? Sometimes a reason becomes obvious if you lay out all facts carefully; think about them; and ask yourself why things are the way they are, and how things would be if certain things were changed. And, you must see those facts and possible changes through the eyes of the other person. Mrs. Martinson told you that. Remember?"

"Yes, I remember," Marty replied to Miss Iniquity. But Marty could not follow Iniquity's advice. Her narcissism wrested control of her thoughts away from seeing things as the other person might see them. She could only think in terms of how her decision would affect her. *"But if I don't go, I'll never know if he's sincere. He's more to me than a business boss. He's a good friend and my confidant, too. We would be in broad daylight, Iniquity, and I'm almost as strong as David. I think you're overthinking this. He mostly does office work. He's not that physical, and I am very well-muscled. I can't imagine he'd*

try to rape me. He knows he wouldn't need to, anyway. If he wanted to have sex, he knows I'd gladly let him have me. After all, we are close friends. I know he has homosexual friends, but I think he likes women too. Maybe, hopefully, he's more of a pan-sexual person, like me. Possibly he's an opportunistic bi-sexual who doesn't care how he gets off. Anyway, I'm not going to tie myself in a knot trying to understand his orientation. If he wants sex, I won't deny him. What kind of friend would I be? Besides, I'd love having intimate closeness with him. Sex might help him trust our relationship more than he already does. After all, just because I engaged doesn't mean I'd stop partnering with David in the murders, or that I'd deny him sex. I hope he wants me. Intimacy would do us both a lot of good. It would prove he believes in me. He'd never doubt my loyalty after that. I'd like that. I don't like going through uncertain days like this one.

"Anyway, Iniquity, what would I do if I didn't go back to the Firm? Yes, my film career takes more of my time, but it doesn't interfere with my work at the Firm. And porn is such a competitive business. I could be upstaged at any time by a girl with better looks and better acts. So, why shouldn't I do both the Firm and my films for another year or two; or even five if I can? When my body fades and my fans dwindle away, what will I have besides the Firm? Why should I leave a job that's secure?

"Besides the money, there's the sex and relationships I've formed with some terrific salesmen. I have better intimacy and physical fulfillment with many of them than with many of my film partners. Naturally I want to continue those friendships. I'd feel a huge void without them. I should hear David out. Maybe he'll offer more than he already has. I need to know my options before I decide about my fetus. Pregnancy has been a blast so far. I've never even had morning sickness. My nipple nubs are extra sensitive. And my libido acts supercharged. Pregnancy has been an erotic sensation. But I must decide something before I start showing. I don't want my body to repulse my porn partners or turn off my fans.

"Think, Iniquity. If I go back, when Mother retires, I could take her place and make Barbara my assistant. I could service Mothers' big clients and some new ones while Barbara did all my tedious detail work. Mother still services her clients. And she's twenty-five years older than me. I'd love doing that, especially since Barbara has her eyes on Bob. I'd work her little ass off. I'd rub it in her face that I service clients while I also have Bob; and she has no one. She's so obvious. She thinks no one notices how she takes everything in, like she's the indispensable office whiz kid. But I notice. She's smart, I'll give her that. She's smart about how the business runs and all that, but I don't need that. I can hire those kinds of smarts. Sales are what make the Firm a business. And I bring in sales. I think that's why David wants me back. He'll lose sales without me."

"It sounds like you've thought of every possibility," said Miss Iniquity, *"but you should think about it some more. And don't let your emotions play tricks on you. Mrs. O'Dell told you to be extra careful about that. You know you're easily swayed when you start to feel someone else's emotional needs.*

"Remember Miss Carboy, your second shrink? Remember how she drew out your feelings about oral sex? Remember when she told you she had those same feelings? You need to remember what happened. Instead of helping you get over your love affair with Mr. Sorber, your geometry teacher, Miss Carboy began kissing your sex, just like he did. She said she needed to compare your feelings while Mr. Sorber gave you oral sex with how you felt while she gave you oral sex. You believed her; but she fell in love with you, just like he did.

"Remember how messy things got when Mr. Sorber's wife came to the admin offices? She screamed and threatened suicide. Then, Miss Carboy begged you to run away to New Orleans with her. Remember how you had to fight her off? Those people were more unbalanced than you are. You finally got up enough courage to tell Mrs. Hugel, the WEX headmistress, about Miss Carboy. That's when she assigned you to Mrs.

O'Dell, your last shrink at WEX. You also had enough sense to keep your mouth shut about Mr. Sorber. He finally took you to motels and stopped taking you to his house; and Mrs. Sorber went back to him. That's when you got smarter about managing your affairs. You met him in hotels and motels, and he paid you for sex all through your senior year and after you graduated. His wife never did commit her threatened suicide. She was bluffing and feeling sorry for herself. She was only playing a control game with her husband.

"Ask yourself: How did you get into that mess in the first place? It's because you never think things through. It's understandable and forgivable though. Both those affairs happened shortly after you got your wings. You were still young and impressionable. You were feeling hurt because Maria left for Montana. But bearing your soul to Miss Carboy about Maria didn't help your sex addiction, did it? No, it made it worse; Mrs. O'Dell said so. Remember what that episode taught you? You must keep a straight face while reading other peoples' facial clues? That's when you learned how to spot subtle signals and respond in ways that move things along.

"When you told Miss Carboy that Mr. Sorber's smile made you feel like lying on your back and spreading your legs, you caught that little lift in Miss Carboy's lips, and you noticed the relaxed muscles of her forehead. Thinking about sex makes some people look beautiful. You read her signal perfectly. She looked pretty. You felt her falling in love with you. You sensed her saliva surge into her mouth. Then, when you asked her if she ever felt like Mr. Sorber did when you returned an inviting smile, Miss Carboy didn't hesitate. Two minutes later she was licking your clitoris. She wanted you as much as he did.

"At least we now know how to manage these people better. And we make money from them, so they weren't bad experiences. But they were awkward, because Mr. Sorber and Miss Carboy were both connected to WEX. They knew better than to get involved with a student. Mr. Sorber turned out to be a wonderful experience. He taught you volumes about

oral sex; helping you appreciate how enjoyable it is when you take your time and let yourself relax. Miss Carboy taught you how to concentrate on prolonging and repeating your orgasms. So, I'm not mad at you; after all, you were just coming into your sexuality then. I forgave you for losing control during those times. I always forgive you; you know that. I've never expected you to be perfect.

"But remember, people usually put their own interests first. That's why you need to be extra careful with chameleon personalities. David's quick about-face was not natural. It came too suddenly. It represents a radical change in his position. That's unusual, even for David. That should trouble you. Think hard about what you should do.

"So, go inside and brew some tea. Make it chamomile, not green. You don't need stimulus right now. You need to relax and think about who you are, where you are, how you got here, and where you're going. Mrs. Martinson and Mrs. O'Dell both told you to do that."

"Yes, dear Mother that I never had, I'll do as you say," thought Marty to her imaginary voice of Iniquity. She went inside to brew tea and have a long sit-down thinking session, like her two best shrinks said she should.

CHAPTER TWO

Tis a chequer board of nights and days where destiny for men with pieces plays.

Hither and thither moves and mates and slays, and one by one back in the closet lays.

(Edward Fitzgerald: Omar Khayydm)

Hearing voices is a signal that you need to pay attention to something; maybe to one of them; maybe to some or all of them; maybe none of them. Maybe you just need some sleep. (Rosemary Ness-Bitner, author)

THE VOICE CLOSET

It was late summer on the high plains. The Rockies' peaks already had their first dustings of snow, and the foothills' evening temperatures were dipping into the upper thirties. Marty's roses had passed their blooms and their petals were dropping. In the huge Douglas fir that towered above her garage busy squirrels padded their nests for the coming winter. A squirrel she'd named Old Fred was the savviest of the scurry troop that laid claim to her Douglas. She'd noticed him hanging face down on the trunk of her Douglas for the last two days. He was eyeing her roses; no doubt gauging the hips crop her canes would soon offer. He was waiting for the last petals to drop, knowing that was when the hips were most nutritious.

'Smart old boy, aren't you' she thought, admiring Fred's healthy coat. Her roses were ending a spectacular year. Their canes had grown at least three feet longer. They'd grown riot wild in every direction; totally out of control. They covered the fence beside her rose beds. They seemed to be reaching for the sky. David's bone chips were working their magic, as he said they would. She had dutifully dug the holes exactly as he had instructed, up close to the base of each plant, and eighteen inches deep. She had poured half of a Mason jar's chips into each hole and covered them with mulch and soil, mixed. David said the mulch held moisture and its slow moisture drip leached calcium and phosphorus into the rose roots.

She wondered where he bought his chips. She got her garden supplies from Dorgino's, the biggest garden supply store in town, but they didn't carry bone chips in huge Mason jars. David's jars were the largest she'd ever seen; huge two-gallon ones. And he gave her six of them! She had one full gallon of chips for each of her twelve rose bushes. She reminded herself to ask him where he got his jars of chips when she saw him tomorrow; if she decided to see him tomorrow.

'Ha, how would all of you, furry squirrel critters, fare if you weren't getting your vitamin C from my roses? Maybe you wouldn't even live here? Maybe you'd move away?' It was one of Marty's idle curiosities. The squirrels nested in the same place, year after year. They got what they needed without making any changes. *'Am I the same? Do I stay with David because he gives me what I need? Nature would take care of you squirrels if you moved. Would nature take care of me?'* She shook her head and gazed up at the high Colorado sky. The bright blue sky helped her stop thinking about the squirrels. There were more pressing things on her mind. She needed to go inside and think things through, like Mrs. Martinson said she should.

Inside her bungalow Marty carefully selected some music for her CD player. Music and tea helped her think. Her favorite sitting place was an oversized Italian tapestry chair. It sheltered her. Sitting in it, next to her fireplace with her feet propped up on its matching footstool, she felt secure. She could see her entire living room while listening to her music. She hadn't made fire yet. It was still warm in the house. Evening hadn't fallen. The lazy late afternoon sunlight was pleasant enough. Her thinking would be undisturbed by fireplace wood crackling and embers popping. She looked across the room at her portrait. Bob had an artist paint it from a snapshot photo of her face. He liked capturing pictures of her in spontaneous settings like that. It was his way of letting her know he adored her.

The portrait expressed her feeling perfectly. She wore her special smile, the one that comes when everything's right. Her face was confident and content, combined with her mischievous hint of victory glow. She radiated her heart's happiness from that smile because she was on top of the world that day. Bob had achieved his breakthrough in their love making that afternoon. He had softly kissed her between her wings for that first time and become smitten by the tastes of her lady flower. His face told her he had experienced reverence and wonderment. His smile had told her that he loved it; and that he felt more connected to her than ever; and that he loved her. That's when she knew she'd taken his love from Barbara. Those were the things she was feeling and understanding when he flashed that snapshot of her smile. When he brought her the finished portrait with the picture of a Monarch butterfly flitting over her head, she *knew* he'd rather make love with her than with Barbara.

"You can't let your mind go backsliding into sex like this," interrupted Miss Iniquity rudely. *"You always do that, and it moves you off your focus. Remember what Mrs. Martinson said. You must lock your sex addiction in a closet and no matter how much it pounds upon the door and screams to be let out, you must keep it locked away in there, even if it feels like the door is breaking down, until it settles down and becomes quiet; and you must think about the important things, about whom you are, where you are going, what you want to accomplish, what this situation is all about, what the facts are telling you, and all the things we talked about."*

Mrs. Martinson was Marty's first shrink. Her advice had been much like Mrs. Schnell's, her third shrink between Miss Carboy and Mrs. O'Dell. Marty tried to forget Miss Carboy. Her sex addictions seemed as bad as Marty's. Mrs. Schnell basically agreed with the advice Marty had been getting from Mrs. Martinson until Mrs. Martinson got married and moved to New York. But Mrs. O'Dell's advice sharply contradicted Mrs. Schnell's and Mrs. Martinson's advice. Mrs. Schnell said Marty should face her voices with courage, challenge them and examine them and their advice, essentially separate them from herself and sit and talk with them like they were real live people. That way, she said, Marty could understand what her voices' needs were and then she could decide whether she wanted to meet their needs. Mrs. Schnell told Marty that drawing out her voices was the only way she'd ever discover stability in her life. Marty liked Mrs. Schnell. Every session seemed better than the last and it felt like she was making a lot of progress. And Mrs. Schnell never made advances to Marty like Miss Carboy did, so Grandmother Bethany Mallory never had to call the school and scream to get her fired like that time she called school admin and threatened to sue them unless they got rid of Miss Carboy.

But Marty lost Mrs. Schnell anyway. Some man left his wife so he could become Mrs. Schnell's lover. He came to the school one day and brought Mrs. Schnell a box of chocolates. The two of them sat right there in her school office where the girls could see them through her glass office window. The two adults laughed a lot while eating their chocolates. The girls that watched them said they stood up after they ate their chocolates and embraced and kissed for a very long time. Soon after that day, Mrs. Schnell divorced her husband and moved away to North Carolina to live with the other woman's estranged husband.

Marty missed Mrs. Schnell's off-campus private office. It had lots of print posters on the wall by famous artists, like Picasso's impressions and Dali's abstracts and flower vases by Tony Curtis. That office relaxed Marty. The pictures opened her mind up and helped her talk about the problems she had with the other girls. The Dali pictures especially aroused her. She thought about them while lying awake at night in her dorm room. She was sure Mrs. Schnell was making a lot of progress with her because lately she was finding it easier to get along with the other girls. Unfortunately, Mrs. Schnell left town after giving WEX only two weeks' notice. All of Mrs. Schnell's WEX cases were reassigned to new shrinks. That's when Marty got sent to Mrs. O'Dell. At her next appointment Marty had planned to ask Mrs. Schnell why the Dali pictures made her feel like touching herself in her beaver lodge, but she never got that chance. She asked Mrs. O'Dell that question and Mrs. O'Dell told her that was a very normal feeling and she should never feel ashamed of touching herself when she had that feeling.

"Yes, I know you're right," she told Miss Iniquity. *"I'm sorry. I'll do that. I'm going to go way back to the beginning when Mother first took me to WEX. No, wait, I'm going to go back even further; as far back as I can remember. I need to feel that time again. It was so good! And then, suddenly, everything went so bad."*

Marty was a highly emotive woman. Music helped her express her feelings. She browsed selections in used CD stores. She was a music eclectic. Her interests ranged from spiritual and religious music to soothing inspirational pop artists, like Abba, to unusual artistically crafted pieces that helped her set her moods. She experimented with audio equipment and pieced together home-made CDs for those times where someone's store shelf album wouldn't match her changing moods. This afternoon she needed something to help her follow Mrs. O'Dell's advice. She needed to put her voices away. She had what she needed. At the beginning of her home-made CD were two songs. The first was the original 'Tubular Bells,' By Oldfield.

The second was 'Dance Macabre,' the Middle Ages Dance of Death song by Camille Saint Saens. The rest of the CD was, oddly enough, maritime songs and ballads from Nova Scotia. The first two songs helped her put her voices into a closet and the maritime songs helped her feel tranquil after her voices fell asleep.

As 'Tubular' began, she imagined her voices coming toward her; and her pushing them back. They became angry at her rejection. That's why the music she selected was off key, and why its movements and counter movements overlapped the theme with changing tempos, deliberately agitating her voices. She imagined hearing her voices. They screamed mournful screams. They tried to kick her closet door down to let themselves out. Then they stomped their feet in anger and went away for a while. But then they returned. Eventually they became quiet in her mental closet. She imagined she could hear their heartbeats. They feigned they didn't care about her anymore. They even became blasé about their separation from her. She imagined they were dancing with each other because they couldn't dance with her. Soon they voiced their indignation at being locked up. They alternately roared at the closed closet door, then pranced about pretending they didn't care. Even listening to the music's church bells didn't calm them down. She imagined hearing her voices plotting their escape. They believed if they mustered their strength, they could overpower the closet door. She listened to them as if they were part of her music.

They stomped their feet faster and faster, until the piano played. That's when their energy peaked and climaxed. Each new instrument coming into the piece made her voices become more tired. They began relaxing and falling asleep when the glockenspiel played, joined by the mandolin and the guitars. Their anger became quelled. They were finally peaceful. They hugged each other, loved each other; and they rejoiced in their sinful lesbo ways. They felt smug about who they were and the sensations of lust they knew they could arouse in men. Then, Marty began to feel peace. She imagined her voices had fallen into a deep sleep.

Listening to the 'Dance of the Macabre,' Marty pretended her voices slid down the closet door to the floor and temporarily died there. She decided she'd let them lie there until she was ready to awaken them and let them out of her closet again. While they were lying moribund in her imaginary closet, they'd be harmless while she did her thinking. Soon, the baleful whaling tones of Nova Scotia began playing softly. Marty's mind was finally undisturbed and relaxed. She believed she could now think clearly.

CHAPTER THREE

(Public) Schools are the nurseries of all vice and immorality (Henry Fielding: Joseph Andrews)

WEX

The Wexler Baxter School for Girls, or WET SMACKS, as boys from the nearby public school called it; or WEX, as its female students knew it, prided itself as the penultimate icon of exclusive social snobbery. Only daughters of highly socially connected and wealthy parents were admitted. Money alone didn't guarantee a girl's acceptance. Social standing, in and of itself, didn't assure a daughter's admission either. Since its state charter in 1851 this iconic monument to slavery and status had withstood every assault on its singular pursuit: Superiority of Image. If your daughter was a WEXER, you were in the in crowd. If she wasn't, you weren't. Mere mention of the school evoked feelings of exclusivity amongst the wealthy country club set. Latent resentments flared amongst the unaccepted who felt diminished, cursed, and relegated to inferiority when they heard the name WEX.

As if to solidify its image, WEX commanded the physical high ground. It arose from its verdant hilltop environ like an unassailable monument to daughters of the privileged. Massive white marble Corinthian columns fronted the main administration building and the main entrance to the education building. Long porticos of rich gold-threaded Italian marble walkways, covered by sparkling white plastered ceilings, sheltered the pampered WEX darlings. Faculty and parents felt cloaked in majesty while walking between these buildings. Red Italian roofing tiles amplified the sense of opulent casual richness. They reinforced WEX's sine qua non; that without a WEX pedigree, your daughter would become a worthless nothing; a doomed social nobody. The WEX board of directors insisted the school's prestige justified its sky-high tuition bills. On this sacred principal, the board was unyielding. Nobody got tuition breaks at WEX.

The driveway up to the hilltop WEX campus was an introduction to visual majesty. A half mile from the school, the state-maintained pothole marked blacktop road transitioned to a perfectly maintained private road. It dazzled with white and gray pebbles; accent bordered by three feet of immaculately maintained Kentucky blue grass on both sides of the road. Beyond these lush grass carpets, edging both sides of the driveway were white fencing posts. These were linked together by heavy gauge, white paint-dipped battleship anchor chains. Nothing suggests security and strength more emphatically than battleship anchor chain. A road sign said: 'CAUTION STUDENTS,' reminding drivers that WEX students are especially precious. A second sign follows. It warns drivers: SPEED LIMIT FIVE MILES PER HOUR; reinforcing the message of the first sign. The warnings prevented speeding cars from scattering the precious pebbles off the roadbed onto the manicured border grass; keeping maintenance costs down. Above the storybook driveway, arching cathedral branches of chestnut, birch, and elm trees tower; all expertly pruned and trimmed.

The color splash of white road, green border and fall colored reds, yellows, blues, oranges, and purples overhead reinforces parents' decisions. When they bring their precious daughters here for their first 'Welcome and Matriculation Day, and the 'WELCOME TO WEX,' Ceremony. It creates the indelible impression that everything about WEX is Godsend perfect. It reassures them that they made the intelligent, loving, best possible choice for their darling little girls;

that they did their very human best for their lives and futures; that they will know and appreciate privileged lives because of this wise choice and financial sacrifice; and to hell with the place's outrageous expenses! They were ready to write those tuition checks.

This heaven on Earth is for *their* daughter, their little Miss Precious. This is their curly golden-haired baby with her heart shaped mouth and her azure blue eyes; the same darling little girl who bounced on Daddy's knee while hearing him recite her nursery rhymes; the same daughter who looks up to Mommy and wears Mommy's clothes so she can pretend to be a real grown-up woman like Mommy; and the same little girl who still loves her dolls and baubles and plays grown up in her very own doll house. She's their one and only darling baby girl; their first daughter; that little bundle of love that kisses them on their cheeks and says her prayers at nighttime, before she goes to bed. Nothing could ever be out of reach of her abilities, or too good or too expensive for her! Parents didn't just read the dazzling brochures about WEXLER BAXLER. They obsessed over them. They were brought to a frenzy over getting their child into this school. It was the very best school, so costs didn't matter. They believed the best, most complete experience for a girl was to start life on the right foot; right away, in first grade. So, here came the Blantons, almost to where their daughter would become transformed into social royalty. They had almost arrived at WEX! They were bringing sweet little Trudy, Marty's future roommate.

"Look, Trudy! Look how beautiful this school is. Here you'll have lots of fun and lots of wonderful friends. You'll learn to play the piano and the violin; and you'll learn how to sing and dance, too. You'll have the very best and the smartest teachers in the world. They'll teach you all sorts of things and they'll explain things very well. You'll learn all sorts of things here; so, you will know lots of things, just like Mommy and Daddy. Your teachers will love showing you lots of exciting new things. You'll go on field trips with your little girl friends; and you'll

see new and interesting places. You're going to love it here, sweetheart. Mommy and Daddy will come to visit you often, so it will be a lot like being at home, except you won't be sleeping at home during the week. During Christmas and Easter and during the summer breaks, you'll be home with us for those important family times. We'll come every Friday afternoon when your last class is finished. And we'll bring you home with us for the whole weekend. We'll do that until you decide whether you'd rather stay here at the school on your weekends. Okay baby?"

"Okay, Mommy," answered Trudy. *"Mommy, if I call for you because I get afraid, will you or Daddy come and get me?"*

"Well, sweetheart, Mommy can't just drop everything she's doing and do that. Mommy might be playing bridge, or she might be at a ladies' party; and Daddy must work. Daddy is a very important executive. You know that. Why, if Daddy dropped everything and came running whenever you got a little scared, all the electric lights would go out all over the world. And then nobody could see in the dark, and lots of people would freeze to death. Now, you wouldn't want to cause people to freeze to death, would you?"

Trudy shook her head. *"No Mommy, I guess not."*

"That's my good girl. Now listen, Friday will come soon enough. If you get scared, you just go tell Mrs. Higginbottom. I've met her. She's a very nice lady. She understands little girls very well and she'll help you lose your fears, right away. You'll meet her soon. I know you'll like her a lot. Okay, baby?"

"Okay Mommy." Little Trudy looked out the window of the family sedan and up at the colorful branches overhead. Thoughts that this place would soon be her new home, and that she'd soon meet new friends ran through her tentative, impressionable mind.

WEX school soon came into view. It was surrounded by a massive iron fence with spear pointed tops that served to keep intruders out and girls in. The front gate was bordered by massive red brick columns capped with white marble tops. Mounted above both columns were statues of white marble lionesses, proudly guarding their marble lion cubs.

"*Female lions. Fierce, protective. Nice female touch,*" remarked Trudy's father, taking in the statues. "*Do you suppose they need anchor chains to keep a grip on the girls' morals?*"

"*It's a girls' school,*" reminded Trudy's mother. "*Those things are meant to make the girls feel empowered. It's good for their confidence, Ed. Isn't it beautiful?*"

"*This place looks even more impressive than it does in their brochures,*" said Trudy's father. He eyed the main administration building. The sun's gleam reflected from white shuttered windows, accenting the three-story brick administration offices, repository of school records and its extensive second and third floor library. He decided to swing past the building for a closer look. Driving under the expansive portico, he slowed the car to read a sign by the main door. NOT A STUDENT ENTRANCE was boldfaced black on white signage.

"*Well, Trudy, I guess they won't let you have the run of the place,*" said her father.

"*Now Ed, don't upset her. There are two side entrances as well. The brochure said this building holds a world class library.*"

"*Let's see.*" Ed stopped the car and got out. "*Come on Trudy. Dad wants to check this out.*"

"*It says no students, Ed.*"

"*Yeah, Marge, but Trudy isn't a student yet. Come on Marge, you too.*"

The three entered the main admin building's cavernous foyer. It had marble flooring and a wide double-circular staircase, going up three floors; and a massive crystal chandelier.

"*These ladies know how to live, don't they?*" quipped Ed.

"*Come on. Ed. let's go up the stairs and look at the library. Then let's leave. Maybe we shouldn't be in here.*"

"They want our money, don't they Marge?" Ed barked his retort and climbed stairs. When the three got to the second floor they opened a large French door entrance to the library. It was stunning; an immaculate showcase every bit as impressive as a college university library. There were stacks after stacks of books. Sections were marked for Literature, Sciences, Biology, History, Mathematics, Physics, Biographies and Autobiographies, Poetry, Young Children's' Books, Animals, Theater Arts, and so on.

"Well, that should convince you, Ed. It is a first-class place. You can see that," Marge opined.

"Yeah, I get it," said Ed. He walked toward the spiral staircase in the center of the second floor and began climbing it.

"What are you doing now? Marge asked."

"Looking, Marge, I'm an engineer, remember? I like to look at stuff, up close and personal. I'll be down in a minute."

After about five minutes Ed came back down the stairs. *"There's three buckets up there,"* he said.

"So? Trudy isn't coming here to study buckets." Marge replied.

"Nobody studies buckets, Marge; but buckets tell you something. If you know about buckets, they'll tell you a hell of a lot. They tell you this place has roof leaks, and they need to fix them. There's molded carpet surrounding two of the buckets, but not the third. That bucket catches a new leak. The roof has had leaks for some time."

"So?"

"So, maybe they are cash strapped, like a lot of schools. Maybe, despite what their brochure says about how financially solid they are, they ain't all that solid; but it's private so we don't get a look at their books, unless we're on their board of directors. I get that. Do you want to go on their board?"

"No, and they wouldn't ask me anyway. We haven't even had Trudy here for one semester."

"Yeah, I get all that, but just keep your ears open and ask unobtrusive questions when you're with some of the other mothers, okay?"

The Blantons drove around the grounds a while longer before they went to the matriculation area. The school's classroom building, and its dormitory building were laid out as part of a triangle, with the admin building as the apex. Behind the admin building was the gymnasium; and behind the gym building was the natatorium building. The school had produced many Olympic gymnasts and swimmers over the years. That was one of its big draws for recruiting students. Every mother dreamed her daughter would win an Olympic gold medal and become world famous. Adjoining the natatorium was a huge athletic field. It was easily a hundred fifty yards long and a hundred yards wide. A cinder and clay surfaced running track bordered the field in a huge oval. There was even a ten-yard square clay-surfaced warm up area, huge sand pits for volleyball, and ten tennis courts. Ed surmised the track bordering the field measured nearly a half mile distance.

"Look, Trudy," exclaimed Marge, *"here's where you'll come to play soccer and field hockey and volleyball and lacrosse and tennis. And you'll be able to run to your heart's content. You'll like that, won't you dear?"*

"I guess so," replied an intimidated Trudy. *"Will I have to do all those things?"*

"Well, I think they'll want you to learn sporting things like that with all the girls your age and I think they'll expect you to give everything a good honest try to see what you're good at. That's only fair, Trudy. Mommy and Daddy are paying a lot of money for you to come here, so it's only fair that you try lots of things to see if you like doing them, sweetheart. You want to be fair to Mommy and Daddy, don't you?"

"Okay. Yeah, I guess so," Trudy sounded resigned to try her best.

"Great," said Marge. *"That's my good girl. Now let's get over to the matriculation place."*

Driving to matriculation, Ed circumnavigated the school's grounds. Near the rear service entrance where food and supplies were delivered, he noticed that the ground rose to form a barrier berm. He got out of the car and climbed to the top of the berm. He noticed there was a sizable gap between the iron fencing and the berm, making it unlikely that anyone would try to climb the iron works from the outside to jump in. The risk of a broken leg or ankle was real. Ed scratched his head when he noticed an eight-foot gap in the fencing. There was a rear gate big enough to drive a truck through. It was locked, but it had a pedestrian gate within the larger gate. The pedestrian gate was wide open. A sign on it said: PRIVATE PROPERTY, NO TRESSPASSING. A dirt road led from the rear gate to a notch in the berm.

Back in his car Ed mentioned that the road through the berm led to two small, padlocked buildings. *"Those must be where they store their supplies and food for the cafeteria,"* he noted to Marge and Trudy. *"But I don't think they're fooling anybody with their berm and their iron fence. Anyone can just walk in and out of the place through that back pedestrian gate."*

"Ed, let's talk about this silly fence business later. We need to get Trudy to matriculation." Marge had a way of moving things along.

"Thank you, Mrs. Higginbottom," said Marge to the portly middle-aged deputy headmistress. The Blanton's and Trudy had finished Mrs. Higginbottom's introductory tour of the campus. *"You've showed us around and signed Trudy up for her classes and showed her how to get where she needs to go. Trudy has seen her new room on the second floor with its views of the grounds and the forest beyond."* Marge turned to address her daughter. *"You like your new room a lot, don't you Trudy? You have your own locker for your things, your own desk, and a very nice sized twin bed with*

a comfortable mattress and a brand-new down pillow. You'll be very comfortable here, sweetie."

"Yes Mommy. It's a nice room," responded a timid Trudy.

"Do you have any other questions for Mrs. Higginbottom, Trudy?" asked Marge.

"No, Mommy. Are you going to stay a while, Mommy?" Trudy was apprehensive and her fear of separation was rising.

"Well, Trudy, if you don't have any questions for me, may I ask a question of you?" Mrs. Higginbottom understood nervous little girls very well. She anticipated this and had just the right remedy. Trudy looked up at the Assistant Headmistress with curiosity in her eyes.

"How would you like to meet your new roommate for your first year at Wexler Baxter, Trudy? I know she's anxious to meet you. She can't wait to have a new playmate. Let's go find her."

"Okay," said a tremulous Trudy. Everything was happening so suddenly. The poor child's head was swimming.

"Fine, then," asserted Mrs. Higginbottom. *"Mr. and Mrs. Blanton, and Trudy, will you please come with me?"* Obediently, the Blanton family followed Mrs. Higginbottom to the third registration table away from their own. When they arrived, Mrs. Higginbottom announced them.

"Ahem," she cleared her throat. *"Mr. and Mrs. Blanton, I'd like you to meet Mrs. Joseph Maloney. Mrs. Maloney, I'd like you to meet Mr. Edward and Mrs. Marge Blanton."*

"Call us Ed and Marge," giggled Marge when the woman at the registration table looked up at them. Mrs. Maloney seemed piqued that she needed to break from filling out a form. She frowned, placed her pen resignedly upon the form, and folded the page over it so as not to lose her place before she stood to meet the Blanton's. She was in a hurry to register her daughter and return to Colorado; and obviously annoyed by Mrs. Higginbottom's and the Blanton's interruption. She wore a tightly fitting black business suit with faint blue pin

striping; a noticeably short skirt for business attire; blue polka dotted silk stockings; a white shirt with opened collar and a gold neckless chain.

Marge noted her heels' length. They were too high and too spiked for an afternoon outing; more appropriate for cocktail hour and evening out. The Maloney woman wore no hat. Her golden blond hair was tied up in a bun knot, fastened atop her head, revealing a stunningly beautiful face that stayed long in male memories. Her lips were heart shaped and perfectly formed. Her cheekbones were highly placed and accented by perfectly spaced, sharply clear, brightly blue eyes. Her frown relaxed and her eyebrows lifted as she offered her hand to Mr. Blanton. Her eyes and mind quickly assessed Ed:

'He's the tall, rugged type. Triangular, muscular body build; early forties; handsome, the guy that gets things done kind of face complete with stunning chiseled jaw; determined to have his way with men, likely women too; an alpha male; confident in himself; a leader. Yum. I want him.'

Mrs. Maloney positioned her body between Ed and Marge, blocking Marge's view of her face. The slow way that Ed took Mrs. Maloney's hand while melting his eyes into hers made Marge Blanton instantly uncomfortable. In the back of her mind a silent alarm signaled her to get her guard up. Marge didn't see the Maloney woman's annoyance vanish; replaced by a warm smile. She didn't see the woman arch her breasts and wet her lips, signaling interest in physical intimacy with her husband. Marge didn't see what happened inside the meeting of hands, either. She couldn't feel the secret soft, circular rubbing motion of a finger against her husband's palm. She couldn't know the lascivious thoughts secretly transmitted through aroused blood, nerves, and eyes through her husband's hand:

'Hey, big guy, my fingers are telling you I want you. I'm serious. I'm a player. I don't want to be standing here in a stupid business suit playing nice-nice with your dumpy wife. I want to be in a hotel room

with you on top of naked me, except for my panties. I want to feel your big hands squeezing my tits and my ass while you're kissing me. I want to feel your teeth tugging on my nipple buds. Yeah, I love to play. And I want to feel that instantaneous thrill surge when your hand reaches into my panties and touches my playful fuck happy hamster for our first time. And then I want you to peel my black lace panties off me and spread me open with those huge hands of yours.

'And I want everything that comes after that, too. I want to feel your tongue strokes over my clit and your cock thrusting over my vag lips and reaching way up inside me. I want to Kegel squeeze your cock; squeeze, relax, and repeat until I drive you out of your mind over me in ways your wife will never understand. Oh, did I forget to mention? I want to suck your cock and make it fall in love with me. I want it to become my personal joy toy. And I want to show you all the ways I can get it hard. I want to do these naughty things with you for hours.

'Hey! You're the big guy. You're the alpha male. That's written all over you by the way you stand, the way you look, and the way you present yourself. You know my information will be on file at the school admin office; so, you know how to find me. I know you'll want me more than this frumpy wife who's hanging on you. Make it happen for both of us, big guy. I'm counting on you. Think of something. I'll be waiting for your call.' Then, using her middle finger, the woman gave three light tap punches into Ed's palm, seductively signaling that her finger rubs were intentional. She spurred her chosen stud horse and expected him to respond.

After her elongated connection pause with Ed Blanton, the Maloney woman stepped back to look at Marge. She extended her hand to Marge and widening her smile. Her broader, convincing smile beamed sincerity and melted Marge's ice. It made Marge feel more at ease. Susan had extremely high emotional intelligence. She was an exceptional seductress, confidence artist and manipulator of others' feelings. She had, in less than a minute's time, captured Ed's sexual desires and transferred them from Marge to herself. She would next communicate a sincere misdirect that Marge had nothing to worry about. And Marge, having no basis to confirm her unease, would be forced to tentatively accept it.

"Please. I prefer to be called Susan. Susan Mallory," said the woman. *"I'm Marty's mother. I'm not married. I've decided to return to using my maiden name of Mallory; although Marty will be registering with her birth certificate name of Maloney."*

"Oh, I'm very sorry, said Marge. Have you been divorced very long?" Marge's presumptive question seemed logical enough to Ed. The alluring woman's dress, movements, and hand signals told him she was a cat on the prowl.

"No, Marge, I'm widowed. It has been a difficult ordeal. I've had to heal my emotions from a terrible loss. I'm trying very hard to find my way in life as a single woman. That's how things are for me now. It's challenging. I can't dwell on feeling sorry for myself. I must find the strength to move forward. I'm putting a sad experience behind me."

"Oh, you poor dear, I'm terribly sorry," Marge voiced her heartfelt sympathy. *"If there's anything we can do, anything at all, please call us. We only live a half hour away from here."*

"Thank you, Marge. You're very kind to offer, but I won't be calling you." Now Susan's smile bore a hint of condescension punctuated by certainty. *"You see, I'm from Colorado. I'll need to be away, working. I'm leaving Marty here, placed in the care of WEX's full-time tuition, room, and board program. I believe that's the very best I can do for her."*

"Oh, I see. Well, Ed and I certainly wish you and little Marty well. We're here for you if you want our help with anything." replied Marge. Her voice betrayed a crestfallen sympathy for Susan's daughter, Marty. At the same time, she felt an inner sigh of relief that this prowling female, who dressed herself to the nines and wore outrageously sexy appeal as business attire, would be two thousand miles away from Ed. But socially conscious, practiced card player Marge

wore her best outwardly understanding face while returning Susan's smile. She didn't want the brazen ally cat to suspect she was secretly saying to herself: *'Thank God you don't live around here, Bitch!'*

Other adults and Trudy had not noticed; but Marty, from her short distance away, did observe the prolonged interaction between Mr. Blanton and her mother, Susan. Child Marty didn't appreciate the significance of that telling moment. Her formative mind only noted that it seemed unnaturally elongated; and she remembered that. Only later would she link it to two additional interactions she would observe between her mother and Ed Blanton. At her tender age, Marty was only beginning to glean insights into the ways of adults; particularly how powerful men behaved around her mother.

Mrs. Higginbottom had great timing sense about awkward social moments. School administration wanted parents to harbor no resentments toward other parents. WEX was one big happy family.

"Trudy, sweetheart, you wait here," Mrs. Higginbottom burbled. *"I'm going to find a special little girl and bring her back here to meet you. You and she will have lots of fun together. She'll be one of your new roommates. She'll stay here with you from Sunday evening through the end of classes on Fridays; and she'll be in most of your classes with you, too. I'm sure you will become great friends."* Mrs. Higginbottom chirped her resolute confidence in her most good-natured voice; then she bustled away to an area where several children were playing in the grass. She grasped a tall, dark-haired girl by her arm and walked her back to Trudy and the three parents. She maneuvered the little girl by her shoulders and placed her squarely in front of Trudy.

"Trudy Blanton," she announced with brimming enthusiasm, as if she was presenting Trudy with a new pony, *"I'd like you to meet your new friend and roommate: Marty Maloney."*

CHAPTER FOUR

I know a maiden fair to see, Take care! She can both fair and friendly be, Beware! Beware! Trust her not, she is fooling thee! Beware! (Henry Wadsworth Longfellow: The Arrow and the Song)

MARTY

"Did you get a good look at her roommate?" Marge couldn't stay silent for long.

The Blanton's were driving away from WEX. For Blanch, it was a momentous time; leaving her precious little Trudy in the hands of strangers. Both parents had their private thoughts about matriculation day.

"Yeah, I saw her. What about her? She's a little kid." Ed was a gruff, plain-spoken man. He often spoke brusquely to Marge. He liked keeping his private thoughts to himself. This was one of those times. He exhaled a noticeable exhale. He did that when he wanted to signal Marge that he didn't feel like talking about something. He suspected Marge was about to go on one of her jags about some nonsensical thing that would end up being a ridiculous waste of time.

"Did you notice how much taller she is than Trudy? She's a good three inches taller, Ed. And did you see how she immediately hugged Trudy; and how hard and tightly she hugged her when they were first introduced, like she was clinging to her? And did you see how she lifted our Trudy up off the ground and bounced Trudy's body against hers while giving Trudy that monster hug? She's a very strong kid, Ed. She

almost crushed our little Trudy. What kind of kid hugs another kid like that?"

"Yeah, I saw that. She looked like a healthy strong kid. Maybe she just had a growth spurt or something, who knows? She seemed genuinely happy to have a new friend, so she hugged Trudy hard. That doesn't mean anything, Marge. She's not in your bridge club where you peck-kiss each other on your cheeks. She's just a kid. I think we saw Trudy getting an honest hug. Look at it as a good sign, Marge. The kid honestly wanted to be friends. If the kid had extended her hand to shake hands, then you'd be complaining that the kid was stiff and unfriendly. I was glad to see Trudy get that hug. It told me the kid really wanted to be friends. Maybe the kid didn't have many friends where she came from. Didn't Higgy say they were from Colorado?"

"Yeah, Ed, they were from Colorado. Ed, I've told you I wish you wouldn't call Mrs. Higginbottom, Miss Higgy. It sounds so disrespectful."

"Geeze, Marge, you are so sensitive lately. Listen, this whole WEX thing was your idea. You said you wanted the best for Trudy. We found the school together. You got me on board with your program. I just wrote them a big check, the first of many, so don't go getting your back up, Marge. They need us, and they need our money. I'm sure of it. Their fucking roof leaks. Nobody who knows anything about building maintenance allows a roof to go on leaking like that. It eventually destroys the entire building. I say the place is great on image and low on money. What would you have me call Higgy, Mrs. Ham Sandwich?"

"Oh, Ed, just stop with this, I don't like to fight with you. You know how upset I get when we fight."

"I'm writing the fucking checks for their glorified shit show, Marge. I'm not going to be lapping up their image bull shit. I'm calling her Miss Higgy as long as I'm writing those checks."

"Okay, Ed, have it your way. Just don't call her Miss Higgy to her face."

"All right. I won't Marge. You know I'd never do that."

"That's my good boy. Here let me kiss your cheek." She leaned over to the driver's side and planted a warm smacker on Ed's cheek. That seemed to settle everything between them. They drove along for a few minutes longer in silence.

"Ed, did you get a really good look at that Marty girl?" Marge's thoughts couldn't stop churning.

"Yeah, Marge, what's troubling you now? I got a good look at her, all right? She looked like a little girl, all right? What in the fuck was she supposed to look like?"

"No, Ed, something was not all right. Didn't you see anything strange about her?"

"No, Marge, I didn't see anything strange about the little girl. She's a little girl, for Christ's sake, that's all. What's gotten into your bonnet about that little girl?"

"Come on, Ed, you saw her. What did you see?"

"Damn it, Marge, I saw a nice little girl who wants to be friends with Trudy. What do you think you saw? How about a dinosaur? Maybe a space alien? Maybe a fire breathing dragon? Maybe a secret witch from Mars? What? Stop all this hinting around bull shit and tell me what's bothering you."

"That girl's hair wasn't normal brown hair, and her eyes weren't normal brown or black, either. And did you notice that red streak in the front of her head, up by the corner of her forehead?"

"So, what's the big deal, Marge? Lots of people have dark hair and dark eyes. Why do you give a flying fuck about what color the kid's hair and eyes are? What's normal about hair and eyes anyway? And, so what if the kid has a small patch of reddish hair?"

"Because her mother's maiden name was Mallory and her married name was Maloney. Those are both Irish names, Ed. How many little Irish girls have dark hair and dark eyes from a blonde mother, like that girl's hair and eyes, Ed? And that red streak wasn't some dye streak.

That was natural hair, but it was different, somehow, like it grew out of a birthmark on her scalp or something."

"I don't know. For Christ's sake, Marge, maybe some black guy got into widow Mallory's woodpile somehow; or maybe some Irish kids do have dark hair and dark eyes like that. Who the fuck knows.... And who cares? I've seen dogs and cats with different hair colors all over them, Marge. Maybe some people have that, too. It must be that we just don't see it that often."

"No Ed!" Marge barked at him. She did that when she was serious about something. *"That hair was not black hair from a black ancestor. It wasn't that kind of black hair. It was not their kind of coarse, thick black hair. It didn't have any trace of kinky curls in it, either. And it didn't have that deep inky blackness like the dark peoples' hair have. It was soft, lustrous brownish off-black; and thin, wispy-stranded, silky hair like a lot of Jewish women have. That girl had that beautifully deli-cate Jewish fineness about her hair. I recognized it immediately. It turns some men on; drives them crazy; makes them want to put their hands and faces in it. I know it does. And that reddish streak will really draw men's attention to her hair. It's very noticeable. It kind of draws you into her face. And she has that Jewish, smooth skin; and a porcelain looking face, Ed. And her eyes were slightly wide set, like the mother's eyes, but hers had that look of soft brown pools that make a man want to dive into them and lose himself in them. That Marty girl's eyes are Jewish eyes, Ed. I'm telling you, Ed, that Marty girl has a Jewish bloodline. I'm sure of it."*

"Marge, for Christ's sake, just hear yourself talk! She's a five-year-old kid. She's not going to be turning men on anytime soon. I can't explain her red hair streak. Who the hell knows? Why must you obsess over this kind of shit? Hell, maybe two different guys were fucking Susan Mallory on the same day that Marty got conceived. So what? She's a nice friendly kid, Marge. Just be happy with that."

But Marge couldn't let go of the subject. When she got onto something, she chewed it like some dogs chew a bone, until there's nothing left to chew. *"Don't be ridiculous, Ed. When a female egg gets impregnated with a sperm it immediately shuts out all the other sperms. The kid cannot have two different fathers. It's biologically impossible."*

"Oh yeah, did you get a good look at the kid's mother? She was like majorly stacked, as in one very hot babe. I could easily see two guys fucking her on the same day. Why not? Hell, a lot of guys would."

"You would too, huh?"

"Come on, Marge, I didn't say that. I'm just saying two guys could have nailed her on the same day."

"That's not possible, Ed. I remember from biology class."

"Oh yeah? Well, it's like this, Marge. If a wide receiver is catching a pass on a slant passing route across the middle, behind the inside linebacker, and he gets nailed simultaneously by both the corner and the safety, he gets tossed up into the air like a helpless rag doll; gets his body bent in half, backwards; then spun around before he lands on his head. He gets his bell rung by two guys at once. He doesn't know who hit him first. It's brutal. Who gets credit for the tackle, Marge? The safety and the corner each get a half tackle, Marge. They both get him. Fucking can be the same way, Marge. Two sperms from two different guys could have nailed that egg at the same time. Sex can be brutal, too."

"Sex isn't football Ed. Is that all you ever think about? Sex and football? That's not how conception happens in biology, Ed. One sperm always wins, and the egg shuts down immediately."

"I'm not buying your biology crap, Marge. I see science guys getting stuff wrong all the time. That's why we engineers build prototypes and test their theories, because the theory guys can get things fucked up. Engineers make sure the final product works for real. That's the real world, Marge. I'm telling you, there were two sperms; two determined little guys that both were dead set on slamming Susan's egg; and they both nailed that little fucking egg at the exact same time.

"Maybe one guy started fucking her in the morning and the other guy nailed her in the afternoon. Maybe he finished her good. Maybe the first guy's sperm ran slower than the second guy's sperm, but both guys got their sperms there at the exact same time. WHAM! SLAM! Just like that corner and that safety both nailed that wide out; exactly at the same time. Those two little fuckers just got in there and hammered that egg like it was a piece of meat wide out; banged it silly before it could shut either one of them down. Those little fuckers nailed that egg, Marge. Nailed it! It happens, Marge. It's like a photo finish in horse racing. Sometimes you have a draw. That's why you get two headed goats and five-legged sheep. I know what I'm talking about."

"That was not my point, Ed Blanton. Could you please take your mind off of how many men were fucking Susan Mallory on the same day, for just one moment and listen to me?" Marge knew it was time to deflect the conversation. *"Mrs. Higginbottom assured me when I first interviewed the school that they absolutely did not have any Jews or Blacks in their school. I'm starting to have second thoughts about their admissions policy, just like you seem to be having second thoughts about their finances."*

"Okay, Marge. Relax, tomorrow I'll call Webster. He's one of my best lawyers. He can check out anybody, even if they are from Colorado. I'll have him run down the Mallory woman, and her dead Maloney husband's family to see if there was another marriage, or an adoption, or a Jew or a Black somewhere in his or her ancestry. Will that make you happy?"

"Yes, darling husband, thank you. I'd feel better if we checked, just to be safe for our little Trudy. I need to be able to tell my friends that Trudy is safe when they see her with that girl. And I'm sure they will eventually see them together. Let's stop at the Country Club for cocktails and dinner, dear. I'm exhausted from all the stress of leaving Trudy at the school without us. I must have a martini."

A half hour later, at the club, the subject of Marty and her mother came up a third time. *"Ed, darling,"* said Marge while sipping her martini, *"didn't anything about Susan whatever her name is, and the way she was with her Marty child strike you as odd?"*

Ed was chewing on a bite of prime rib. He spoke with his mouth full. *"Oh, Jesus Christ, here we go again!"* He slammed his knife and fork down on the table. Their plates lifted slightly and clattered back into position. A few neighboring diners looked at them from their tables, paused momentarily, then resumed eating. *"Now what, Marge? What? What?"* Ed's voice was elevated. Nothing annoyed him more than Marge's incessant questioning while he was trying to eat.

"It's the way they were with each other, Ed." Marge's voice was soft and pleading now, as if she was trying to make up for Ed's outburst. *"There was no affection between them. Susan is Marty's mother. She was leaving her daughter off two thousand miles away from home, and she showed no sadness about the two of them separating. And Marty hardly even looked at her mother. When she did, she gave her mother a 'How can you do this to me?' kind of look. I saw that look in little Marty's eyes, Ed. And that mother, Susan; why Ed, she couldn't wait to get those forms filled out and get away from there. It seemed like she couldn't stand being with her own child for a minute longer than she needed to. Susan never even referred to Marty as 'my daughter.' She only mentioned her to us as 'Marty.' Now, that's a mother who doesn't care about her child, Ed. And, ask yourself this, Ed, what kind of mother sends her kid to a school two thousand miles away?"*

"A mother who wants the best school for the kid," quipped Ed.

"I'm not buying that, Ed. There are plenty of good private schools out west."

"Maybe they aren't as expensive as WEX," quipped Ed a second time. He shrugged his shoulders and cut into another piece of prime rib.

"Wrong, Ed. Some of those mountain schools are just as expensive or more expensive than WEX; and they are just as exclusive as WEX. But, if you drew an arc of schools that were over fifteen hundred miles from Plaintown and selected only those schools that charged the top one percent of tuition rates, you'd only find one school: WEX! What does that tell you?"

"That the woman has money to burn, what? Who gives a shit about why some mother sends her kid two thousand miles away?" Ed was getting cynical.

"Partly right, dear. She has money. And she wants to be as far away from her child as possible. Marty is a hindrance to her somehow. Her daughter gets in her way. And we do need to give a shit, Ed, because that woman's kid is rooming with our daughter. We are Trudy's parents. Ed, please pay attention to me. I wish you'd stop eating and talking with your mouth full. And please look at me when I'm talking with you, Ed. You are being very rude to me, Ed."

Ed calmly laid down his knife and fork, finished chewing and swallowing a mouth full of steak, pushed back his chair, and looked at his wife. *"So, am I supposed to dislike this Marty kid because you think that somehow, she's a secret Jewess; a planted spy, encroaching on your country club turf, Marge; or are you telling me I should feel sorry for the kid because her mother is dropping her on her head? Why are we even doing this? I cannot do this female-world, brain-game, mind-flipping bull shit. You and your friends are like a bunch of cats, tiptoeing around on your little paws, sniffing at each other's asses, trying to figure out what one cat thinks about some other cat. It's all female fucking bull shit! I want to finish my steak and go home and watch football."*

"Stop it Ed. This is serious. Trudy is our only daughter; that's why we need to know what's going on here. We must love her and protect her, Ed. I need to know our little Trudy will be okay at WEX with that Marty girl being in the same room with her. She might try to corrupt

Trudy; teach her to lie and cheat; or even mouth breed with vaginas and penises. You know how they are, Ed."

"Stop it, Marge. Jews don't lie and cheat any more than anyone else. And what is this mouth breeding shit you're talking about?"

"It's when girls excite each other by kissing their vaginas, Ed. It's a dangerous trend. I don't want Trudy learning about it or doing it. I wish you'd worry more about your own daughter, Ed. Please take me seriously, Ed."

"Jesus! Enough! If you want something to worry about, Marge, why don't you worry about something real? That fencing and berm by the service entrance won't stop anyone from walking onto school grounds. There's a big gate back there for supply trucks. And there's a pedestrian gate within the vehicle gate. That inside gate stays unlocked. All it's got is a no trespassing sign on it."

"That's terrible! What should we do? Should we go back and get her?"

Ed was relieved. He thought he had successfully changed the subject. He cut another piece of prime rib and tortured Marge, making her wait until he chewed it and swallowed it before he answered her. *"Well, I think it's probably okay. I'm not that worried about it. That must be how the cleaning people and the cafeteria workers come and go. They have a night watchman and a Doberman dog that walk the grounds at night. Likely, if there's a prowler, the watchman would intercept him. He packs heat. He should be able to handle anything. Besides, lots of schools we looked at had no fencing at all. Also, Trudy is on the second floor with the younger girls, so it's not likely some intruder would go to all that trouble when he'd have better pickings with the teen-aged girls on the first floor. So, I think, at least for now, our Trudy will be safe. But if you want to get your nose into things, why don't you go to the school offices tomorrow and tell them you want that pedestrian gate padlocked."*

"This is all very upsetting to me, Ed. You know how much I hate to get upset. I'll go ask them about the gate, but then how would the

servants come and go? Wouldn't everyone need a key? So, what would be the point of it? Someone could just forget to lock the gate behind them. It would just slow people down. I'm sure they've thought about all this gate issue, Ed. Now, darling, will you remember to call Webster in the morning?"

Ed exhaled again. Marge was back on her jag about the Marty girl, His diversion had failed. *"Okay." He spoke softly and nodded, "okay, Marge. I promise you that I'll get Webster on it first thing in the morning. You want to worry more about the Marty girl's influence on Trudy than about Trudy's physical safety. I get it. We'll soon know more about Marty and her mother than we know about our own sisters, okay? Can you be okay now? Can we please drop it now? I want to eat. I came here to eat, Marge. I mean, Geez Louise, Marge. I just wrote the check for half a year's tuition. It's nonrefundable, so unless Webster finds out that Trudy's roommate is an ax murderer, our Trudy is going to do at least a half semester at WEX. I refuse to take her out of there and put her in another private school. It's too late to change."*

Ed was a huge man. He had big hands, a massive head and an outsized appetite and ego to match. He angered quickly and cooled down slowly. He understood corporate politics and how to get things done. Unlike Marge, he was firm and decisive. If you were his friend, he could be the world's most lovable teddy bear. But if you became his enemy, he could be relentless, merciless, and brutal.

"We need to do what's right, Ed, you know that. You're Trudy's father."

"You don't need to remind me that I'm her father, Marge. Now you listen to me," he gruffed. *"If you take her out of WEX, Marge, she's going into public school; and that's final!"* Ed snarled. Now he was getting angry. He decided to provoke her. *"And by the way, Marge, in those dirty public schools they's got lots of 'dem little black nigger kids. They run around with their lunch boxes full of greasy fried chicken that they rub into their hair to make it even blacker and extra slick,*

greasy-messy and kinky; and all of them jig-a-boo kids play jungle bunny music on their boom boxes, and smack bubble gum; and they get that gum all over their faces." Ed waved his hands around his head, mocking Marge, as if he was rubbing imaginary grease into his hair.

"And all 'dem black boys with their big, fat, extra long dicks and their pants hanging down around their knees are all day lifting all the little white girls' dresses up and pulling down their panties, and finger fucking them while they sit and squirm on those black boys' laps." Ed lifted the tablecloth and peaked under it, mocking her further, as if he was a boy looking up a girl's skirt. *"And when the boys aren't fingering the little white girls, they're throwing their schoolbooks at their teachers and fighting with each other. And when they finish fighting, they chase all the poor defenseless little white girls into their girls' bathrooms where they can take down their panties and take turns fucking them really, really, good, Marge.*

"So, you can make your choice, Marge," Ed raised his voice to shouting. *"You decide where you want our little Trudy to be. I can only indulge so much of your society horseshit piled on top of your bridge club's bull shit in my one lifetime. God Damn it, woman, we have made our decision! And now we're going to stick with it!"* Other diners looked at the Blanton table again. Marge brought her napkin to her lips. It was her automatic default response whenever she felt embarrassed.

"You had eyes for that Susan woman, didn't you, Ed? Be honest."

"Hell no, Marge, why would I even think about screwing some beautiful dame who looks and acts like all she wants to do is fuck her brains out, when I can be having these ridiculous conversations with you about all your neurotic bull shit?" Ed's cynical voice had gotten louder than permitted in the country club's dining room. He didn't care that some neighboring diners began coughing uncomfortably. Ed lived by one mantra only. When he paid his good money for a membership to something he assumed he owned the place. And he acted like it. He rose from humble beginnings in a rough neighborhood.

He enjoyed a good brawl and he didn't let anyone push him around. He was a smart top executive at a major utility company. He worked with many Blacks and Jews, and he liked and respected all of them. He flatly rejected unjust falsely stereotyped categorizations. And he hated silly stupidity.

But Marge was from the newer Old South. She was rooted in post carpetbagger era rural Georgia. She never understood the racial and ethnic forces that coursed and blended in Ed's native Maryland. Her prejudices annoyed Ed. But he tried to be patient with her; continually trying to educate her about societal change. He'd married her. She bore him their precious darling Trudy, and for the sake of marital peace he normally indulged her. But tonight, he had reached his boiling point. She was no longer the romantic sexpot that he'd married. Tonight, after seeing Susan Mallory, comparisons between the Colorado woman and his wife played regrets with his mind.

He didn't care one iota whether the Mallory woman had a relationship with a Jew or a Black. The woman was hauntingly beautiful and mysterious. He'd gladly trade away Marge for Susan Mallory, if he could. That brief encounter, the way the Mallory woman played his mind with his hand, opened his eyes to his own reality. With each passing year, it was becoming harder for him to overlook Marge's hidebound prejudices; her constant double guessing and her endless whining and complaining. Their interests were fast diverging; his toward business, hers toward social status. Two double martinis after a long day of listening to Marge had brought their marital tensions to the surface. He desperately wanted her to shut up. Gin had that effect on him.

CHAPTER FIVE

I must be cruel only to be kind. (Shakespeare: Hamlet)
The joys of parents are secret and so are their griefs and fears (Frances Bacon: Of parents and children)

MOMMY'S MEAN

Marty had graduated from WEX School ten years before. Today she was inside her home, seated in her Italian tapestry chair, the one she called her thinking chair. Her thoughts traveled back in time to when she was a little girl. They were slowly coming back to her. Tomorrow, she needed to see David or else make up her mind to stop playing head games with him and just leave the Firm. Her eyes closed. Her voices were all temporarily silenced. She had locked them away in her mental closet, in her imaginary one room beach house on her imaginary shore. She was mentally at sea now, hearing only the soft folk tunes and songs of fishermen and lobstermen, rowing and sailing their boats while singing about whales and herring. She was losing her thoughts in the lives of working people who had tasks to do. Here, on her imaginary ocean, her mind and her memories came alive. She could be her real self. Her voices had no control of her anymore; not out here, far away from them and everyone on her imaginary isolated sea. She smiled, congratulating herself that she had found some peace time while her inner turmoil stayed quelled. Slowly, the memories she wanted to relive and cherish returned to her.

The back yard of her childhood home reappeared, exactly the way it had been. Everything about it was vivid in her memory. There was Mommy's cactus and rock garden. Marty had never liked it. It frightened her. It was unfriendly and threatening. She stayed away from it. She looked beyond it to her swing set. She imagined Daddy was there with her, pushing her on the swing. He pushed her higher and higher; until she could look over her shoes and see the sky. She deeply inhaled the imaginary smell of freshly cut grass. Daddy had just finished mowing their long green lawn. At the far end of it was her sandbox with her toys. The sand was slightly crusted, orange-brown. It had rained that last night.

"Will you cut the grass before you go?" Her mother had shouted the request, phrased as a question, to her dad about an hour before. Now she called again. He was pushing Marty on the swings. The two of them were having fun when Mother called.

"You can swing by yourself for a while. Don't go so high that you scare yourself. And remember to hang on," Father said. That was the last time her dad had pushed her on the swings. She let her swing come to rest; then she spun herself around in circles until the two chains that suspended her swing got bunched up into a big twisted stem; then she let herself go. She spun around and around until she made herself dizzy. When the chains unwound and her seat started to steady, her dizziness went away. Then she spun herself around in the opposite direction until she had the chains all bunched up again. Then she let herself go again, and spun around the opposite way until her head stopped spinning.

She heard Dad start the lawnmower. She felt like she needed to walk beside him that day. *"Now Marty, you can walk along with me, but you must stay back a little behind me and on this side of me, away from the direction that the lawnmower throws the cut grass,"* he cautioned. *"Sometimes a lawnmower can suck up a stone and throw it out really fast; and that flying stone could hit your eye."* Dad was good like that. Whenever a situation arose, he explained things to her. She trusted him. She knew he looked out for her.

The smells of freshly mowed grass came back to her. When her dad finished mowing, he always put the mower in his tool shed at the far end of the yard, in the corner opposite her sandbox. She had gotten tired of walking behind the mower. Now she sat on the back porch step and waited while Dad finished mowing. He smiled as he walked to the house; took a tennis ball from his pocket. Then he opened wide the back door.

"Here Baron! Fetch, boy! Fetch!" Dad's voice boomed. He held the door open as he threw the tennis ball far down the yard. Then Barron came. She heard him coming from the bedroom, deep inside the house. He howled and barked his distinctively sharp Barron bark. If a strange man heard Barron's bark, it would send shivers down his spine and make the hair on the back of his neck stand up. When Barron barked at strangers at their back gate, Dad would come and explain that Barron wouldn't hurt them; he was just being protective of her. This remembering day, Barron had come running. She remembered hearing his toenails clattering on the kitchen floor as he skidded around the corner from the family room. His sliding, skidding sounds gave way to his claws gripping their wood floor sounds as he propelled himself forward. Mother hated the scratches Baron made on the wood, but Dad didn't care about them. Most things that bothered Mother didn't bother Dad at all. Then, like a rocket shot from a cannon, Baron bolted through the back door and hurtled down the newly mown grass, chasing the ball. He was magnificent! She cherished her memory of that precious sight. Barron was in his glory. His muscled body rippled. His alert ears pointed forward. He was such a happy dog! He knew he had a purpose. He was important. He needed to fetch his ball. Barron was life as life should be.

'He's so fast and strong,' she thought at the time, *'Barron is the mightiest dog in the whole world.'* It gave her feel-goods to watch

Barron run like that. She knew he'd always protect her from every-thing and anybody. He was her wonderful, great, good dog and her best friend.

Barron wriggled his behind constantly whenever she came near him. *"His wiggles give you giggles,"* Dad often told her. *"He does his doggie wiggles because he's happy when he's with you,"* Dad told her that, too.

Dad told her that about Barron at least twenty times. Dad loved watching her and Barron playing together. He was an exceptionally strong, powerful dog with a very thick, muscular neck. He was so well muscled that his neck and body rippled like ocean waves when he wiggled and when he ran.

Marty smiled in her memories now. *'Barron must have wrig-gled his body so much because he didn't have much of a tail to wag,'* she thought. *'He was a magnificent animal and so friendly. He didn't understand his own strength. Sometimes he knocked me down when he played with me, but I didn't care. I laughed about it and Barron did too, in his smiling, playful boxer-dog kind of way. He drooled a lot too. But I didn't care about that either, even when he drooled all over me. He loved me. Love just burst out all over Barron. He couldn't help himself. He was always rubbing against me and licking my face. He'd run and twist his body, bending himself into half circles and rubbing up against me whenever I was near him. He showed his love that way.'*

He jumped into the air when her dad, Joseph, threw tennis balls to him. He'd catch the balls in mid-air; or he'd run them down and bring them back. Barron never learned to drop the tennis balls. He just held the balls in his mouth and refused to part with them. Even-tually Joseph reached into Barron's mouth and forcibly pried the ball away. Then he'd throw the ball again. Barron would fetch it; and he and her dad would repeat the entire process. They did their pitch and fetch game many times in a single afternoon. And when Barron wasn't chasing down a ball, the three of them would roll around in the grass hugging each other. Marty loved those moments. Mother was a damper to their fun. She always complained that they got their clothes grass stained and messy.

She remembered the times Daddy took her, Barron, and Mommy to the lake. They'd rent a cabin and Daddy would build a fire. In the first evening when they got there, they would always roast marshmallows in the fireplace. Daddy would read bedtime stories to her. Mommy sat in her chair, reading too. Mommy read business books to herself; but she seemed happy. Daddy would tuck her into bed and put Barron in her bedroom with her. He'd whine at the door for a while. He loved Daddy because Daddy played ball with him and gave him treats. Eventually, Barron understood that Daddy wasn't going to open her bedroom door to let him come out. That's when Barron stopped whining and jumped up onto her bed. Then he'd settle himself down and sleep by her feet. She loved knowing Barron was there with her. He made her feel safe and loved.

During the daytime she swam in the lake with Barron. He'd swim past her into the deep water to retrieve tennis balls that Daddy threw. He'd bring them back to Daddy and shake himself dry, sometimes shaking water all over Mommy. Mommy didn't like when Barron did that. She sometimes got mad about it. She even yelled at Daddy to move further away from her so Barron wouldn't shake his water onto her. Neither Marty nor her father gave much thought about Mommy's upsets at the time.

Memories of those good times became sparse after their last time at the lake. Father still played with her and Barron in their yard; and he still played horsey with her. He pretended to neigh and buck while on all fours with her on his back. He still read to her and took her places on weekends. But during those last few times she was with Daddy, the two of them went alone. Mommy didn't want to come along anymore. Marty remembered going to the zoo and seeing the animals. She remembered Daddy taking her for ice cream, lots of

times. They both loved ice cream. The last good memory she had
was how much she looked forward to going horseback riding with
Daddy. He told her about it. He had arranged everything. They were
going to go riding the next weekend. She was really excited about
going riding with her dad with Barron running along the trail beside
them. That's when her memories became terrible.

"*I hate you.*

"*You're stupid.*

"*He is a better man than you.*

"*Just try it and see what happens to you.*

"I wish you'd fall down the steps and die. I wish the rats would
come and eat you.

"You're not sleeping in my bed anymore. Go away on your stupid
road trips and stay away longer.

"Find yourself a whore while you're away from me, out on the
road. I don't care.

"Marvin will have security remove you from the premises. You'll
get thrown in jail.

"We're through, Joseph.

"I don't care what you do, just stay away from me. Leave me
alone.

"Do me a favor, Joseph. Please just go away and die someplace."

These were the sorts of upsetting things Marty heard when
Mommy and Daddy fought. She remembered covering her ears so
she wouldn't hear the mean things her mother said to her father. Then
Daddy went away on one of his road trips, but he didn't come back.
The next thing she remembered was coming home from a friend's
house. And Barron was gone!

"*Where's Barron, Mommy?*" she asked.

"*Well. I don't know, dear,*" her mother said. "*Did you look for him
in the yard?*"

"*Yes, Mommy, I've looked everywhere for him and I can't find him.*"

"Well, let's look again. I'll go with you." Mother said as they walked into the back yard together.

"Look, Marty! The back gate is open. Did you leave it open?"

"No Mommy. I didn't"

"Well, somebody must have come here and opened the gate then, because I didn't open it. It looks like Barron has run away from home."

She and Mommy put up signs in the neighborhood for people to see that there was a reward for Barron, but Barron never showed up. Barron disappeared about two weeks before the sheriff came to their door and told Mommy that Daddy died in a car accident. In that very short time, she'd lost both her father and Barron, her two best friends. She remembered feeling terribly lonely. She also noticed that Mommy seemed happier than she'd been in a long while.

Mother took her along to the office for a few days after that. She sat on the reception area floor and put picture puzzles together while Mrs. Rodriguez watched her. She remembered how Mother was always busy in her meetings with Marvin, the man who owned the place. Marvin even started coming to see Mommy at their house sometimes; and she remembered Marvin bouncing her on his knee a few times. He was okay as a person she was supposed to be nice to, but he wasn't like her dad. Marvin was much more interested in being around Mommy than in playing games with her. That made her feel uneasy somehow. He didn't much care about her, nothing like the way Daddy did. He never even put one single puzzle together with her. He just gave her hugs and kissed her on her cheek or forehead, but he never *did* anything with her. She remembered he always told her to be a good little girl. She didn't think he had any business saying that to her, but he always said it. He was just a different kind of man than her daddy was. But Mommy seemed to like him better than she had liked Daddy.

Then things got terrible for her. She felt like Mommy didn't want her around anymore. It seemed like Mommy had turned into a kind of cold person that she didn't know anymore. It was like Mommy's heart had left her. Then, Mommy picked her up from Grandmother Bessy Mallory's one day and told her that she found a wonderful school for her where there were lots of little girls her same age to play with. She remembered that everything happened fast after that. Life became a kind of blur. She sensed that, in Mommy's mind, Mommy had stopped living with her. Mommy's mind was living in some other place now; somewhere away from the two of them being together. Soon after that, she remembered being on an airplane with Mommy; then they were in a taxi cab and she was very tired; and soon after that they were at the Wexler Baxter School for Girls. She was introduced to Mrs. Higginbottom and Trudy that first day; and then Mommy left. So, except for Trudy, she was suddenly alone. She had no Barron, no Daddy and now, not even Mommy; and she didn't know anything about Trudy, this strangely quiet, shy girl that she was going to be living with for a good part of every week.

She first tried to make herself believe that Mommy was leaving her at WEX because Mommy had no other choice. She desperately wanted to believe that Mommy really loved her more than anyone or anything else in the world. But in her heart of hearts, she kind of knew she was only pretending and hoping that was true but that it really wasn't true. The realization began to sink into her mind that Mommy had ditched her here at the WEX school. Then, that realization began to stalk her thoughts. Then it started to eat at her. It made her feel sick at first. She kept asking herself if there was something wrong with her. She wondered why Mommy didn't love her anymore; but she couldn't figure out why that would be. Then, the realization started making her angry and resentful of Mommy. Whenever they talked, in the few times they did talk, Mommy kept saying how busy she was and how she needed to make all this money; and how Marvin was so demanding on her time; and that she'd call and write; and that they'd be together for Christmas; and how Christmas would come in no time at all. Marty remembered trying to have the best outlook about everything that had happened. But in her little girl gut, she knew she was missing something very important. That's when she started to believe that nobody loved her; that she had been dumped off and abandoned like a piece of trash that nobody had any interest in. She had come to understand that nobody loved her. And she was right.

Marty's young heart of hearts tried to come to grips with the fact that she was unloved. And that was a profound feeling for a little girl to have. She knew she needed to find a way to accept her circumstance and prepare herself to go through life on her own, without love or help from anyone. That's where her good memories ended. Her transition to naughty girl began.

At first, she didn't understand why she had sudden panic attacks and fits of crying. She wondered whether she was different; inferior somehow to the other girls. She chewed her nails. She created imaginary friends in her mind so she could talk to someone about her feelings. She didn't create names for these new friends. Those came later in the personas of Miss Promiscuity, Miss Shameless, and Miss Iniquity. But these imaginary friends arrived, complete with separate, distinctive voices, during Marty's emotional transition. Her rational mind tried making logical sense of the happenings that confused her and made her feel helpless.

She first tackled why nobody loved her. Was she, herself, the reason? Was it the way she looked or the way she moved or acted or the things she said? Was she forgetting to brush her teeth or comb her hair? Did she sound funny when she talked or when she seldom laughed? She considered whether she was perfectly normal, but everyone else was not. She considered that might explain why Mother rarely contacted her. She next turned her focus from herself to Mother. When she started asking herself about Mother, she began making progress. That led to discovering her own identity.

She tried to understand why Mother made her feel alone and apart as a child after her father died. Why did Mother make her feel unwelcome? Why didn't she feel the same closeness to Mother that she felt with Father? Why didn't the other WEX girls feel abandoned? Why did their mothers love them? Other girls' parents came to see them and take them away from WEX to do things with them. Why didn't Mother do those things? Why was she at WEX? Why couldn't she be in Plaintown so she could see Mother and go home with her? She didn't understand why other little girls' parents called them at their dormitory and talked with them on the phone for fifteen minutes to an hour; and laughed with them about family things; and made them feel like they were part of a family; and why Mother never did any of those things. Why did Mother want her kept out of her life? Why didn't Mother accept her and love her? Why was she made to feel she had no family?

Even Grandmother Bess stopped calling her. Marty had always believed Grandmother Bess loved her and cared about her. There were things about Grandmother Mallory that Marty didn't understand. After her father died there were days when Mother took her to stay at Grandmother Bess's while Mother went to work. Several of those days Grandmother Mallory went into her bedroom and closed the door, leaving Marty to play by herself in the living room. Grandmother Mallory screamed out loud behind her closed bedroom door. Then Marty heard Grandmother pound her fists on the top of her little secretary desk. When she came out, Marty could see that Grandmother had been crying. She would wipe the tears from her eyes and mutter that the devil ruined her family. Grandmother never explained why she said that.

Grandmother Mallory talked to herself. Marty often noticed her lips moved but she didn't put words in the air. One day, Grandmother Mallory grabbed Marty by her shoulders and looked, serious like, into her eyes and shook her back and forth. Then, Grandmother said that Marty's mother, Susan, was sleeping with Satan. That didn't make sense to Marty. She understood from her church school that Satan was the Devil. But she knew that her mother slept in her own bedroom, by herself. She even sneaked into Mommy's room one night to look for the Devil while she was sleeping. She looked all around Mommy's room and under her bed and behind the curtains to check for herself. She didn't see Satan anywhere. Now, far away at WEX, it became obvious that Grandmother Mallory didn't care about her anymore. That hurt in an especially hurtful way, like a connection to someone who loved her was broken. She thought maybe Grandmother Mallory had lost her mind or that possibly she had never cared about her in the first place.

Marty began wondering whether Grandmother Mallory was a phony sort of person. And that made her wonder whether Mother was also a phony person. Marty considered that possibly Grandma Bess had her Devil notions because she was crazy and that, possibly, Mother was crazy, too. For a time during her first WEX year, Marty wasn't quite sure what to think. Mother called sometimes; but she sensed that Mother called because she felt guilty about leaving her at WEX. She could tell that Mother didn't actually want to make those calls. After a while, Marty didn't like taking Mother's calls because she knew Mother was a fake sort of person who just talked about loving her, while not meaning it.

Marty noticed that Mother was more animated when she talked about her own life, especially about the things she did with Marvin. Mother was always telling her how she had to do this or that for Marvin, and how she had to go here or there with Marvin. It seemed like Mother, herself, had become a little girl and that she, Marty, had become Mother's Mommy. When Mother talked to her about how smart Marvin was and how much she was learning from Marvin, and how much money they were making together, and how she believed Marvin was falling in love with her, Marty felt like she wanted to throw up. Everything Mother said was about Marvin this and Marvin that. Whenever she heard the name Marvin, she felt like hanging up.

About this time, Maria, an older girl who became Marty's friend, told her that she wasn't thinking about her mother in the right way. Maria told Marty that her life would become more understandable when she started thinking of her mother, Susan, in the same way that Maria thought about her own mother. Maria told Marty that she should think of her mother, Susan, as if Susan was somebody's asshole. That made Marty laugh. It was the best laugh she had in a long time. Her new personality took root.

For the next several months she tried to understand what love was and the reasons Maria told her she should think of her mother, Susan, as somebody's asshole. Marty finally became objectively critical. She noted that her mother had stopped calling every week, like she had promised; and that her mother's letters stopped coming. Mother's behavior fit with Maria's assessment of both mothers. Maria had a philosophical maxim. She often looked at Marty, opened her hands, smiled, shrugged her shoulders, and nodded her head when commenting on one of their mother's behaviors. Maria then confirmed her maxim to Marty: *"Never expect or depend upon an asshole to do what a real person would do."*

With Maria's help, Marty marginalized the importance of her mother. This revised assessment happened at the same time that Trudy began playing more with Evelyn and Courtney and less with her. Those three played together every day after classes let out. They were 'weekday' WEXERS. Their mommies picked them up on Friday afternoons. Marty remembered how their mommies planned social events so their daughters would grow up socializing and partying together. The weekday girls went to each others' houses for sleepovers. They watched movies together on Saturdays and went to their Episcopal church together on Sundays. Trudy told Marty that

Episcopalians were Catholics that had money; and that she, Evelyn, and Courtney were Episcopalians, while Marty was merely an ordinary Catholic.

Maria gave Marty a retort for Trudy's uppity comment. Maria told Marty that all Episcopalian girls were assholes, too; like their own mothers were. Sometimes one or more of the Episcopal girls' dads took the three weekday WEXERS to a museum, or sporting event, or a fishing or sailing day on the Chesapeake Bay. Then, when Marty and Trudy were back in their room after Monday classes, Trudy would effusively babble on about the wonderful weekend she had with Evelyn and Courtney. Marty was never invited to join them. She remembered how hurtful that was. She felt depressed about her isolation; but those depression days happened before she began palling around with Maria.

She met Maria one day at Swim classes. Maria told her she stayed on campus, same as Marty. Her parents lived in West Virginia. Her father owned several coal mines. He had to stay near his mines to make sure everybody kept working, or else he could lose money; so, Maria's parents rarely came to see her. Maria was already in third grade, but she didn't care about their age difference. Marty was thrilled to finally have a true friend. Being older and wiser, Maria told her all sorts of things that Trudy, Evelyn and Courtney didn't know anything about. Maria said she knew a lot about a lot of things because she was seeing a shrink. Maria explained that shrinks know all kinds of things and that her shrink explained how older girls and parents thought about things. Shrinks understood everything about peoples' feelings, too. Maria saw her shrink every week. She liked seeing her shrink.

CHAPTER SIX

Fair as the rash oath of virginity which is first love's first cry; oh, baby Spring which flutteriest beneath the breast of Earth before thy birth (Coventry Patmore: The unknown Eros)

Maria, there's something mystical and inviting about your name (Unknown)

MARIA

Marty remembered how she befriended Maria. They didn't have the same classes together, except for Swim. Maria had difficulties with Swim, especially her butterfly stroke. Mrs. Raybenald, her instructor, held her back. Mrs. Raybenald was an imposing tower of lean, muscular physicality and a former Gold Medal Olympian. She was a physical fitness and swim fanatic. When she wasn't instructing her classes, she worked out on weight machines. She made Maria swim extra time with the First-grade girls after she finished swimming in her pre-Olympic class. That's where Marty and Maria first met.

"You're crying, aren't you?" asked Marty.

Maria was crying crocodile tears. Marty had come to class early. She heard Mrs. Raybenald screaming at Maria because Maria couldn't get her legs into the proper rhythm with her breast stroke. Her legs separated on her down push, preventing her from thrusting forward. She simply could not coordinate her leg movements with her back arch and arm extension to pull water under her.

"Get rid of that baby blubber," barked Mrs. Raybenald, *"then you'll move your legs better. You're not trying. Remember what I told you. When you're doing the Butterfly, you must believe you are a butterfly. Your arms must go way out, like butterfly wings, to pull the water toward you and push it under you. Feel the water lift you up like you are a butterfly. You must flutter up and fly forward. Your legs are together and straight behind you, pushing the water down, like the tail feelers of the butterfly. Out! Pull! Push under! Push legs down! Now out! Pull! Push! Legs down! Together, down hard! Push! Push! Push!"* Mrs. Raybenald was relentless and merciless. She drove her Swim girls hard, especially Maria. *"Keep your fat legs together, tightly close together. Push them down very hard. Push! Make your body ride over the water that your butterfly wings just pulled under you. Push! Push! Push! You can't be a big baby all your life!*

"Think before you take your next bite of food. Every time you have a spoon of food in front of your fat face, I want you to ask yourself, 'Do I want to have a fat uncoordinated ugly body all my life? How will I ever get my legs together to do the butterfly, unless I lose my ugly fat?' Every time you sit down to eat, ask yourself: 'Why am I so fat and ugly?" quipped the cruel instructor. Maria got out of the pool and sat on the cement, her legs dangling in the water. Marty came and sat down beside her, putting her legs in the water.

School administration knew their Swim instructor drove the Swim girls mercilessly; relentlessly, to near exhaustion. But they accepted her domination over the Swim girls and the inflexible rigidity of this iconic woman. No one dared to challenge Mrs. Raybenald or her methods. She walked with strident erectness. She was confident and sure of her methods. She believed that she knew everything that could be known about competitive Swim. She often remarked that it takes hard work to earn gold. And, she had produced five Olympic Gold Metal swimmers from WEX school. That was a majorly huge drawing card that admissions trumpeted to new parents and their daughters.

Hopeful mothers had starry eyes, visualizing their darling daughter taking the Olympic high podium to receive her coveted gold.

But Marty didn't care about Mrs. Raybenald's success at producing Gold Medal Olympians. She sat next to the crying Maria, feeling sorry for this sad, blubbery girl who had just had her persona crushed and kicked into the trash. *"Don't cry, Maria. She's just being mean. You can swim, all right? Many girls can't even swim at all. Don't let her make you feel bad. She's just being mean. She's just nasty to everybody."* Marty put her arm around Maria's shoulder, helping the older girl feel better about herself.

"I know. Thank you," sniffed Maria, looking at her new found friend. *"Mother brought me here because she wants me to become an Olympic swimmer. But I don't know how that will ever happen. I'm too fat. I can't get my legs together tightly enough to do a perfect butterfly. It's impossible. And I can't push them down hard enough to even do a good butterfly. I float higher in the water than the skinny girls, so when I reach out my wings to pull in water, I can't pull enough water under me to ride my body up and over the top of my water flow.*

"I'm afraid I'll never be able to perform a championship butterfly. Mom thinks I'll do great if I just keep working harder at it, but I can't get my coordination right and I can't get my weight down. She keeps me in Mrs. Raybenald's Olympic group and tells me to try harder. I get yelled at by Mrs. Raybenald here at school, and when I get to go home or whenever Mother comes here, Mother yells at me too. Mother says I don't try hard enough, but I do. I really do! I can't try any harder than I'm trying already. I keep messing up. I can't get my legs together and when I down push, the water always pushes them further apart; and I simply can't pull enough water under me with my arms to lift my body above my water flow. I'm sick of getting yelled at every time I have Swim class. I'm starting to hate Swim. I used to love Swim. I hate Mrs. Raybenald. I just hate her. All she does is make fun of me and yell at me. She's just another asshole!"

"And what are you two geniuses talking about? Huh?" barked Mrs. Raybenald. She had moved behind the girls without being noticed. Now she stood behind them. She overheard their whole conversation. The girls realized she was there but they didn't answer her.

"I don't ever want to hear you say the word 'can't' again Maria." Mrs. Raybenald's voice was rising. She did that naturally. It was her self-reinforcing anger amplifying personality trait. *"You can do anything you put your mind to do. You know that. I've told you that, haven't I?"* Maria just sat there at the edge of the pool, staring out over the pool, being completely unresponsive. *"WELL, HAVEN'T I?"* screamed Mrs. Raybenald.

Marty felt she had to do something to stop Mrs. Raybenald's merciless haranguing. She felt extreme, heartfelt sorrow for Maria's plight. She looked up at Mrs. Raybenald and voiced what she believed Maria surely felt in her own heart.

"Fuck off, you fucking bitch!" There, Marty had said it while looking directly at Mrs. Raybenald's startled face, speaking her command loudly, emphatically and with meaning. Maria looked at Marty. Her eyes widened and her jaw dropped. No one ever spoke to Mrs. Raybenald that way. Maria was shocked, but inwardly gleeful. Marty said what Maria herself had wanted to say for months. Mrs. Raybenald's sensibilities were shocked as well. No girl had *ever*, in all her years at WEX, confronted her this way. Not even a parent had ever challenged her authority this way; yet here was this skinny impertinent first grade child smacking trash street language. At her! The great Mrs. Raybenald! The Olympian! This impudent child had dared to reprimand her, the great, famous Olympic swim coach; the crown jewel of the WEX faculty. Her jaw dropped as her anger rose. Then her anger seethed until it boiled over. She couldn't restrain it for one second longer. Then she did it. She slapped Marty hard, right across her defiant little face, with its jaw set hard and its lips drawn tightly together.

"You will NEVER speak to a WEX faculty teacher like that again, Miss, Miss......."

"It's Mallory, Mrs. Raybenald," answered Marty, continuing with her defiant unflinching face as if the stinging sensation in her cheek didn't bother her one bit. She had begun calling herself by her mother's surname, thinking it might shame her mother into showing her more love. *"My name is Marty Mallory, Mrs. Raybenald."*

"Well!" snapped Mrs. Raybenald. *"You come with me right this minute, Miss Marty Mallory smarty pants. We are going straight to administration and you are being placed on report. You do not speak to a teacher that way, do you understand?"*

Defiant Marty refused to signify that she understood. She continued the confrontation. *"Fine, I'll go to detention, Mrs. Raybenald. But Admin is going to hear from me about how you bully Maria. They are going to hear how nasty you are to her. She can't do what you are telling her to do, and you know that. You are mean to her, Mrs. Raybenald. You know that, too. You just like to be mean."*

Undeterred, Mrs. Raybenald yanked Marty up by her arm that rested over Maria's shoulders, marched her to administration and placed her in detention for insubordination to a faculty member. Marty's pleas for Maria's well-being went unheeded by WEX administration. Mrs. Raybenald held high cards at WEX. Marty was only a student. She went to detention to serve the first hour of her ten-hour sentence. Mrs. Raybenald returned to the natatorium where she reigned supreme. She continued to bully Maria; now with an even greater determination to make Maria do what the poor girl physically could not do. Maria absorbed even more focused abuse from Mrs. Raybenald. But all the while she was absorbing Mrs. Raybenald's abuse, she thought about the skinny little kid from Colorado who came to her defense by speaking up for her. After Marty served her ten detention hours, Maria sought Marty out. Thereafter the two girls spent most of their free time together.

Marty thought back to that time, remembering that incident, smiling now and recalling how she and Maria became best friends at WEX. She remembered the many times they played together, went into town together to the general store for ice cream and flirted with boys from the nearby public school; and how they sometimes went to the beach when they got offers from boys that had cars; and the times they laughed and cried together; and when they compared notes about their puberty and their mothers.

CHAPTER SEVEN

Yet still we hug the dear deceit (Nathaniel Cotton: Visions)
Come forth into the light of things. Let nature be your teacher (William Wordsworth: The Tables Turned)

THE SCAM

Marty was at a tender age when her mother enrolled her at WEX. Her mother, Susan, gave little thought to the long seductive pause that her handshake had communicated to Ed Blanton. Certainly, Susan didn't contemplate that little five-year-old Marty would catalogue that fleeting interaction. Marge Blanton had noticed the pause. She noted that it was oddly unnatural. It made her uncomfortable. But she dismissed it from her list of things to harp about when she heard Susan declare she was returning to Colorado that afternoon. But Marty remembered the interaction. Her emotions still stirred over the loss of her father. Seeing her mother intentionally holding a strange man's attentions reinforced her sense of unease.

'Mommy didn't act right. What she did with Mr. Blanton was weird.' The interaction had disturbed Marty's impressionable mind. *'Mommy's eyes met and held Mr. Blanton's eyes. She smiled at Mrs. Blanton, but quickly turned her eyes back to Mr. Blanton. And Mommy seemed to turn her back to Mrs. Blanton so she could stand between Mr. and Mrs. Blanton and look at Mr. Blanton. Mommy was much friendlier to Mr. Blanton than she was to Mrs. Blanton. Mommy seemed to be letting Mr. Blanton know that she didn't want Mrs. Blanton there.'*

It was a little thing. The adults seemed to pass it off as a simple oddity to be quickly forgotten; but to a little girl who had just lost her daddy, and who had been whisked off to a boarding school two thousand miles from home, it was highly significant. And it was. It opened a peculiar type of wedge in Marty's mind. It was the beginning of her real-world education about how to read people. *'Mommy doesn't even pay that much attention to me,'* thought Marty. The interaction raised a concern, and she paid attention to it. She was too young to label it as a red flag; but it stirred something. It was Marty's first inkling of evil's presence. It resonated with what Grandmother Mallory said about Mommy sleeping with Satan. She thought more deeply. Something about her mother's explanations about why she lost her father and her dog, Barron, hadn't felt right. And her mother's interaction with Mr. Blanton didn't feel right either. Marty's first taste of distrust was served by Mother.

ED AND SUSAN

Two years after the Blanton's enrolled Trudy at WEX, Ed Blanton wrangled his way onto the WEX board of directors. He insisted whatever WEX did they did wrong. He assured them there were ways to do everything better. After hearing Ed harp about their leaky roofs, ridiculous fuel bills, outrageous tuition expenses and WEX girls' disappointing acceptance rates to the nations' top colleges, the school relented and offered Ed a seat on their board. Ed was not a typical passive board member. He aggressively looked for ways to improve the school, while subtly carving out a benefit for himself.

He discovered why WEX scrimped on everything except the cosmetic appearances of the place. The faculty members who controlled the board had adopted a Rabbi Trust Deferred Compensation plan. It allowed them to make maximum contributions into the plan without causing the school to deduct those contributions from the school's income. They wanted to take out huge salaries and make huge contributions to their deferred compensation plan. The pain of taxation for payments coming out of the plan would fall upon the plan's participants after they retired and began taking out money from their individual plans. Most of the faculty were near retirement age. Questions about their plan came up frequently at board meetings.

"I just don't think our investments will do well enough at this rate to allow us to retire anytime soon," opined an older math teacher.

"I have the same concerns," said an English teacher. *"I can't imagine how we'll take out enough to match our current salaries and have enough to live on after we pay the tax bill on our withdrawals. The plan was great for the deductions we got up front, but we'll get killed getting our money out of the plan. These investments just didn't do well. Look at poor Harry's case. He can't afford to retire. He's eighty-seven with stage three Parkinson's Disease; wheelchair bound, and still teaching ninth grade civics. We'll all end up like Harry if we can't find a solution to this."*

Ed listened with intensity. Most meetings were boring recitations of inconsequential expenditures and complaints, but this one was a door opener. Ed saw his opportunity. *"Let me make a few calls and get back to the board on this one,"* offered Ed.

His gut told him who could tackle the problem. He remembered the woman who intrigued him on Trudy's matriculation day. He had pegged Susan Mallory as a player. After Ed got the board's nod to solve their financial dilemma, he made the one call he'd been wanting to make ever since he first met Susan.

"Hello, Sustack Advisors, I'm Ed Blanton from Maryland, from the WEX School. I'd like to speak with a Ms. Susan Mallory……. Yes, she'll know who I am. Tell her I met her some time ago when our daughters matriculated at WEX. That's Okay. I'll hold for her. I can wait."

After a short while Susan picked up the phone. She remembered Ed. Her voice was very friendly. He posed the school's problem to her and asked if she could get back to him with a solution. She took his office number and told him she'd get back to him shortly. After two days, Ed's phone rang. It was Susan Mallory.

"Ed, I've worked through the WEX faculty's situation, and I have come up with a proposal. It will involve you forming a limited liability company as the managing director with investment authority. Can you handle that?"

Ed: *"Of course."*

"Very good." Susan went on to outline the details of her plan. Then she got the question she expected.

"And, as the plan's investment authority, I believe I'd be entitled to account meetings to explain how we're doing. Isn't that correct?"

"Absolutely correct, Ed, I'll be your account representative. You're entitled to four meetings a year; more if there are specific questions you have about our strategies. We could meet at least twice a year in Maryland and twice a year in Colorado. I'll be happy to make the arrangements for those meetings to be overnight meetings, if you'd prefer; and I only think it's fair for me to travel twice and for you to travel twice. Would that be acceptable?"

"Very acceptable," grinned Ed into the phone. Susan was speaking his language. Following the call, she sent him all the necessary paperwork to accomplish the scheme she planned. Ed would present the plan for ratification at the next board meeting.

Coincidently, Trudy Blanton and Marty still roomed together; and Marge Blanton had phoned Trudy the previous evening, telling Trudy that her father would be at the board meeting the following day. When Trudy heard about the board meeting, she told Marty. The two young girls decided to sneak into the admin building and listen while the grownups were talking. Trudy's plan was to rush her dad after the meeting, surprise him and give him a big hug. Marge Blanton expected Trudy to tell her what the board members talked about at the meeting. And Marge had her reasons. She had overheard

Ed talking with Susan on their home phone days before. Her radar warned her that another of Ed's extramarital affairs was headed her way. She would wait patiently to hear confirmation of her suspicions. The following evening, unbeknownst to the WEX board members, four little ears in the adjoining anteroom attentively listened to their entire conversation.

"Fellow board members," began ED, *"you are not going to pay taxes on your withdrawals from your deferred compensation plans. You are all going to retire as soon as we can find a buyer for WEX."* Ed went on to explain Susan's plan. It was ingenious. The school would be sold and the new buyers would agree to pay the tax bills of the retired employees' withdrawals from their deferred compensation plan.

The four little ears tried to follow what the adults were saying. It seemed complicated, but they understood the gist of it. The WEX board was going to screw the new owners. They continued to listen while Ed Blanton summed up the scheme. *"And in the hour after the examination room closes, Harry will insert our unanimous board approved resolution regarding WEX's tax liability for deferred compensation plan withdrawals into the board minutes, before the signature page. After the closing documents are signed, the new owners will be on the hook for your taxes."*

"But, isn't this illegal?" asked one of the members.

Marty and Trudy looked at each other in amazement. Trudy frowned. She wasn't following as well as Marty was. Marty whispered, *"They're screwing the new owners and they're making sure their paper trail is perfectly legal. Your dad put this together. He's very smart."* Trudy nodded her head. She was getting sleepy; but Marty stayed alert to the very end of the meeting.

"Well, actually, no. It isn't illegal," said Ed. *"The taxing authorities have recourse to the new WEX owners. It's not our responsibility to ensure that the buyers' lawyers do a thorough review of the minutes. The minutes will be available to them in the review room until the day*

of the sale. The room will close an hour before the sale is finalized so Harry can get all the books and records bundled together for delivery to the new buyers. That gives Harry a full hour to slip our approved tax resolution page into the minutes, before the signature page. Likely, the minutes will not be pulled out and reviewed again by the buyers until long after the sale. They'll have their new board and a new minute book. Likely, they'll just file the old board's book of minutes."

Marty looked at Trudy. *"Your dad is slick,"* she whispered.

"Wait a year before you make any withdrawals," commanded Ed.

"Why must we wait?" one member asked.

"We don't want the IRS to ask the school why they didn't get their tax money until after a full year has passed."

"Why?" The same member asked.

"Taxable year reporting reasons," replied Ed, sounding knowledgeable.

"Oh," said the member.

"What if something goes wrong? Who takes the blame?" asked another member.

"Harry," said Ed. *"He's in the late stages of his terminal illness now. By the time anyone figures this out he'll be unavailable for testimony and he won't remember a thing. Isn't that right, Harry?"*

Harry, the oldest, most ill board member, nodded.

"Will we be sued?" One board member had anxiety about such a scallywag plan.

"Possibly. But we'll win," explained Ed. *"The burden to disclose was met by allowing review of the minutes up to the time of sale. The burden of discovery and objection to terms of the sale is on the buyers."*

"What if they want a final look at the minutes?" asked the skeptic.

"Then we'll show them the final version and there will be no deal. We'd just be back to where we are right now. But it's not likely that they'll want a final look. That would show distrust and it would look like bad faith, especially since we'll be throwing a party to congratulate

the new owners and their legal team. We'll be having an open bar with great hors d' oeuvres. I'll open the bar an hour before the sale is finalized. I think their minds will be focused on great food and drinks, not on taking one last-second peek at our board minutes. Remember, when you are at the party, don't drink much. Smile, be friendly, and above all, keep your mouths shut."

"What about this LLC we're all buying shares in?" asked the skeptic.

"I've known them for a long time. They're a first-class outfit. I've been in contact with Marvin Sustack, the Firm's president and a Ms. Susan Mallory, the corporate secretary. They're very good with money, administration, and service. I'm certain of it. They're creative, too. This plan to save you from your tax hits was their idea. I'll be meeting with their representative four times a year and I'll be keeping a close eye on our investments."

When the little ears heard Susan Mallory's name spoken by Ed Blanton, little eyes opened widely. The two roommates stared at each other. Their little jaws dropped. Marty immediately suspected that there was more to this arrangement than simply a business transaction. Trudy was unsuspecting initially; but then Marty spelled out the implications of the arrangement for the two of them. Both girls now understood that they were now connected to each other by something bigger than being roommates. Marty's mother and Trudy's father would be seeing each other, regularly.

"Your dad and my mother will be working together. Can you believe that?" said Marty. She had a sinking feeling in the pit of her stomach. It turned her little girl's dismay into anger thoughts: *'How can Mother find the time to work on a deal with Mr. Blanton but not have the time to even call me? She must not want me anymore. If she loved me, she'd stop at WEX and see me, and she'd call me and write to me. Well, I'll show her. I know boys think I'm pretty. I bet I can get some of those boys to love me, even if Mother doesn't. I'm sure I can do that. Maybe boy*

love will make my hurt feelings go away. I won't be needing you either, Mother. You'll see. When I grow up, I'll prove it to you, too.'

Trudy dutifully reported her juicy bits of information to her mother during their phone conversation the next evening. Marge Blanton was displeased by what she heard from her daughter, but not shocked. She knew Ed often behaved like a dog off his leash. Nevertheless, the reality of this new unsettling circumstance pounded her mind repeatedly, like tidal waves from a tsunami shoving their flood ever harder against the shore. She retained and sifted Trudy's information for future purposes. She understood that Ed's new arrangement would likely continue for several years. She now saw her husband for the uncouth, unfaithful, lying lout that he was; a no-good son of a bitch. Her anger began to fester.

Marty was uncertain about the meaning of what she heard. She was still at an impressionable age, but the board meeting affirmed in her mind what she'd previously heard about her mother. Mrs. Rodriguez, Sustack's front office secretary, had told her that her mother, Susan, was a winner in business. Mother knew how to use board minutes and transactions and corporate structures to outplay her opponents and the tax authorities. Marty felt a tinge of pride. *'Mom is smarter than all these guys,'* she thought. She was prescient enough to usher Trudy away from the anteroom and her father, and out of the building. Marty thought it might be most unwise to allow Trudy to rush her dad and hug him. Something instinctively told her that could be a huge mistake. Her sense was to let adults do whatever it was they were going to do; and, as children, stay quiet about it.

There were no further questions. The measures Ed proposed were all adopted by the WEX board and their meeting was adjourned. *"They went for your plan, unanimously,"* beamed Ed on his follow up call to Susan. *"Congratulations, brilliant work. There will be about ten million dollars in the new LLC, coming your way for management."*

"The congratulations are all yours, Ed. You sold them on it. Great work yourself!"

"Thank you."

"And, Ed?"

"Yes?"

"I'm very excited about being your account servicing representative."

The WEX account was not Susan's first servicing arrangement. She had established four similar arrangements before this. Susan had come to WEX twice times during Marty's first three years at WEX, but then she had stopped coming. Her calls to Marty diminished steadily until there was no contact between parent and child; none at all.

In Marty's first six years at WEX she flew to Colorado for Christmas and summer breaks, but in her last six years Marty stayed every day at school. Maria became her best friend and constant companion during this prolonged time of abandonment. Together, the two girls tried to make sense of the adult world and boys. In the final six years that Marty was at WEX, Susan came to Maryland twelve times to see Ed about the investment account. She stopped to see Marty once.

One spring Sunday Marty and Maria had just walked around the corner of the natatorium, when Marty saw her mother. Ed's car was the only one parked in the WEX faculty parking lot. Susan drove a rental car up to Ed's car. She got out of the driver's side. Ed got out of the rental car's passenger side. Susan opened her car trunk, took out a folder and handed it to Ed. Ed placed the folder in his car's front passenger seat. Then he turned to face Susan. She walked forward, placed her arms around him and gave him a long soulful kiss. Ed grabbed Susan's ass through her silk tweed skirt, held his hand there and squeezed. Susan responded by pressing her body even closer to Ed's. They held their wanton embrace for a full half minute or so. Then, both Susan and Ed got into their respective cars and drove away. Marty's eyes were opened wide. She had observed the entire event. Suddenly everything about her mother made sense.

'I've watched you, Mother. I understand. You're very smart. You never cared about Daddy or me, did you? You know everything about a situation; then you work it to your advantage. You learned every possible detail about the WEX account. You worked with Ed Blanton to make the account fall your way. You put your feelers out to him years in advance. I still remember that day the two of you first met. You were patient. You waited for your opportunity. How many Ed Blanton's are there in your world, Mother? How ruthless are you, Mother? Does Mrs. Blanton know what you're doing with her husband? Your business is sex, isn't it, Mother? You trade sex for business, don't you? Does your precious Marvin know what you're doing? Is he okay with it; or is he a part of this? I see what's important, Mother. You're about money, aren't you? I now know I don't count; but you wait, Mother. I'll show you. You just wait.'

CHAPTER EIGHT

But love is such a mystery I can not find it out; for when I think I'm best resolved, I then am most in doubt (Sir John Suckling: Prithee, send me back)

PARENTS

"Can you take your mind back to remember what Maria said about her parents," asked the voice of Miss Iniquity.

"Yes, I try very hard to hold onto her words. I don't want to ever forget what she said," replied Marty.

"I'm not just trying to dredge up bad memories Marty, I'm only trying to reason with you."

"I know that. I wish I could talk with Maria right now."

"You can't. But if you can remember the things that she said, you can take away some lessons from her. People can be unpredictable. Just when you believe you know what they are going to do they can surprise you and do the unexpected."

"You're talking about David."

"You bet I am."

"Well, he already did the unexpected when he came to my door and told me he was going to rehire me."

"You make a good point there; but remember this is David we're talking about."

"Yes, I know."

"Do you?"

"I think so."

Marty's mind slipped away from Miss Iniquity. Thinking about her friend Maria was sweeter, lovelier, and more comfortable than thinking about David. Her mind traveled back in time to embrace Maria's words:

"When Mrs. Raybenald screams at me, she reminds me of my mother." whined Maria. *"I'm sick of Mrs. Raybenald. No matter what I do, she never stops screaming at me. Have you noticed how her whole voice changes when she's talking with me? It rises as if she's yelling at an animal that did something bad, even when I'm not doing anything."* Maria was fifteen then, pouring out her frustrations to her thirteen-year-old friend, Marty. It was that warm fall afternoon after swim classes. Maria wore blue pedal pushers and a pink moo-moo top. She looked good in moo-moos. She had blossomed out like a tasty looking bon- bon. Her moo-moo covered up her baby fat pretty well. When she dressed this way, attention was naturally brought to her face. And Maria had a beautiful oval face that hosted her little girl smile and soft blue eyes. But today the smile was gone. A puzzled little girl frown had taken its place. She and Marty were walking along the front entrance drive to WEX, kicking at the fallen leaves that would be raked into piles and carried off by the grounds people later that day. The road's border grass had not yet been cut and manicured to accent the majesty of WEX. It was still in its natural long blade condition with leaves on it. The two girls were enjoying their feelings of power, kicking up fallen leaves as they walked.

That was the time Maria finally unburdened herself to Marty about her parents. Until that day Maria had been secretive about them. Kicking at leaves seemed to help her open up. *'Must have been she was feeling a power thing,'* remembered Marty.

"I remember talking with Tommy Horn about my dad," recalled Maria. *"Dad left me with Tommy whenever Dad took me to the mine with him. I liked Tommy a lot. I always felt good about myself when*

I was around him. He always treated me like I was a real person and a friend. He was the mine manager for the Big Jenny. The Jenny was Dad's largest coal mine. It produced more coal than his other two mines combined. Tommy worked out of a little shack at the mine mouth. Dad left me with Tommy that day while Dad went into the mine with some engineers. Dad was upset about something that had to do with a new decline ramp the mine development crews had constructed so the production miners could access a lower seam of coal. I remember Dad was excited about this project. He said some things to Mom about it at dinner one night. It was supposed to make Big Jenny's output more than double. But the engineers had overestimated the water draw down rates; and the dewatering pumps weren't getting the water table to go down fast enough, like they were supposed to. So, Dad wanted to go deep into Big Jenny, himself, to look at the lower-level pumping station with his engineers. Dad never let me go into the mines because he said it was too dangerous for a little girl to be down there. I didn't want to go in there, anyways. Everyone that came out of the mine mouth was always totally dirty with black coal dust all over their faces and hands. So, I was inside Tommy's shack, talking with Tommy and studying the way he moved a big gold coin between his fingers while he talked. He did that constantly, automatically without looking at it, like he did it without thinking; almost as if he could do it in his sleep. I asked Tommy why he did that with that coin. He told me it was to remind himself to always be honest. I didn't understand what the coin had to do with being honest; but Tommy said that someday I would understand. He told me to come back and see him when I was older and graduated from WEX. Then he said he'd explain it to me. Whenever Dad was deep inside Big Jenny, I always asked Tommy a lot of questions; and Tommy always took his time to answer my questions between the times when his phone wasn't ringing. He got lots of calls from his mine foremen who were working miles away, underground, deep inside Big Jenny; ripping out coal from the faces of Jenny's coal seams.

"Tommy's shack had a padded chair for Tommy and two simple metal chairs for anyone else. The shack was up high on a hillside near the mine mouth. Tommy could look out his windows and see the area near the mine. Sitting in Tommy's shack I could hear the steady humming sounds of the huge conveyer belts bringing their steady streams of coal out of Big Jenny. The coal was loaded into huge trucks with wheels three stories high. Then the coal was trucked to the rail loading area where a steady stream of railroad coal cars passed under the loading tipple, getting filled to their tops with coal. After hundreds of rail cars were filled, the long coal train would slowly pull away and another coal train would come under the tipple to take its place. This loading of coal trains went on twenty-four hours a day, three hundred sixty-five days a year. It never stopped. Tommy said there was enough coal in Big Jenny to keep the coal trains filled for another three hundred years. Tommy told me that the Big Jenny produced enough coal to power the electric lights for the entire world. He said Jenny was the most fantastic mine in the world. Above ground, Dad owned hundreds of acres of land. There were acres after acres of coal stored in piles of coal ten stories high. The piles of coal went for several miles. Huge front loaders with monster sized front blades were always busy. Surface crews lifted the coal, then carried it to a ramp where they dumped it onto another conveyer belt that took the coal up to the loading tipple. Tommy said Dad wanted some coal kept in contract piles and some coal kept in spot piles. That way, Tommy said, Dad could always meet his contracts, and make money on his spot coal when Dad thought the prices for spot coal were good. Tommy told me that my dad was the reason the country's electric lights stayed on at night. I liked being with Tommy in his shack. I could watch the huge coal trains come by below us and slowly pass under the tipple as Jenny's coal poured into the railroad cars. It gave me a sense of power to watch that. And I felt good, knowing that my dad was doing important work, keeping America's lights on.

"Tommy always had a pot of coffee going in his shack. Sometimes men would come into the shack to talk to Tommy and the men and Tommy would study maps of the underground levels of Big Jenny. These were men that worked very hard and they knew what they were doing. They knew how to rip coal out of Big Jenny. They talked about tonnages and mine supplies. They checked with Tommy to make sure that they were doing things the way he wanted them done. And they liked Tommy's coffee. He always had a half-cup of coffee in his hand or on his desk. The smell of fresh brewed coffee made me feel like Tommy's shack was a place where important things got done. I loved the working smells of that old shack. There were men in the shack in their work clothes. Phones rang a lot and men talked mining talk with other men: hydraulic shovels and dozers; rock and rotary drills; blasting caps; dynamite; rope shovels, pullers, graders, face bolts, roof bolts, frames, cages, scrapers, whackers, main pumps, level pumps, vent shafts, and which men were down there. I was only a little girl, but I knew big things were going on inside Big Jenny and these men were doing important things; looking at their maps and charts; making and taking phone calls and talking to other men who were working deep underground. These weren't men that talked about their opinions and attitudes. They were men that got things done. All over Tommy's desk and shack walls were blueprint maps of the vast underground workings on all the different levels, deep inside Big Jenny. The underground of Big Jenny was like a huge city that went on for twenty miles on different levels, Tommy said. She had people and coal cars and conveyer belts and railroad tracks, and electric cables, and lots of people and equipment moving around inside of her all the time, day, and night. The work never stopped.

"Tommy looked at his maps. His mind visualized where all the men were working, deep inside the mine; what they were doing; what equipment they were using; where the mine cars were with mine crews and supplies in them; where the conveyer belts were; how much water the different pump stations were lifting to the surface; and how much *coal the production crews were moving out of the mine. Tommy was a tall skinny man with very strong hands. He always listened carefully to the questions his men asked. Then he made his decisions and gave his orders to the men who had called on the phone. None of the foremen questioned Tommy's decisions once he made them. He was a wonderful mine manager. Dad had complete confidence in him. Everyone trusted him. Dad said Tommy was the final word on the day-to-day operations of Big Jenny. I always liked being around Tommy. He explained things to me. He could talk to me in ways that I could understand things, like Dad never did. I always felt like Tommy cared about me. There was just something about him that I liked. I can't explain it. Other men swore; but Tommy didn't swear. He said he didn't see much use in swearing. Tommy just made things happen. I guess that's what it was.*

"I decided that, when I grew up, I wanted to be married to a man who was just like Tommy. I told Dad that. Dad just laughed. He told me that Tommy wasn't the kind of man that got married. He said that Tommy believed men and women were too different to live together. And Tommy believed women had strange chemicals in their brains that made them think about things differently than the ways men think about things. Dad said whenever Tommy felt like he needed to have a wife he would go to see either Sharon or Julia. Those two women understood that Tommy only wanted to be with a wife occasionally. So those women played wife with Tommy for about a half hour or an hour at a time; and Tommy paid them to play wife with him. And that was all the wife time that Tommy wanted. I remember thinking that, if I was Tommy's wife, I'd be so much fun to be with that he'd want me to play wife with him all the time. He wouldn't even think about renting a wife by the hour anymore. I told Dad that, and Dad just laughed again. He said Tommy needed to keep his mind on mining coal; and told me that I should not try to make Tommy think about marrying me."

A hush settled over the little girls' conversation. Marty's eyes searched Maria's, sensing that their life's paths would someday diverge; that they would bear each other's experiences as their own. A bittersweet sadness befell Marty. She wanted to grow up and have the freedoms that big girls had. She wanted that for Maria, too. But Maria was her psychic armor that shielded her from the hurt of abandonment. And now Maria was telling her that she would, someday, marry a man and devote her loyalties to him. She wondered: *'Will everyone abandon me?'*

"Why do you want to get married?" Marty sought to learn if Maria was serious about her goal.

"Because it's so beautiful," Maria's eyes affirmed her words. Her face glowed just thinking about marriage. *"Mother took me to a cousin's wedding. I saw the whole thing. The bride was so beautiful. She walked down the aisle with this beautiful music playing. She was dressed all in white with a long wedding train and a veil. And the preacher had them say these promises to each other. Her groom promised to love her. And then her groom gave her his ring; and he kissed her and hugged her right there in front of all of us. And a lot of women cried because they were so happy for her. And then they walked out of the church together while this wonderful music played. And people threw rice on them so they'd have babies. It was so wonderful. It made me cry."*

Marty remembered the times when her mother had berated her father. She didn't understand why their marriage wasn't working. She wondered whether Father had done something that somehow had hurt Mother. She was very confused and uncertain about the concept of marriage. She didn't share Maria's faith that marriage would guarantee that one's partner would always love you. She remembered her mother telling her dad that she hated him and wanted him to die. The idea of marriage frightened Marty. It seemed very risky and uncertain. She wondered whether there was anyone like her father who would always be good to her and whom she could rely upon and trust enough to marry. From these inner ruminations Marty's inner resolve was born. She would always love Maria, but she would chart a different course for her own life's direction, than Maria's life. She would be Maria's steadfast friend and protector until Maria married Tommy, or some other dream man. But she would steel her own resolve, depending upon no one else to supply her with lifelong fidelity. She would shape her own loves in ways that suited her need to experience the feelings of being loved; but she would only allow her loves to be close to her and share her love as she felt the need to be loved. Now she sought to test Maria's sincerity about marrying the older man that held her fascinations.

"Do you think Tommy will wait until you grow up; then marry you?" Marty felt sorry for Maria. She could see that Tommy was at least thirty years older than her friend. He was more like the dad that Maria wished she had, instead of the dad she did have.

"I think he might," sounded a hopeful Maria. *"He's already taken me on a date."*

"He did? When?"

"After we finished talking in his shack one day. He walked me all the way to Dad's car. He even opened the door for me and made sure I got in okay. He held my hand the whole time so I wouldn't stray away and get run over by the huge dump trucks and front loaders that were moving piles of coal around in the coal yard."

"Maybe he was just making sure you didn't get hurt?"

"Oh, I think it was more than that. He knows I can see the big trucks moving around. He knows I'm not just a little girl that can't look out for things." Maria nodded her head and smiled to Marty, as if that would make her assertion true.

"Wow, Maria. You are so lucky to have a man like Tommy who loves you and who is waiting for you to grow up. You're special." Marty decided it was harmless to go along with Maria's dream.

"I know it and I'll be good to him, too. I'll let him kiss me and hug me whenever he wants." Maria's eyes were filled with a young girl's wonderment. This time, her nod to Marty was more like she was

making marriage pledges to Tommy, her imaginary future husband. *"That day he walked me to Dad's car was the day I decided I should understand Dad's thinking better. So, I asked Tommy: 'Why does Dad need to get that lower seam opened? Dad once told me that there is enough coal in the upper seams of Big Jenny to power the entire United States for the next hundred years. Why do we need more coal than that?'"* Marty remembered feeling relieved that Maria had stopped talking about marriage. Her notion had seemed impractical; the pointless fantasy of a whimsical childhood dream.

"'That lower seam coal has more energy in it than the coal from the upper seams,' Tommy told me. 'Every ton has twenty five percent more thermal energy in it than the upper seam coal has. That makes that next lower seam's coal worth almost twice as much money than other coals.' Tommy explained: "he told me that Jenny's deep coal burned hotter, longer, and cleaner than the upper seam coal; and that Dad could get better contracts for it. That meant that everybody would make lots more money because Dad was a good owner and when his mines made more, he paid bonus money to his miners. Then Tommy explained that they had to first lower the water table in the mine to get to that higher quality coal; and that they then had to vent the methane from the mine faces before Dad could let the development and production crews go down there. That's when I asked Tommy about methane. He told me it's a gas you can't see. When you breathe it, you can't breathe oxygen; then you die. I knew from Dad that some of his miners died deep inside Big Jenny every year.

"When I asked Tommy why men wanted to mine coal if they know they can die down there, he said that every man that goes into Big Jenny knows he could die. But everybody knows they've got to die sometime, anyway. Everybody's got their time to die, he said; and some of us know when that time is and what it'll be that causes us to die; and some of us don't know when that time will be, or why it will be; and that's just the way it is. He said when a man loves his woman enough, he'll go into

the mine and risk death to make money for her. He's willing to die for her and their kids, if his time comes. When you really love somebody, you must be willing to die for them. That's what Tommy told me. He said that's what real love is. That got me thinking that maybe Tommy didn't want to get married because he was afraid being married would make him die, somehow. I don't know too much about men, yet. But since Dad and Tommy are so different, I think there are probably lots of differences between different men."

"Yeah, you're probably right about that, *Maria*." Marty nodded her head. Her frown indicated that men were a mystery to her, too. But Marty supposed that Maria should be older and wiser than she was. And Maria made a great deal of sense when she explained adult world things, like she was doing that day.

"Tommy said he was glad to work with Dad because Dad was a good owner and a safety minded owner and he paid top money. Tommy helped me understand Dad better than I could ever understand him by myself. I remember asking him why Dad needed his other two mines and why he was buying a fourth mine if he could double the coal production from Big Jenny."

"'It's not just about money for your dad,' Tommy explained. 'He does what he does because he must do it; because somebody must do it; and if your dad didn't do, it would be somebody else doing it. And your dad can't let that somebody else be anyone other than him. Your dad must be the man in charge. He must be the owner and the man who gets the coal out. He's one of those men that must be a leader of other men. He can't rest knowing that there's more coal down there. He must get to it and attack it, because it's there. And if the day ever came when there wasn't anymore coal to discover and attack and rip out of Mother Earth, your dad wouldn't have a reason to be alive anymore. He must be the leader of the men that attack the coal. If he couldn't be that man, he wouldn't know what to do with himself. Why, he'd probably just sit on the front porch of your house and whittle little animals out of wood.

He's not wired up to be that kind of man, so he leads other men. It's just your dad's nature, Maria. Each of us is made to be different in some way, that's all.'

"I told Tommy that I wished Daddy stayed home more because that would make Mommy happier. Tommy explained that, with a man like Dad, that wasn't possible. He needed to be out there in his mines with his men, leading them, making sure they were doing things the right way. He couldn't help himself; that's the way he is. He explained that the coal comes out of the mines, day and night, every day of the year, never stopping. The men moving into the mine and the coal coming out is, for Dad, like blood going into a heart and the heart pumping the blood back out. Dad's got coal in his blood was how Tommy explained it. And if his mines ever stopped pumping out their coal, Dad's heart would stop pumping too. Tommy said what Dad does is very import-ant. And because the country needs coal to keep the lights on, Dad needs to always be with his mines.

"But I wasn't sure if I believed Tommy about that. I think Daddy stays away from home because he doesn't like to be around Mommy. She drinks a lot and she gets really mean when she drinks. My brother John died when he was twelve and I was only five. That was the year before my parents sent me to WEX. Mom blamed Dad for letting John have a big twenty-six-inch bicycle. She said he couldn't handle the bike and blamed Dad for giving it to him before he was ready for it. John was walking his bike along the side of the road when a car ran over him. Dad had told John to walk his bike on the side of the road when he was on a curvy road or when he was going up hills. Dad figured John couldn't fall off the bike or lose control of it if he was walking it. Neither Mom nor Dad ever imagined that a man would drive close to the road-side, like that driver did when he ran over John. That driver had been drinking. He went over the shoulder of the road and hit John. And he went to court over it. And the judge let him get away with killing John. He only had to pay a fine because it was his first time drinking and

driving. Mom couldn't believe that the judge let that man off without sending him to jail.

"Then Mom screamed a lot at Dad about John's death being all Dad's fault. That's when Mom started drinking all the time and when Dad started staying away from the house. Dad only came in a few times during the day or night, usually for an hour or less, to make himself something to eat; then Dad went back to his mines. Dad even slept at the mines rather than come home to Mother. I only knew when he sometimes came home because he'd come into my room and kiss me on the forehead while I was sleeping. Sometimes I'd wake up and he'd hug me for a minute, before he went back to his mines. But he never stayed to talk with me. And he never talked about John with Mother. He avoided her. Dad just worked. He loved to work.

"After about a year of Dad being gone most of the time, Mother started yelling at me about everything. She told me I moved too slow. And I didn't comb my hair the way she wanted me to comb it. And I didn't brush my teeth good enough for her. She didn't like the clothes I picked out to wear, either. I got yelled at when we were the table, too. Mom said I ate too many sweets, but never enough good food. She told me I was too fat for a girl. She was always picking at me about something or other; and I got tired of hearing it. That's when I started disliking her. It got so that I didn't like being around her. So, I started eating more. That helped me from getting upset over her bitching about my weight. I understood how Daddy felt. I wanted to stay away from her, too. She started drinking constantly. And she cried a lot. She complained she didn't want to live in our little town anymore. Nothing suited her. Nothing was good enough for her. I got tired of hearing Mother complain.

"Then, one day she looked right at me, straight into my eyes like her eyes wanted to melt me away; like she really meant the nasty stuff she was about to say. Then she told me that she wished I had been the one that had gotten killed on that road instead of John. She told me that she had always loved John more than she ever loved me. She said she wasn't sure whether she could ever love me at all, because I was just a fat little pig; and she didn't think she could ever love a fat pig.

"Later, she cried about what she said to me. She told me she didn't mean to say those mean things; but that she was only trying to let me know how much other people would hate me because I'm fat. But I didn't believe her. I still don't believe her. I kept asking myself why she would tell me she wished I'd been killed instead of John. I believed she must have really meant that. I still believe that. I remember her words and how she looked at me. Her eyes were filled with hate. If killing me could have brought John back to life, I believe she would have killed me. I've never felt the same about Mother since that day. Before, I had always felt sorry for her because we lost John; and because she took it so hard; and she couldn't stop her drinking. But after she said those things to me, I thought of Mom as my enemy. I was afraid to be around her.

"Soon after Mother said those awful words, I was sent off to WEX. I liked WEX okay at first, but I missed Dad. I remember crying in class those first two years at WEX. That's when I was sent to Miss. Carboy. She's a shrink. She seemed to feel sorry for my situation, so I told her about everything and especially about how I felt about my mom. Miss Carboy told me that I should pretend that she was a Mommy substitute for me, and that she loved me just as much, probably more than Mommy did; and that if one parent loved a child, the child didn't need the other parent. She said that since I had her as my new mom, I didn't need my dad; and that he was too busy to be with me anyway.

"Miss Carboy said she wanted me to trust her with my feelings. She said she wanted me to imagine that I was her newborn baby. Then we spent many sessions pretending she was my mommy. She had me take all my clothes off and sit on her lap. She hugged me and pressed her cheek against mine and she kissed my cheek. She asked me how I felt. I told her I didn't know how I felt; so, we repeated this mommy and baby therapy many, many times. She'd rub my legs and tell me she didn't think I was fat. She squeezed me hard around my waist while she kissed *my cheek. Then she had me sit naked with my legs around her waist; and she had me hug her with my arms around her neck; and putting my cheek against hers while she patted me on my back. I told her I was starting to feel kind of weird about taking my clothes off for her sessions.*

"That's when WEX admin sent me to Mrs. Martinson. She was a different shrink. She listened to me much more carefully than Mrs. Carboy did. She's an okay shrink, except that she made me think a lot. But we didn't play Mommy kisses Baby, like Mrs. Carboy did. Mrs. Martinson told me I was a good person, and I would have a good life, even if I was fat. She told me to pay attention to my good feelings and hold my good friends close to me. That's when I decided that you were my best friend, Marty; and that I could always trust you.

"I felt good about my life then, sort of; unless I started thinking about Mrs. Raybenald. Mrs. Martinson even went to admin and had them call Mother. They told Mother I'd never be an Olympic swimmer, but Mother didn't take their word for it. She called Mrs. Raybenald and Mrs. Raybenald told Mother that she remained convinced that I could make the Olympic swim team if I could get my weight down and do a better butterfly. She said I had years to work on getting better and told Mother not to worry. She guaranteed Mother that I was a powerful swimmer and I had what it takes to medal at the Olympics. All she needed was Mother's permission to push me a lot harder. Mother agreed.

"So, admin kept me in Olympic Swim with Mrs. Raybenald's group of elite swimmers and Mrs. Raybenald screamed at me more than she ever did. She was pissed that I tried to get out of her program by using Mrs. Martinson to go to admin for me. So, I sort of screwed myself. From then on, Mrs. Raybenald had me at her mercy. And she punished me hard for going to admin. She worked my ass off. She never let up on me. She screamed at me every single class, all through the class period. My times got a little better, but not quite good enough to qualify for the Olympics. Mrs. Raybenald continued pushing me for a faster time every Swim class. When I was a younger girl, I loved Swim. Now, I hate Swim."

CHAPTER NINE

Your Maiden Modesty would float face down, and men would weep upon your hinder parts (Aldous Huxley: Leda)

BOYS

"Weren't you afraid when it wouldn't stop?" asked twelve-year-old Marty. She was trying to understand what her first flow meant.

"Yes, a little," answered Maria, *"I heard that boys could smell me down there and that the smell would make them want to do it to me. So, I kept myself really clean, by always changing my napkin and washing myself off really good, so no boy could smell me."*

"But, what about the blood?" Marty asked. *"I've been bleeding for three days. It's bleeding just as much as it was yesterday. When will it stop?"*

"It should stop in another two days or three days."

"But what can I do if it doesn't stop? It's really bleeding. It makes me feel kind of weak. It scares me because it doesn't want to stop."

"No, it stops. It always stops. It's just flushing out an egg, that's all."

"What takes it so long; and what happens if the egg decides to stay in there? Do I just keep bleeding forever?"

"I don't know," Marty's questions stumped Maria. *"Maybe it sort of slows down a little until the next egg comes. Then maybe the second egg flush flushes out both eggs. Why don't you ask your mother?"*

"I can't ask her. I'd be too embarrassed to ask her. I don't feel like I can talk with her about stuff like this. She doesn't like to be troubled

by questions from me. I'd just leave a message and she'd wait until I'm asleep before she calls back; then we'd never even talk. That happens all the times I call, so I stopped calling her. But you could ask your mother, couldn't you?"

"Yes, but she'd tell me I'm being stupid. She'd probably be shitfaced drunk anyway. I hate talking with her when she's drunk. She slobbers all over the phone and has hic-ups and forgets what we're talking about. Then she says how sorry she is about everything and how everything that happened to the family is her fault. She asks me if I love her. And I say 'yes.' Then she says: 'Good girl,' and hangs up. It's a total waste of time."

"Maybe you could ask your shrink? She might know about it."

"No, I don't want to ask her. If I do, she'll want me to take off my panties. Then she'll feel around me down there while she explains it. Anytime I ask her about boys or sex she tells me to take my panties off. Then she touches me there and puts her fingers inside me while she explains things to me. She gets creepy about sex things, so I'd rather not ask her. You shouldn't worry unless it goes longer than seven days. Mom told me that once, so you're probably okay."

"Will that blood smell make a boy want to do it?" Marty wanted to move on to a new topic.

"I don't know. I think some boys are attracted to the blood smell; kind of like boy dogs go after girl dogs in heat; but I think most boys are turned off. I think it scares them. The older girls say it does, except when a boy loves you and can't get enough of you. Then nothing stops him. It's confusing."

"So, you wait to do it until you're not bleeding?"

"Marty, I haven't done it, even when I'm not bleeding. That way I don't need to think about it."

"You haven't done it? Not even once?" Marty looked puzzled.

"No." Maria lifted her chin, proudly. *"I've been very good."*

"So, what would be so bad if you did it with a boy?" asked Marty.

"Well, I think it might hurt and I'm not sure I want to find out how it feels. There's a membrane down there and it hurts when a boy breaks it. Boys call it popping a girl's cherry. I still have my cherry."

"But sooner or later a boy is going to do it with you. So, why not let one do it now?" asked Marty. "Are you afraid you might have a baby?"

"No, I'm not afraid of the baby thing. I know where I can get birth control pills for that; but I don't want some boy laughing at me because I'm fat. I don't want him telling all his friends that it didn't feel good while he did it with me. So, I think I'll wait until I lose weight."

"You haven't even tried to do it, have you?"

"No, I haven't. I'm afraid a boy would make fun of me afterwards. And I don't want the boys at the public school thinking I'm a bad choice for a date."

"You haven't dated yet, have you?"

"No. I would like to go on dates with boys so I can get out and see things, even football, baseball, and basketball games. I'd love it if a boy would ask me to go to the movies with him, but so far no boy has asked me."

"I don't believe a boy would make fun of you, Maria. After a boy gets inside you, it probably feels the same as when he's inside any other girl. Trudy said her mom told her that. If you smoked a cigarette afterwards the boy might think you've got experience doing it. If you act like you're comparing him to your other lovers, that might make him want you again; and he'd try to get good at doing it with you."

"That wouldn't work, silly. If he just popped my cherry, he'd know I didn't have other lovers."

"Oh, yeah, right. So, you just need to get that first boy to do it; then you can become popular. Some boys might like having you under them, instead of a skinny girl. I think some boys would like that."

"Are you being honest? Do you think some boys would want me, as fat as I am? Honest, Marty, do you believe that?" Maria's hopes were rising.

"Yes, absolutely I do. I wouldn't say it if I didn't believe it. I see men with fat women all the time, Maria. Most of them look like they're having fun. They walk together and go to stores together. Many of them hold hands. I see men kissing fat women all the time. I think some guys love fat women. We just need to find the right guys."

"You're serious about this, aren't you? You'd help me get a boy?"

"Yes, I've told you yes. I think we should find two boys to do it with us so we can find out how it feels, for real. Some of the older girls do it with their boy friends and a lot of them say they like it. Even girls that don't like it, do it anyway because their boy likes it; so, it must not be too bad. I've heard them talk about it in the cafeteria. Let's try to find a boy that will want to do it with you. Maybe he'll like you so much he'll pick you up and take you where you can do it with nobody around. He'll probably like you so much, he'll fall in love with you. He'll probably want to take you places. You'd get to see movies, sporting events; go to picnics and the beach; who knows? The seniors at my table talk about boys a lot. They say boys are hard to predict. They try to figure out which boys to trust; what boys mean when they say things; and how different boys act differently.

"I know some boys love being with girls; but lots of boys fear us. They don't know how to act around us or what to say. They play sports and work at making their cars go faster to impress us. Some work to make money so they can take girls on dates. If we find boys that like us and if they have money to take us places, maybe they'll want to do it with us, too. I think we should try it."

"Maybe you're right," said Maria, "It's not fun listening to the other girls talking about boys and wondering about them. Except for you, I don't have fun being around other girls, anyway. They're always jealous about something or picky about something. They don't want to be my friend. They believe they're better than me. The only girls I get along with, besides you, are three girls in my chemistry class. They study and talk about chemistry; never about boys. They think boys are a waste of time."

"I know the three you mean," said Marty. *"I've seen them. They wear white socks and plain dresses down to their ankles; never skirts or leggings; and they always wear sneakers, never shoes. What is it with them?"*

"I don't know. I've watched them kiss on the lips. It's weird, seeing them do that. I wonder if they are, you know, different; like they'll never let a boy do it, but they do it with each other. I like them, all right. But I don't think they like me. They treat me like they've got some big secret. I think they've figured out how to do it with each other, without needing a boy. I don't want to ask them about it. They scare me. I'm afraid if I try to be friends with them, they'll want me to be like them. I'm not sure I want to be like them. I just don't know. It's confusing."

"I don't want to be like them," said Marty. *"I want boys to do it with me. I love the way boys look at me; and I feel like I want to do it with them. Boys make my insides flutter and I feel like kissing them. Don't you feel like that?"*

"Yeah, I do, but you aren't shy. I'm shy. I know I'm fat. And boys know it. And that's a problem for them. They're afraid to do it with a fat girl. I think they believe I'll smell bad or that they'll get stuck inside me. Maybe they're afraid their friends will make fun of them for dating a fat girl? I don't know. Maybe their friends will think they can't find a girl with a better body. Maybe that's why boys, that want to do it, won't ask me out. If we do this, I'm afraid my date will make fun of me."

"Don't be afraid. You'll never know what it's like if you don't try. Like you said, it's hard to know what boys think. We just need to find the right boys."

Years passed. Marty and Maria were still having the same conversations about how to get boys to ask them on dates.

"Listen to me. If we stick together, and tell them they must do it with both of us, or neither of us will do it; then maybe they'll decide to take us someplace where we can both do it." Both or neither was Marty's idea.

"You'd do that? Do you think it would work?" Maria was encouraged that Marty would deliver an ultimatum to help her get a boy.

"Yes, I'm pretty sure. Anyway, what have we got to lose? I think I'll like doing it and I'm pretty sure you will too, okay? Let's go to the Trading Corner General Store on Saturdays and hang out there until some boys ask us out. We'll just sit outside on a bench eating ice cream and drinking sodas until some boys find us. What do you say? If we both go, we'll have a better chance of two boys asking us out. We could go on double dates to lots of places. And, if the boys want to, we should just do it. You get us birth control pills; in case we start doing it. Okay?"

"Okay, I'll get the pills." agreed Maria.

"Remember, we're not trying to get pregnant. We'll just have fun. We'll go places and see things. Okay? Nothing serious like falling in love or anything. Okay? Listen to me, Maria," Marty looked her in the eye. *"You are a very sweet person. I know there are boys out there that want that in a girl. You're smart. You're witty and funny. You are good natured and honest. Believe in yourself. Don't let your weight stop you from going out. Once you get a boy to do it with you, you'll see. He'll want to be with you all the time. Maybe he'll want to go steady. He'll give you a pin or a ring. Lots of boys like going steady. He might fall in love with you. You'll never know what might happen unless you try. I'll be there with you, so nothing bad will happen. Okay?"*

"Okay, let's try it." Maria giggled. She imagined a special boy would soon be all hers. They would go to shows and picnics. He'd kiss her and do it with her. He'd see how sweet she was; and he'd fall in love with her. Maria agreed to Marty's idea.

CHAPTER TEN

Urge and urge and urge, always the procreant games of the world (Walt Whitman: Song of Myself)

If it feels good, do it (Advice from a bartender)

BEACH GAMES

"Here come two boys," said Marty. *"Quick, lift your skirt above your knee and put your head back. Pretend your ice cream cone is a cock and lick it real suggestively, from the bottom up. Then kiss the top of it before you bite some off. After you swallow, smack your lips slowly, like you loved licking it. I'll do the same. See if they'll talk to us."*

Marty and Maria were sitting on a bench outside the General Store, baiting boys. These two looked promising. Marty guessed that they were eighteen or nineteen. The girls performed their penis licking pantomime for good looking boys that were well dressed and old enough to drive. Marty guessed correctly that these two were either eighteen or nineteen.

"Are you girls waiting for someone?" asked Donny.

"Oh, my God, You are twins!" shrieked Maria.

"Yeah, we are. My name's Donny. Meet my brother, Billy." Both boys politely bowed to the girls. They were very handsome; both six feet tall with dark, curly, neatly cut hair. They wore identical clothes: casual sandals, tan trousers, and blue shirts. They were eye candy for girls.

"Would you girls like to go to Ocean City with us? We've got all afternoon. It's only ten in the morning. We've got a Shelby Ford Cobra convertible with a big engine. We can get there in an hour. What do you say?" The boys didn't waste any time. Their offer to party came shortly after the introductions and small talk.

Marty whispered in Maria's ear: *"Jackpot. We've got a two-fer, with fast wheels. I think they have money, too. What do you say?"*

"Let's go," smiled Maria, looking up at the twins.

The foursome got into the convertible. They swung by WEX to pick up the girls' swim suits; and they were off! Donny was anxious to get to the beach. He drove at a blistering pace. Marty rode next to him in front. She slouched back with her skirt hiked high above her knees and bare right leg propped over the passenger door. Her naked foot dangled outside the car, feeling the rush of cool wind. She loved hearing the full-throated roars that came from the Cobra. Donny showed off the car's power by popping the clutch and peeling rubber from its oversized wheels. That maneuver had the desired effect on Marty. She believed the car and the twins were invincible. Maria sat beside Billy in the back, her head resting on his chest. He draped his long, strong arm around her shoulder and let his hand dangle over her breast. Occasionally, his hand slipped onto it. He would then squeeze it softly. At first, she gently lifted his hand away, but Billy persisted. After a while she figured *'what the hell. Why not?'* She let his hand stay there. She closed her eyes and concentrated on the wind blowing through her hair and her thoughts of the ocean.

Donny' eyes left the road to glance at Marty. She was beautiful, smiling and enjoying the sun. *"Her face; those eyes! She's a living dream! It's hard to keep my eyes on the road. I want to look into her brown pools. She has the eyes that they write songs about; like they are magnets for my soul; like I want to lose myself in them; dive into them and love our lovemaking and never come out. I want to hold her face in my hands and kiss her lips. They pout, naturally; like they expect to be kissed; like they deserve all the passion I could ever put into a first kiss. And then kiss her again, and again; and never stop kissing her. Sometimes she moistens her lower lip with her tongue. I can't get my mind off that first time I saw her tongue; the way she licked that ice cream cone from bottom to the top; and then her slow, deliberate mouth-bite off the top; the way she prolonged that bite; like she wanted her lips to stay there. Was she signaling she loves to lick and mouth the cock? Yeah, I'm sure she was. That had to be what she was telling me; and the way she smiled so naturally and innocently, after she took that bite. Was she letting me know that she feels completely guilt free about performing fellatio; that she loves the naughtiness of it? Yeah, I think she was. She said lots without saying a word. She's a special girl, all right.*

The wind was lifting Marty's dark silky hair from her face. Her skirt was high above her thighs, revealing her pink silk panties. *'No modesty. She's inviting me.'* Donny took his right hand off the wheel and touched her leg. She didn't push his hand away. She looked at him and smiled, as if she expected him to do that. *'She's confident. Her eyes are saying she wants to be touched. She wants me to go further.'* He slid his hand higher. *'She's not pushing me away.'* He moved his hand still higher, until he could feel her mons through her panties. He let his hand rest there. *'She needs to know that I'll respect her wishes; that I'll stop any time she signals me to stop. But she's not signaling me to stop. She's smiling. Her smile is widening! She's letting my hand rest on her vagina. She's letting me know that she trusts me; that she knows I'd go further, only if she signaled that she wanted me to.'* Marty smiled to him. *'Sweet Jesus! I believe she can read my mind!'*

Marty was thinking of Donny in a new way now. He was no longer just her ticket to fun times with his hot car and good looks. He was the one. She wanted him to be the first boy to make love with her. *'He respected my mood time. He's waiting for me to tell him yes. I like that about him. He thinks of me as a person with needs; but also, with the need to be a partner in our petting and what comes after;*

not just some girl he can use and forget. I feel my body transitioning. I'm accepting him in that partnering way. His touches are titillating. I like his closeness; and I want him to do more.' A thousand nerve endings stirred inside her. Donny touched her! Not on her arm; but there! Her primal hormones awakened. She felt urges she'd never felt before; urges to open her legs; urges to discover what came next. She loved these feelings of flooding passions. *'I hope he keeps his hand there. I hope he's unafraid to do more. I want to know what comes next. I'm not afraid. I want him to know I like this.'* After a brief while and getting no objection, Donny began gently caressing her mons.

"Do you have a name for her?" He slightly pressured her vagina with a gentle circular motion.

"No. Some girls call her 'Pussy.' But I haven't given her a special name. Do you think she should have a special name?"

"Oh, most certainly, I do. Especially, if she's as beautiful as you."

"They say beauty is in the eye of the beholder, don't you know? You'll have to behold her to know whether you believe she's beautiful, don't you know?" Marty giggled. She was enjoying her teasing. She correctly assumed her challenge would make Donny desire her even more than he already did.

"I'm dying to behold her. May I name her first, before I officially meet her?"

"He, he! Marty giggled. *"Sure, you can. She and I would both feel honored. What would you like to call her?"*

"Well, let's agree to call her Miss Muffy. How does that sound?"

"Delightful; like she's a very proper, dignified, and highly respected lady. That is an excellent choice. Miss Muffy, she shall be."

"Wonderful. And may I have your permission to become better acquainted with Miss Muffy and become Miss Muffy's very good friend?"

"Oh, yes indeed, Donny. Miss Muffy very much wants you to be her very close friend." Marty placed her hand on Donny's crotch, feeling

for his penis, emphasizing her immodesty and desire. Ever so gently, she squeezed his cock. *'He needs to know I want to go all the way.'* Marty's heart beat faster. Her libido had ignited her natural feminine desires. Her eyes widened and her face relaxed. Her signals were unmistakable. She wanted nature to take its course. She wanted to have sex with him. Donny's hand modified its circular stimulations. Marty's mons now received gentle, squeezing caresses.

"Oooh, that feels nice. Miss Muffy and I feel all wonderful inside. I think you're trying to tell us something. We loving what you're doing. Can you do that, and drive, too?" asked Marty. Her words clearly confirmed what her eyes had already told Donny.

"Yeah, I can. If I have one hand on the wheel and my eyes on the road, we're okay. Are you sure Miss Muffy is okay with my hand doing what it's doing?" Donny stole a quick look at her face.

"Absolutely," said Marty, batting her eyelashes quickly. *"I already told you; we are both loving it. "I think your little friend would like to get better acquainted with me and Miss Muffy,"* she said, after locating his cock and holding it firmly with her fingers. She continued smiling at Donny. He responded by stimulating Miss Muffy's crown through her panties. His gentle squeezing and rubbing were accompanied by the subtle, low vibrations of Donny's Ford Shelby Cobra's modified, thousand-horsepower engine. Her libido craved more of Donny and his wonder car. It's vibrations carried her thoughts away. She daydreamed of lying in a place where Donny was peeling down her panties; opening her; penetrating her; all the while kissing her lips and eyes. Feeling the vibrations of unbridled horsepower excited Miss Muffy, making her hotter, slipperier-wetter. Marty's smile widened, returning her to the present. She rapidly batted her eyelashes and giggled, encouraging Donny to continue massaging her mons. Donny read her mind. He kept his hand on Miss Muffy; continued stimulating her. His squeezes were less tentative now; firmer because he knew she enjoyed them; and that she enjoyed capturing him with

her sex appeal. Marty knew they were at the beginning of something wonderful. She felt certain that Donny would be the first to have her. It was only a question of time. She let her head fall back against the headrest while casually stroking his cock, as if she was practiced from stroking many cocks before. She closed her eyes again, imagining what sex with Donny would be like: *'How will it feel to have his swollen hard cock pressing against my vaginal walls and sliding over my clitoris? I can't wait to know how that feels. How will it feel to wrap his naked body in my arms and hold him clasped in my legs? Will he respond when I kiss his forehead and his neck? Will he grab my ass and pull me hard into him? Will he love me more, when I turn animal and dig my nails into his back? Will he come inside me? I hope he will. I want to feel what it's like to have a boy's hot cum inside me. I'm sure he will if I ask him to. That will make us so close. He'll love me for wanting him to do that. I'll tell him not to worry. I'll tell him I'm on the pill. If I get pregnant, I'll just get an abortion. I'm not even going to worry about all that. I just want to feel his cock inside me. Will he love me more, after he comes inside me? Will he love hearing the sweet things I'm going to say to him about how wonderful it made me feel? Will he want me again, after we fuck; often? Yes, I'm sure he will. I'll tell him we're good together; good for each other. Yes; I'll make him mine. And I'll fuck him so good and so lovingly, I'll get him addicted to my vagina and I'll totally ruin him for all other women.'* Marty felt sure of herself; right with herself; and wonderful. This day at the beach held great promise.

A trip that normally took others an hour and a half only took Donny's Cobra less than an hour. Marty loved feeling the combination of speed and sexual stimulation. Her precious Miss Muffy had become hot and wet.

"I think we have a live one," said Donny to his brother. The foursome had gotten out of the car. They had changed into their swim suits and their oversized towels were spread on the beach. *"Let's run*

into the surf," said Billy. Everyone agreed to take a running plunge into the ocean. But when the girls took their tops off, Maria's fat was revealed. It was unmistakable. Her tummy roll fell over her belly; her breasts bulged against her bikini top, straining to burst free of it. Her legs were noticeably chubby. Otherwise, Maria was beautiful. She had a stunning face. One could see that with a little body work or concentrated exercise, she would become a ravishing goddess. Marty, on the other hand, already personified a feminine dream body. She was splendid, mouthwatering, magnificent. Her's was a body that should rightfully grace magazine covers. The twins realized their good fortune. They had a sex goddess in their midst. Both boys wanted her. The twins looked at each other. They knew that whichever one of them got Marty would hit the jackpot. But whichever one got Maria would feel short changed. When the four of them got into the water Billy whispered to his brother. After everyone splashed around a while the foursome went back to the beach to lay on their towels.

"I've got a fun idea," said Billy. *"Let's did a big hole in the sand and take turns sitting in it. We'll bury each other in sand; and then we'll dig each other back out. Then we'll all run into the water and splash off. Would you girls like to do that?"*

Marty and Maria looked at each other. Marty shrugged her shoulders. The girls understood that boys could act goofy. So, they decided to play along. All four dug a huge hole. Once it was deep enough and wide enough, Billy said to Maria, *"Maria, how about being a good sport and being the first one to get buried in the sand?"*

"Okay," giggled Maria. She stepped into the hole and sat down. Then Donny, Billy and Marty covered her with sand until only her head showed above the sandy beach.

"Okay, that's really good Maria," said Billy. *"Now just stay in there for a little while. You'll soon feel nice and cool."*

"Okay," said Maria, smiling. She was being a good sport. Their stretch of beach was nearly deserted that day. The life guard's tower

was over a hundred yards away. Between the surf breaking and the umbrella that the twins had put up, the lifeguard could neither hear nor see Maria. Billy motioned to Marty to come closer to him. When she did, he grabbed her around her waist and pulled her down onto his blanket. The blanket was behind Maria. She couldn't see what was happening.

Donny immediately lied down on Marty's other side. She was bookended by the twins. They began touching her breasts and her legs. She was astounded by how aggressive they were, but pleased to have their attentions. Soon, the twins were taking turns kissing Marty on her cheeks and full on her mouth. She enjoyed that too. This was her first encounter with boys of a sexual nature. Donny's hand returned to where he had placed it while they were in the car. *"Are you sure you're okay with me touching you there,"* he asked her.

"Yes. Absolutely. I love how you made me feel. Miss Muffy and I love what you're doing. If no one sees us, I'm fine with it. But if some-one comes by, then I think you should stop, okay?" Marty was thrilled for the attention the twins gave her. She loved feeling all four hands touching her over her entire body. The twins took turns sliding their hands down inside her bikini bottom and entering her vagina with their fingers. Their experience showed. They took turns stimulating her crown while kissing her full on her mouth, massaging her breasts, and gently tugging her nipples with their fingers. Their foreplay was gentle and seductive; unhurried and loving. They appreciated being blessed with the presence of a truly beautiful, sexualized Madonna.

Marty felt electrifying thrills course through her body. She wanted more. Her impulse was to remove her bikini bottom, clasp Donny between her legs and guide his penis into her. Then, much like a human octopus, her arms would hold his torso in place while she engulfed his penis inside her vagina's pink lips. She imagined thrusting wildly while holding his penis inside her, appreciating its full magnificence; amplifying the delicious sensations craved by her vaginal sensory nerves. Reminding herself she was in broad daylight on a public beach, she checked her responses to their touches; but continued giving them lusty kisses.

But her libido guided her thoughts further along promiscuity's path: *'If only this were a bedroom, I'd do it with them. I'm sure of that. I want to. Oh my God! Yes! I know that's what I want. Their touches feel so wonderful. I don't want them to stop. Not ever. I love feeling their fingers inside me. I love how they are stimulating me. They are making me feel fantastic! I want to do so much more with them. I'm certain that I want to do it with them. Yes, I want to make love with both of them at the same time; on the same day. They are very handsome; such well chiseled bodies; so well-muscled! How lucky am I? Everything they are doing with me feels wonderful. I feel like they love me and they care about me. And they respect me, even though I want to be totally slutty with them. I don't want to stop them. If we weren't in public view, I'd fuck them right here, right now.'* This hot sensual petting went on for some time. Meanwhile, Maria estimated that Marty had been by herself with the boys for a good fifteen minutes.

"Hey, let me out now. I want to get out and splash off. I want this sand off me," shouted Maria. *"Where are you anyway? Marty, what are you doing?"*

Marty didn't answer, Billy did. *"She's just having a little fun with us,"* he answered Maria.

"Marty, what are they doing to you?" Maria tried to turn her head around, but she couldn't get it all the way around. The three of them were directly behind her. She became mildly concerned for her friend, and for herself. It occurred to her that they might abandon her; leave her stuck in the sand.

"I'm okay, Maria, Ohhh, Heee, Heee, Ohhh, Billy, Donny, how am I ever going to stop you? That feels wonderful! Oh, oh, that tickles." Marty was laughing, literally behind Maria's back; behind her head, to be precise.

"Marty, please make them get me out of here. I want to get out," shouted Maria.

"In a minute, just a few more minutes, okay? Heee, heee, ohhh, oh, I love what you're doing. That feels so good Billy. Yes. Yes. Oh, Donny, kiss me more," said Marty. The two boys were aggressively kissing and licking her nipples now. They were unconcernedly stimulating Miss Muffy with their fingers, eagerly gliding their fingers over her clitoris; pleasuring Marty with sexual stimulation, and alternatively kissing her mouth and rubbing her sides and stomach. Miss Muffy was becoming transformed into Miss Sex Craving Pussy and loving what the twins were doing. In her subtle animalistic way, Miss Pussy began purring. Thousands of nerve endings inside her were responding to the boys' stimulations, signaling her hormonal glands to prepare her for coitus. Her blood felt surges of heat and lust rushing to her; preparing her. Her clitoral tendrils became electrified with desire. The urges to fuck raced through her upper thighs. They were incredibly real; relentless and demanding. They were insisting that she have sex. They needed to be slaked. Now! Marty entered another world. Her behavior was controlled by a higher power. Instinctively, she yearned to spread her legs widely open and welcome her first male penis. She wanted it to share her wonderous, euphoric feelings.

She'd never experienced ecstasy before. She loved receiving the boys' attentions. The twins began taking turns lying on top of her, gripping her tightly by her ass and pretending to have sex with her; with their swim trunks on. She whispered she wanted to do it with them. *'I want to fuck both of you. I can't wait. But I can't do it here, on a public beach with Maria here, right in front of me. Maria's my best friend. It wouldn't be right.'* As if to prove her eagerness for sex with them, Marty slid her hands into their trunks and stroked both their penises. She temporarily brushed aside all thoughts of Maria. Her own pleasure; the promise of more dates with the twins; and more trips in their hot convertible car meant more for these few moments than Maria's friendship. She was excited about having actual sex. The prospect of becoming the love interest of both these twins fascinated her. She was enthralled with the possibilities. *'Probably, I'll often be asked to date one or the other of them; sometimes I'll probably be asked to date both of them at the same time. Likely, one or both of them will have sex with me, whenever I want.' It would be a wonderful arrangement.'*

"Get me out of here!" Maria screamed. She'd figured out what was happening, and she didn't appreciate being left out. Marty reacted grudgingly.

"Okay, okay, Maria, we're coming," Marty said, giving one last soulful kiss to each of the twins; and one last hard stroking squeeze of both penises. *"Until our next time, okay?"* she whispered to the twins as she got up. The three of them dug Maria out of the sand. They all waded into the water. Then, Billy kick-blocked Maria behind her knee joints. Awkwardly, she fell backwards into the ocean surf. Billy pushed her head under with his hand. Billy was the insensitive twin. He delivered his revenge to Maria for cutting short his fun with Marty. Maria's head bobbed up from her dunking. She was upset and sputtering. Marty was appalled. She tried to help Maria get up, but her friend pushed her away.

"Just leave me alone," sobbed Maria, regaining her footing by herself. *"I thought you were my friend,'* she screamed in Marty's face. *'How could you do this to me? How could you?"* Maria bared her teeth at Marty. Her anger was palpable.

"I didn't do anything, Maria, I just kissed them a little, that's all," fibbed Marty, opening her palms to profess her innocence.

"Bullshit! I heard you behind me. You were doing more than kissing. You were stealing my date from me. You couldn't have just one boy, could you? You had to have both of them, didn't you?" Maria's hands were akimbo. She was beet red and furious.

"It's what 'they' wanted, Maria. I didn't decide that. 'They' did."

"But you didn't 'do' anything to make one of them come and kiss me; did you?"

"Maria, I did the best I could. The rest was up to you. You had all that time with Billy in the back seat. Didn't you do anything to make Billy want you?"

"Shut up! Just shut up!" screamed a sobbing Maria. *"I never thought you'd abandon me like that."*

"I didn't abandon you, Maria. I've been right here the whole time."

"Oh, yeah! Sure! I'll bet you were. If it was nighttime, you would have done it with them, right here on the beach. I know you would have. I don't trust you anymore, Marty. Just stay away from me." Maria was sputtering and sobbing like a wet hen. Her hair had gone straight. Her wet bathing suit made her look even fatter than before. The boys simply looked at each other and shrugged, as if the day's event was like a football play that hadn't executed well. They merely shrugged it off, figuring they'd try something else. On the way home Donny drove slower. And everyone kept their hands to themselves.

CHAPTER ELEVEN

The ruling passion, be it what it will, the ruling passion conquers reason still (Alexander Pope: Moral Essays)

JUMP

Maria had been held back two years; forced to repeat her tenth-grade classes twice, because Mrs. Raybenald had repeatedly given her an 'F' in gymnastics and admin had given her an 'F' in conduct and deportment because she refused to perform her butterfly strokes to Mrs. Raybenald's satisfaction. Maria had given up and stopped trying. Being a larger bodied girl, Maria stood out among the others in her class. Other girls snickered behind her back, making fun of her large body. Some called her '*Blimpy.*'

Intentionally inflicting punishment upon Maria for her body, became Mrs. Raybenald's obsession. She convinced Maria's mother that giving Maria extra time in Swim would correct Maria's attitude about the importance of achieving proper weight. After Maria's mother signed off on Mrs. Raybenald's accelerated program for Maria, Mrs. Raybenald had ordered Maria to join her Olympic Dive group.

"Well, Maria, since you refuse to lose weight, I've decided you need more incentive to get those ugly pounds off," barked Mrs. Raybenald at her favorite victim. *"You'll learn to perform every dive that everyone in my Olympic Dive class performs, from the low board and from the tower's high board. If you refuse to do a dive correctly, your body will*

hit the water flat on your fat, ugly belly; or flat on your back. And that will sting you, Maria. A botched dive will hurt you, but it won't kill you. You'll get over it. Everything is totally up to you, Maria. When you make up your mind to lose weight, you'll be able to get your body all the way around and make a perfect water entry from your front flips and back flips. And you'll stop landing flat on your fat belly or on your back. You are going to realize I am serious about making you into an Olympian. Now get your big fat ass up there."

Maria had just done some back flips off the low board. She had hit the water partially on her stomach, every single time. She was unable to swing her legs completely through her flips and enter the water standing upright. Mrs. Raybenald demanded that she perform signature perfect, no splash, water entries. Her belly's skin was stinging. She hurt from her last three botched tries. But Mrs. Raybenald showed Maria no mercy. She became sadistic and cruel. She decided to bully her hapless victim more today than she had ever bullied her before. She ordered Maria do a double back flip off the high tower.

Marty stayed after her own Swim class to watch Maria dive. Since their beach incident the week before, the two girls had become good friends again; just like old times. Maria was good natured that way. She did not hold grudges. She forgave Marty for her indiscretion at the beach. She understood that Marty had a natural hormonal response to nature's most compelling need.

Up, up, and higher, to the very top of the high dive platform, climbed terrified and bullied Maria. The Olympic Dive girls watched. Fright and awe showed on their faces. They intuited that Mrs. Raybenald's experiment might end terribly. Marty also watched while lapsing into a suspended dream world. She was having her own special thoughts about making love with both twins while observing Maria ascending the tower platform. Mrs. Raybenald ordered Maria to climb all the way to the top; then walk the plank to the edge of the ten-meter-high board. Maria was thirty-three feet above the water surface. Her dive would be like a jump from the roof of a ten-story building. While Maria climbed, Marty daydreamed:

'I wonder if those twins will want to see me again? They might think Maria has to be included. They may never call me. I hope they will call. I'd love to feel their stiff cocks in my hands again. They were so large and hard! Maria said a boy's cock is like a barometer. When it gets hard that means the boy loves you. I wonder how it feels to suck a hard cock, while stroking it? I've read about fellatio. I'm sure I can do it. I believe I'll love doing it. I think it will be exciting. I know I'd love to try it. I'm sure I'll feel like I have an intimate connection with Donny while my mouth strokes up and down on his cock. I'd love kissing the heads of both twins' cocks and licking them. I want to study their faces while I do that. I want to see if they like it.

'If they do call me, that means they'll want to make love. I'm sure of it. I wonder how they'll react when one of them pops my cherry. I acted like I knew all about making love while we were at the beach. They'll discover I was faking it when my cherry pops. I hope they won't laugh at me or think I'm too immature to make love. I desperately want to do it. I can't wait to feel a real cock inside me. I want to thrust up and down on it, like the ways their fingers stimulated me. I imagine a stiff cock feels much more powerful. I imagine it feels more wonderful than finger stimulation. Please Donny and Billy; please, please, call me. I want to fuck both of you. I want to make love with you in so many ways; for hours at a time. I don't want you taking out other girls. I want both of you to come inside me. I want your beautiful cocks to fall in love with me and Miss Muffy's hot honey pot. You'll never regret fucking me. I promise. I'll be a fantastic lover for both of you, I double promise. I want you to teach me everything you know about love-making. I know you can do that. Won't you please, please call me?'

One of the Olympic Dive girls snickered. She opined that Maria would go all the way around once, but then be unable to control her body. She predicted Maria would continue her body rotation, uncontrolled; and not enter the water feet first. The girl commented that Maria had poor body control; and was unable to control her dive spins. She believed Maria would land flat on her back, resulting in a very painful, possibly even a fatal ending to the dive. The girl commented: *'This is not about teaching Maria anything. This is about something else altogether. Mrs. Raybenald is so frustrated with Maria she's willing to risk killing her.'* Everyone watched as Mrs. Raybenald blew her whistle. Maria had reached the top of the tower. She now stood at the very edge of the high board, afraid to flip off backwards. Marty came back into the natatorium and stood closer to the dive tower. She stopped her obsession over the twins and focused her attention on Maria. She wanted to watch Maria's dive, up close.

"Jump up and off! Just jump, damn you! Do it! Do a back flip!" screamed Mrs. Raybenald. She blew her whistle a second time, hard. But Maria just stood there. She was shivering; obviously frightened. She was a swimmer, not a diver. *"Jump, Maria; or I'll force you off!"* screamed Mrs. Raybenald. She blew the whistle a third time; this time as shrilly as she could. Her face was an angry, beet red.

But Maria did not respond. She just stood there, trembling. Clearly, she was terrified for her life. She feared if she dived, she'd possibly hit the water flat; and that would feel the same as hitting hardened cement. She knew the dive could kill her. *"I can't do this Mrs. Raybenald. I'm afraid. Please don't make me."* Maria began crying.

"I don't ever want to hear you say the word can't, Maria. You can do this. And you will do this. Now, JUMP!" Mrs. Raybenald stood, her arms akimbo, glaring at Maria, waiting for Maria to jump into her double back flip.

But Maria didn't budge. Her cries were more like bawling now. She faced Mrs. Raybenald from her tower platform board and pleaded: *"But, I've told you I can't do this. I'm not a diver; and I don't want to be a diver. I want to come back down."* Some of the girls in the Olympic Dive class snickered. It amused them to see someone challenge their coach's orders.

Hearing some of her girls snickering agitated the coach. The two things she insisted on in her classes were respect for her instructions and discipline. This situation was an affront to her authoritarian mindset. Maria's plea to climb back down stoked Mrs. Raybenald's anger. The coach regarded Maria's plight as an impudent student's personal challenge to her authority. *"All right, damn you!"* Mrs. Raybenald's scream now carried a threatening tone. *"You are not going to get away with this. I am damn sick and tired of your defiance and your whimpering, you fat little bitch! You are going to take my classes seriously, if it's the last thing you do! "Get back out there, you. Do as I say, fatso! God damn you! You ARE going to do this dive. You WILL do as I tell you. I am totally sick of your insubordinate attitude. Don't push me. This isn't funny anymore."* Mrs. Raybenald had screamed her frustrations forcefully at terrified, trembling Maria. The Olympic Dive girls heard Mrs. Raybenald's lack of professionalism. They knew their coach was taking this situation personally, and way too seriously. Some of the girls looked at each other. They sensed that something about this impasse between Maria and their coach was terribly wrong; but they had no authority to interfere, nor did any of them know what to do if they did. Mrs. Raybenald intimidated all of them. None of them had ever dared to challenge their coach's instructions. But Maria? What, they wondered, would Coach do? Perplexed; frightened for Maria, they just sat and watched. Marty also watched. She didn't comprehend what could happen if Maria jumped; but she intuited that, likely, it would not be good. She thought she should, at least, say something; speak up for her friend.

"Stop shouting at her! She's afraid! Can't you see that?" screamed Marty, trying to come to Maria's defense. But it was no use. Her caution only further hardened Mrs. Raybenald's resolve. The coach's muscles tensed. Her jaw clenched. Her face broadcast her determined

anger. She was not about to pay heed to cautions shouted at her by impudent Marty Mallory. That troublemaker was not going to dissuade her from forcing Maria to perform a double back flip dive. Coach now turned toward Marty and glared.

"SHUT UP! YOU JUST SHUT UP!" screamed an outraged Mrs. Raybenald. *"YOU MARCH YOUR ASS OUT OF THIS BUILDING RIGHT THIS MINUTE, MALLORY! YOU'RE NOT EVEN SUPPOSED TO BE HERE. YOU KNOW YOU ARE NOT IN OLYMPIC DIVE CLASS! GET OUT OF HERE, YOU NOSY BITCH! GET OUT!"* she shouted. Marty walked slowly to the exit door and through it, deliberately emphasizing her sexy sashay hip hitch as she walked, certain that flaunting her sexuality would taunt and further infuriate Mrs. Raybenald. Marty held the Swim coach in contempt. The woman did not intimidate her in the slightest. Marty held the door open to watch while Mrs. Raybenald turned her attention back to Maria. Meanwhile, Maria had walked back to the dive station, far from the edge of the board.

"YOU GET YOUR FAT ASS BACK OUT THERE, YOU FAT ASSED BITCH! GOD DAMN YOU, YOU FAT ASSED SISSY!" Mrs. Raybenald bellowed. *"YOU WILL DO THIS DIVE,'* she screamed so hard her voice cracked. *"YOU WILL DO AS I TELL YOU! YOU ARE GOING TO PERFORM THIS DIVE. THIS IS NOT OPTIONAL! YOU MUST DO IT! I'M SICK OF YOUR ATTITUDE. YOUR DEFIANCE IS NOT FUNNY ANYMORE!"*

Maria inched her way back onto the edge of platform board. She stood frozen, terrified, and crying; her back to the open air and the water far below. She shivered, not from being cold; but from honest fear for her life. While standing high above the water, her eyes looked up. The roof of the natatorium seemed unnaturally close. Maria breathed in a deep breath. She understood this was an ominous moment. The water appeared to be a distant mile below her. She thought she might as well be diving to Earth from a space satellite.

She was so high! She mused that she could possibly jump up and clutch the steel girders that supported the roof of the huge natatorium. Then, she wondered, would she be able to climb into the girders and be safe from Mrs. Raybenald? Would anyone come to get her down? Would she fall from the girders? Would that be even worse than a backflip off the dive board? She wondered if this building was the place she was going to die. Again, she shivered. Her crying was uncontrolled. She felt like she had become a mere insignificant spec; poised high above the water; a small, vulnerable, worthless human being, captured in the enormity of this impersonal cold building. She felt overwhelmed and dizzy from her increased sense of vertigo. This dive demanded way too much. She was afraid to do her backward leap push off.

Her back faced the open air. The cold impersonal water waited below; defying her to jump. She trembled, not from cold; from fear. She was obviously afraid to dive; physically and emotionally incapable of performing the challenge Mrs. Raybenald demanded. But Mrs. Raybenald refused to relent. She viewed this moment as a contest of wills. And she, the great Olympian, was not about to give in to a fat, obstinate girl. She had no empathy for sissies. She identified them; broke them down; and rebuilt them into women after her own image. She believed she possessed the innate power to mold her girls into champions. She was like God that way.

Now this self-appointed female God gathered up three life rings. She set two rings by her feet and picked up a third ring. Her Amazonian physique whirled around in a circle to create lethal momentum for the life ring. When she had the necessary kinetic energy, she captured it as velocity. She aimed the life ring directly at Maria and launched it. It sailed past Maria, missing her face by less than a foot. Maria screamed. She was shocked and terrified. Meanwhile, Marty ignored Mrs. Raybenald's order and returned to the group of girls. She stood beside the dive platform. She looked up at Maria.

She noticed her friend was standing on the edge of the dive board, trembling. Marty's lips curled inward and pressed together against her teeth. Her hand made a fist which she brought up to her mouth. Her eyes widened. Her skin became clammy. She was horrified for her friend.

"Don't, please don't throw things at me, Mrs. Raybenald." Maria pleaded and cried. *"I'm afraid. Please don't do that,"* Maria's plea was earnest. If she didn't jump, Mrs. Raybenald was likely to keep hurling the hardened polyurethane ring missiles at her until one of them hit her and injured or killed her. And if she jumped, she knew her double back flip would likely result in a bad angle water entry and severe pain. Poor Maria was afraid for her life

"THEN YOU HAD BETTER JUMP, YOU FAT LITTLE BITCH. DAMN YOU!" screamed Mrs. Raybenald at Maria. She bent down to pick up a second life ring. *'This fat bitch represents my failure to create an Olympian out of a girl who has great potential. I refuse to accept this. How many times did I fail to get another gold because I hadn't made the extra effort? But then, through immense effort and hard, persistent work, I pushed on and I finally won my second gold! This is doable!'*

Maria represented Mrs. Raybenald's failure to create an Olympian. Failure was inconceivable to the iconic coach. She refused to accept it. In her mind, the helpless shivering girl on the dive platform personified defeat; and defiance of her best efforts to produce another Olympic champion. Maria represented those times in the coach's past when she, herself, had failed to win the gold. But through masochistic perseverance, Mrs. Raybenald overcame her shortcomings and went on to win her second gold. But Maria, despite the girl's best efforts, was failing to become an Olympic champion. Mrs. Raybenald tried every way she could and with everything she knew to motivate Maria. She had spent extra hours with her to squeeze out every possible improvement in Maria's technique. She had gone to great lengths to explain nutrition and muscle tone; often begging Maria to change her eating habits. Coach saw an Olympic gold in Maria, but for her weight. But Maria had no self-discipline. Coach had even resorted to spying on her; and saw her eating chips and candy; spoiling her chances for gold. Coaching Maria had become a thankless, impossible task. The girl just didn't care about getting the gold; not enough to take her training seriously. Now, Coach had turned against student. Maria's very existence and her baby fat represented the ultimate insult to Mrs. Raybenald's supreme abilities.

Everything finally came into focus. This was the seminal moment. The highly vaunted WEX Swim Coach stood seething with hatred of her overweight student. She could no longer even stand the sight of the terrified fat girl. *I'm going to throw another life ring at you. And I'll keep throwing them at you until I hit you and knock you off; so, you'd better jump! JUMP, YOU FAT LITTLE BITCH! DAMN YOU, JUMP!"* Mrs. Raybenald was now screaming maniacally. Her systolic blood pressure had exceeded one-ninety-five. She was so furious with disobedient Maria that she was perilously close to giving herself a stroke. Her arterial blood vessels were plainly visible. They bulged out noticeably from her face and neck. Her fists now clenched with determination; she looked up at Maria. This had become more than a simple contest of wills. It was a visit to insanity. Mrs. Raybenald snarled like a vicious dog, showing terrified Maria her coffee-stained teeth. The instructor was in a psychotic rage state. Any sane adult would have noticed it and immediately stopped the madness.

But no adults were allowed in the natatorium during Olympic classes. No adults were ever allowed to observe the raving Olympian's brutal coaching methods. She, alone, made all the rules for Swim and Dive classes. And Admin always acceded to her demands. Student and parent complaints were never investigated and always dismissed. Mrs. Raybenald's version of truth was always accepted over a student's version. Admin never interfered with their prized faculty member. Success, Mrs. Raybenald often emphatically declared, required that she be allowed to coach her classes in complete privacy. Mrs. Raybenald ruled the WEX natatorium, and the school itself, with supreme, unchallenged authority. She was a power crazed, unchecked tyrant. And this day, she had gone temporarily insane.

"YOU HAD BETTER JUMP, YOU FAT ASS. DAMN YOU!" threatened Mrs. Raybenald. This time, her threat voice was delivered with a touch of promised, gleeful evil. She bent down to pick up a second life ring. The sane thing to do would have been to allow Maria to climb back down. But Coach had lost all rational reason. *I'm going to throw another one at you, fat ass."* Mrs. Raybenald's determination voice promised Maria she would perform as ordered. Coach's voice tone had changed. It was lower now, as if it didn't matter that Maria might die from this dive. This was about making a fat girl jump when Coach told her to jump. The matter of Maria's dive had devolved into a contest of wills that Coach willed herself to win, regardless of the consequences to Maria. *"I'll keep throwing rings at you, until I hit you and knock you off. And I will hit you and knock you off! I'm going to get you, fat girl. Either way, you will go into the water! So, you'd better jump! JUMP! DAMN YOU! JUMP!"* Mrs. Raybenald screamed maniacally.

Finally, Maria jumped. Everyone watched. There was a long, eerie moment while her body lifted. It first hung momentarily, grotesquely suspended in mid-air, like it knew it was way out of place and did not belong perilously high above the water below. Silence gripped the natatorium. Maria was alone in space. Now, a slow-motion sickening horror unfolded. The observing girls noticed that Maria's torso was not rotating. Her body was not coming around! She struggled, trying to get rotation started. The girls held their collective breath, spellbound by the unprecedented spectacle. Their silent, collective thought was that Mrs. Raybenald overdid it. This time she had risked the life of a defenseless student who was trusted to her care.

Marty stood by the tower, watching. She grimaced. Maria's body had partially spun around; but it had no centerline balance. It careened sideways, out of control, mid-way through Maria's drop. Maria knew she was in trouble. Her worst fear was happening. Her arms flew out of her dive tuck. They flailed wildly, trying to help her body gain its balance; desperately seeking to achieve a near upright entry angle. But it wasn't working! Her arms batted empty air. The dive was a pitiful sight to watch. Maria panicked. She knew there was precious little time to correct her ill-fated dive. Her legs also began flailing helplessly. Coach Raybenald, watching, thought Maria's dive was comical. She felt inwardly gleeful that the chubby fat girl was getting her just punishment for refusing to eat properly, refusing to perform a perfect butterfly, resisting her commands to jump; all of it.

Girls watching Maria's desperate struggle were seeing a dreadfully sickening sight. They were observing a slow-motion train wreck; knowing nothing could stop it from happening. Everyone watching the macabre spectacle saw the obvious. The dive was going to end horribly; tragically; possibly fatally, for Maria. Finally, water's unyielding surface met Maria's body. Human vengeance forced Maria's jump; water's vengeance ended it.

"CRACK, SLAM!" The natatorium echoed from the sound of Maria's horrifying finale. Her body crashed into the unforgiving surface. From her thirty-three-foot dive height, Maria's still accelerating speed upon hitting the water was akin to landing splat on solid cement. She hit the water at the worst possible angle; no angle. Her body was flat on its side when it slammed into the water. Her ill-fated dive had suddenly become a serious life or death matter. Maria lay in the water, stunned unconscious.

Long seconds passed. Maria's body lay suspended dangerously long below the surface. Precious seconds ticked by before it slowly bobbed up. She lay on the water's surface, face down, motionless and limp. Her arms and legs dangled pathetically below her body's trunk. A collective gasp sounded from the Olympic divers. They had watched the failed dive. They saw Maria's horrifying body-slam onto the water's unforgiving surface. Now they were observing the foreseeable result of their coach's tragically inhumane bullying.

Screams of *'No!"* and *"Somebody! Do something! Help! Call 911! Do something!"* sounded from this group. But everyone simply stood there. All were afraid and paralyzed by collective fear. More precious seconds ticked by. Maria still hadn't moved. She was out cold. Was she dead? Many of the watching girls began to wonder if the dive had killed Maria. They started jumping up and down. They were anxiety crazed; screaming maniacally now; realizing that Maria could have been one of them. They were suddenly terrified for Maria's life. Clearly, she was in imminent danger of drowning. *'She may have broken her back or neck! She could be paralyzed for life! She could drown before someone gets her out of there!'* Those thoughts ran through everyone's mind, including Mrs. Raybenald's. Suddenly, her bullying was no longer mere theatrics to slake her monumental ego; no longer the default outlet for her contests of wills. This was a deadly serious matter.

Mrs. Raybenald realized, belatedly, that she had caused this tragedy by her bullying. She dimly comprehended that she might have killed her student. She visualized her illustrious career slamming into a brick wall; bursting into flames. She feared she might be sued by Maria's parents; possibly face imprisonment. Responsible people did not abuse students placed in their charge in the ways that she had abused Maria. Mrs. Raybenald's beet red face suddenly turned ghostly white. Her anger blood escaped to somewhere else. Her obsessive mind began dimly processing the real possibility that, deservedly, her storied career had just crashed and burned.

Marty was the first to snap out of group disbelief shock. She dove into the water and quickly swam to Maria. She immediately lifted Maria's head over her crooked arm; and, keeping Maria's head elevated, swam to poolside. Mrs. Raybenald finally regained her senses and went into damage control mode. She reflexively dived into the water after Marty to help. *"Girls, get in here and help us lift her out,"* she screamed. After a desperate struggle, four girls and Mrs. Raybenald hefted Maria onto the pool's cement border. Maria didn't move. Her entire left side was a ghastly bright-blood, bluish-red. Her blood vessels had burst through her split-opened, bruised skin. Raw meat-flesh hemorrhaged blood, pumping steadily through Maria's crushed arteries, vessels, and cells.

Mrs. Raybenald stood over the girl, shocked again; apoplectic. Was she dead? That horrid unthinkable thought filled everyone's mind. Swim Coach feared, for the first time, that she had trapped herself by overstepping common sense boundaries; that this poor girl, placed in her care, and at her mercy, had human limitations that could only be pushed so far. Possibly, Maria would bleed out or be paralyzed for life because of her incessant bullying. Now, Coach's lips quivercd. She feared losing her job: feared being sued by Maria's parents; but she was still not caring about Maria. Swim had always been about the greater glory of Mrs. Raybenald; never about the successes of her students. Her mind was absent any feelings for what she did to Maria. She believed her entire world was about herself and her iconic image. Even this tragic human moment did not untangle Mrs. Raybenald's internal wiring from her narcissism.

Thankfully, Marty possessed a mature presence of mind. She was the proverbial adult in the room. She saw that Mrs. Raybenald was self-absorbed, non-compos mentis; effectively useless. Furious, she pushed Mrs. Raybenald out of the way and took charge.

"Quick! Everybody! Give me your towels, blankets; anything to get her warm. Now! Right now!" shouted Marty to the other girls. Soon, towels and a blanket covered Maria. Marty then gave her shocked friend mouth to mouth resuscitation for a long minute. Finally, Maria spit up a volume of water; then coughed out water, bile, and

blood. Marty eased her friend's head to its side and pumped her chest, hard. Maria coughed and spit-sputtered. More water came out. Then, revived, she looked up at Marty, puzzled and dazed. *"Call 911. Tell them we need an ambulance. Now!"* Marty barked.

"How did I do? Wasn't I great?" Maria asked with a wan smile.

Marty didn't take time to answer her friend. She was taller and stronger now than she was the last time that she had a run in with Mrs. Raybenald. The intervening years had given Marty the chance to study the swim coach's methods. Marty disliked Mrs. Raybenald even more than before. She had no respect for the woman. Marty glanced up from her injured friend. Her eyes caught Mrs. Raybenald. The swim coach's face had changed from a look of apoplectic fear to a wan contemptuous smile. Marty read the twisted mind behind that face. Now that Maria would survive, that sun-wrinkled face signaled pleasure. Coach was inwardly pleased that her bullying had injured Maria; nearly killing her. That smile made Marty furious.

Years of Marty's accumulated frustrations boiled over and exploded. Her mother's abandonment and neglect; her mother's betrayal of her father; her mother's seedy business ethics; and now this senseless injury to her only friend, triggered an adrenalin blood rush. Suddenly, Mrs. Raybenald became a lightning rod for all despotic authoritarian abuses in the entire world. And Marty became the lightning. Marty's adrenaline rush seized control of her brain. She seethed from her flash of hot, fierce anger rage. Her eyes laser focused on the power-crazed psycho who had nearly killed her friend. Instinctively, she wanted to destroy Mrs. Raybenald.

Coach's eyes caught Marty's; and locked on them. Her wan smile of contempt vanished quickly. Sheer terror swept over her prune face. Goose bumps rose on the back of her neck. She wore the panicked fight or flight look of a trapped prey animal that suddenly realized there was no escaping imminent danger. There was no way of escaping Marty; no time to find words; nowhere to run; and no way to prepare herself for what was about to happen. Marty rose from Maria's bleeding body. She ran straight at Mrs. Raybenald, accelerating to full force. She slammed into Coach's chest with fully extended arms. The kinetic collision knocked Coach off balance; pushed her back, faster, and faster; back further still, until she could no longer back pedal fast enough to maintain her footing. Coach Raybenald flew over backwards, conking her head on the natatorium's cement floor. After long seconds. she propped herself up; revived but dazed and with a ferocious headache. She looked up, timidly. Marty stood over her with clenched fists, glaring eyes and bared teeth, daring her to stand up so Marty could have the satisfaction of thrashing her. Marty was a well-muscled young woman now; no longer the skinny little kid that Mrs. Raybenald had yanked over to Admin, years ago.

"You almost killed her; you sick bitch!" Marty bent over Mrs. Raybenald and shouted directly into her face. *"If you ever throw anything at her again; if you ever yell at her again, I will personally beat the living shit out of you. And I don't care WHO YOU THINK YOU ARE! ..... BITCH!"*

Marty shouted her final threat inches from Mrs. Raybenald's face, making an indelible impression; showing the coach no respect whatsoever; and no fear of being sent to Admin. Marty dished out raw street talk, woman to woman. Mrs. Raybenald inched her body back. She was frightened. It was a pathetic attempt to put some distance between herself and Marty. She feared that the young woman in her rage state would pummel her with her fists. Maria's young friend was now her serious, formidable foe. She had just stripped away Coach's authority and dismantled her bully pulpit. Coach's lips quivered, uncontrollably now. For the first time in her life Mrs. Raybenald felt visceral fear of being thrashed; and of being exposed.

She knew her best hope of escaping a thrashing was keeping her mouth shut; not agitate Marty further; and hope the incident would blow over. No adults had seen what had happened. If so, she knew she would lose her job. Perhaps today's near tragedy would never come to the attention of Admin? Perhaps she got lucky? She sat quietly, slowly coming out of her daze, shaking her head, hopeful of surviving this disaster with her position intact. She shook her head, pretended to feel contrite about the whole thing. Inwardly she fumed that Maria's fierce protector had challenged her authority.

"Class is over for today girls. Meet here tomorrow. Same time." Coach said blandly, while getting up. It was a clever ploy. She hoped it would keep her position and power. The ambulance had arrived. They told Coach they were taking Maria to the emergency room at Community Hospital. She told the paramedic that Maria had a simple diving accident. *"That's all. It's all over now.'* Coach turned to her students and spoke matter of factly. *'Maria will be fine. Everyone, go to your rooms."* She looked at Marty, measuring her as a serious challenge to her authority. Marty had relaxed her fists; but she didn't flinch.

"I meant what I said, Mrs. Raybenald," said Marty, stepping forward into the coach's personal space. She spoke with an unflinching, threatening voice; her jaw thrust forward; eyes glaring into Mrs. Raybenald's eyes. *"Your bullying stops now."*

A cognition chill shivered through Swim Coach's spine. It was a primeval sensation, one Mrs. Raybenald had never known before; but one she instinctively understood. She stood face to face with a young woman who was unlike the other girls in her classes. Marty Mallory lived by her own moral code. She did not place rules, or law and order, above her code; rather, beneath it. It was a simple code: Don't harm her or her friend, Maria. If you did, Marty would fight you. The two girls were inseparable. They were a loyal gang of two.

Coach knew this sudden adversary had no reservations. Marty held nothing back while meting out her version of law and order. Once the young wildcat decided to act, it would be impossible to slow or stop her. Neither detention nor fear of criminal punishment deterred her. She could attack, without remorse, anyone who violated her code. Beneath Marty's outwardly placid persona lurked a restless, bloodthirsty fierceness. Mrs. Raybenald correctly intuited that Marty Mallory was conscience free, willing, and capable of doing her harm.

CHAPTER TWELVE

For the preacher's merit or demerit, it were to be wished the flaws were fewer (Robert Browning: Christmas Eve.)

A flawless person is a dull person (Rosemary Lightfoot Ness-Bitner, Author)

PERFECTION

Maria sat on the edge of her bed, looking at pictures of her mother and father. Her bandaged side had been badly lacerated and bruised from her near fatal collision with the pool. Days had passed, but she was still sore and in pain. Tears filled her eyes. She wondered how her mother could have betrayed her love by forcing her to stay in Swim? How could her mother be so disconnected from her feelings and so unconcerned about what Mrs. Raybenald was doing to her? She tried to make sense of what had happened. Her thoughts hearkened back to the time her mother said she wished she were dead; and that she wished Maria had died, instead of John, her brother. The devastating emotions Maria felt while her mother spoke those hurtful words came flooding back to her. She knew her mother spoke the truth, despite her subsequent denials. Maria stood up. She winced. Moving pained her. Her bruises were deep. She was a slow healer. Today, she was determined to write. She forced herself to her desk and sat down to write. Her first letter was to her parents.

'Mother and Father,

'I know I'm a terrible disappointment to both of you. Dad, you never said as much, but I know it's true because you've never wanted to be with me. Mother, why did you want me in the first place? You only wanted John. Nobody gets everything out of life that they want, do they Mother?

I know how important money is to both of you. But I have learned that money is not the only thing in life that matters. I wish you would take some of your money and go on a vacation together; and after that I wish you would adopt a perfect child; not one who is too fat. I sincerely do love you both; but I am tired of being your daughter. Honestly, I'm sick of being your daughter. I'm done. It's time to stop pretending that we are a family. I will not go through the rest of my life thinking about what's wrong with me or what I'm doing wrong. I'm done wondering why I can never please you.

I'm leaving. I'm going away forever. I'm going where I'll be away from the two of you. I don't want either of you in my life anymore. Understand what I have been trying to tell you for years. Not that either of you care, but I'm going to a special place where everyone does a perfect butterfly, and where everybody loves everybody else. I will finally do a perfect butterfly. You will see. Despite your best efforts, you could not defeat my spirit. I'll show you.

Love,
Maria, your perfect butterfly,'

Her second letter was to Marty.

'Marty,

Thank you for your friendship over our years at WEX. You were the only true, honest friend I've ever had. If I hadn't met you, I would never have known what a good friend was. I forgive you for being so *stunningly beautiful; and for being the girl that all the boys want to be with. I know you can't help being the way that you are around boys. I understand that everything in life is, ultimately, all about nature. After all, when you strip away all the pretenses, sex is what men and boys really want, isn't it? I wish and pray that you will have all the sex partners that you could possibly want; and I want you to know that it's okay with me that you are that way. If I had a beautiful face and a perfect body, I'm certain that I'd be the same way. Honest. I mean it. If I had been graced with your gorgeous your face and fabulous body, I'd become the world's most famous porn star. Millions of men would chase after my gorgeous face and my hot panty hamster penis magnet.*

But I'm crying, Marty. I'm crying because I hurt. Not because of my crash into the pool. I'm crying because I wish you could be in my life forever. But I'll be graduating soon. I'm supposed to go back to West Virginia to live with my mother again. What a joke! You know and I know that I can't do that. I can't stand being around her. After all the abuse she's put me through, I'd rather stab a knife into my heart than even talk to her. What can I do? I don't want to go to college. It would be like WEX, except there'd be boys there; and they'd all make fun of my fat. I'd never get away from their scornful eyes. I hate thinking of being trapped in that situation; just hate it! Yikes! I can't bear any more judgmental ridicule. This world was not meant for me. There is no place for me.

I love you, Marty. I very sincerely hope that you love me too. I believe that you did love me. I believe that you are the only person that has ever loved me. I hope you will always remember me as the fat girl who finally did a perfect butterfly. I'll always be 'The Butterfly You Love.'

With all the love I can give you,
Maria.'

Late that afternoon, Maria was ready. She forced her pained body to walk to the natatorium. She sneaked into the building and hid behind the high stacks of life rings until the custodian locked up the building. She sat quietly, staring at the lifeless concrete floor while thoughts of self-loathing, negativity, and worthlessness surged and reverberated through her mind:

'Why did I get stuck with an asshole for a mother? Why won't Dad see what she's done to me? Why must I be the chunky fat girl; the one cursed with a double chin? Why couldn't I have a sleek racehorse; come ride me; come fuck me, body like Marty's? I am so alone; but I am not afraid of dying! Hell no! I am afraid of living! I want no part of it. No more! No more ridicule; no more trying to hide my body in baggy clothes; no more hearing people snicker behind my back. I'm too good for this shit life. I want out. I'll do one final butterfly. I'll show them what they did to me. Fuck them! Fuck everybody! I am leaving all of you. I'm done!'

After she heard the custodian lock up and she was certain she was alone in the natatorium, Maria taped her feet together with duct tape, so her legs couldn't spread apart. She believed Mrs. Raybenald and her mother would notice that. It would send them her 'fuck both of you' message. Around the back of her ankles, she taped a ten-pound weight. That would hold her feet down, keeping her legs level with her body. She taped another ten-pound weight to her left wrist. Finally, in the palm of her right hand, she used fast drying glue to affix the third, ten-pound weight.

Maria was alone now. She wanted to end it this way; all alone. Stars shined their twinkling brightness through the glass dome of the natatorium. She looked up and stared at the entire Milky Way above her. It was a beautiful night to leave. She moved to the edge of the ten-foot-deep pool and sat by its edge, her feet in the water, thinking her last thoughts:

'I'll get down to the bottom and flatten my body. Once I'm down there, I won't be able to change my mind. I won't be able to come back up. That's how I want to end it. I can't change my mind after I slide in.'

She thought these thoughts while staring into the water. She thought
of the water as her eternal resting place; her final home:

'*After I get to the bottom, I'll spread my arms way out; really,
wide. I'll keep them positioned like that. I'll be brave. I will not flinch
or struggle or curl up to a fetal position. I won't give them that satisfaction. I refuse to feel sorry for myself. I will do this the way I want to
do it. This way, my form will look perfect. Maybe the paramedics will
take a picture of my body while it's still under the water. Yeah, they'll
do that. They'll preserve their photos for the coroner. Mother will see
that I finally performed a perfect butterfly. She'll realize what she put
me through. Fuck her! Worthless drunken asshole bitch! I know I won't
be able to change my mind after I go into the water. After I slide in, I
must to go through with this. I must be committed to go all the way. If
I panic, I'd just botch it and drown anyway.*

'*I'll need to make myself perfectly level with the bottom of the pool.
I won't have much time to get my body lined up perfectly. I'll need to
concentrate. I'll need to think: perfect butterfly. When I take my final
deep breath, water will fill my lungs. I must be ready for it. That will
drown me. It happens quickly. It's painless. I hope I have a spirit soul. I
want to come back to life again as a person who has a beautiful body.
'Maybe I'm a human version of a lowly caterpillar, leaving the world
I know. Maybe I'll return, someday, as a beautiful butterfly. I'll flutter
in my beautiful new world. Yes, while I take my last deep breath that's
what I'll believe will happen to me. I'll close my eyes and believe with
all my heart and mind that that is what will happen to me; and that
I'm doing this for the best; for myself; for everybody. Now it's time. I
must go into the water for my last swim. I'll concentrate on my breathing, like Mrs. Raybenald said. When it's time for me to take that big
gulp of air through my nose and my mouth I'll need to take in all the
water into my lungs that I possibly can. I must do this right, completely
fill my lungs with water, or it could hurt. I'll have to pretend it's a big
gulp of air. I must completely fill my lungs with water. I don't want to*

float back up. I can't become afraid. I must breathe in deeply and hold my butterfly position, one final time. There's no use waiting any longer. I have no reason to wait. This is what I've decided to do. It's time for Maria to become a butterfly. It's now........'

Dawn broke slowly. The last evening stars had departed the sky. Before sunrise broke on this mist-hazed morning, some Robin birds were already on the lawns of the Wexler Baxter School for Girls. They hopped about, listening for worms; blissfully unaware of Maria's body in the natatorium, or her travails of the previous night. Quiet morning. It seemed like just another day; life going on. The WEX day custodian was making his rounds. He walked the grounds and checked the parking areas for unauthorized cars, before he opened the gym and natatorium buildings. Inside the natatorium, it took him a minute to realize that something didn't seem right. A sensation overcame him. Something was terribly wrong! *'What! What is this?'* The custodian reeled from his initial shock. *'How could this have happened? Is that? A body? A girl's body? It is! It's a girl's body! It's lying on the cement beside the pool!'* He recovered his initial shock and wondered: *'Is that a real girl lying there? She's naked. How did she get in here? How did she end up this way? What's that in her hands? Why are her legs taped together like that? Did someone try to kill her?'* Maria wasn't moving. His shock and curiosity turned to fright. Panicked, her ran to cold, naked Maria. *"Are you alive?* He shouted and shook her arm. *What the hell did you do?"* he shouted, frustrated, at the motionless body.

Maria was still alive but barely breathing. She was unresponsive when the custodian shook her. Her body temperature had dropped. Her skin was blue and cold to his touch. The custodian called for emergency services and covered her with his jacket to keep her body warm. Soon, WEX campus was awakened with sirens and flashing lights from police cars. An ambulance sped over the manicured WEX lawns making ruts in the grass. It pulled up to the natatorium's main door.

"What have we got here?" asked the police officer. He took pictures of Maria's still body before the paramedics loaded her into the ambulance.

"I found her this way. She must have gotten in here after the last swim class yesterday. I locked up at five. I swear I checked around. I didn't see or hear anybody. I thought there was nobody here. She must have slipped inside during the few minutes before I locked up and left. I don't know how I missed her. I looked around before I locked up. I always look around. I'm telling you, there was no one here."

"Look over here," said the officer, *"behind this stack of life rings."* The police officer showed the custodian a tube of fast drying glue, a roll of duct tape, a scissors, and a girl's bathing suit.

"Jesus, Mary and Joseph," whistled the custodian, *"I never saw that stuff. She must have held it in her hands while I walked around, checking the place. She must have hidden behind these stacks of life preservers while I checked everything before I locked up. She must have taped her legs together with that ten-pound weight. She must have taped her left hand with a ten-pound weight in it; and then glued another ten-pound weight to her right hand. What do you make of it?"*

"I'm not ready to conclude anything." The officer shook his head grimly. *"Homicide needs to investigate this one. It looks like she was going to go into the water all weighted down so she couldn't come back up. It looks like this one was going to commit suicide, but it also could have been an attempted murder. Were there any fights in here recently? Did this one have enemies? Do you know?"* The cop leveled his eyes at the custodian.

"No, not that I know. I just open and lock up. I don't know what goes on in here. I don't know who the girls are, honest." Frightened eyes and a head shake indicated that the custodian could not help further.

The officer expanded his possibilities from murder to include attempted suicide. *"It appears that she was hell bent to do it; go all the way with it. But something must have changed her mind. That, or maybe someone almost got caught and panicked; then left her lying there. Don't know. But she had no head bruises. It looks, to me, more like she was attempting suicide. This one got close. Lots that get this far go all the way with it. They just can't turn back from it. It compels them; haunts their minds and draws them into it. They start having crazy thoughts like there's some next life that they're going to go to, where all the shit in this life stays behind them.*

"*It looks like this one got way past the thinking about it stage. Her swim suit is lying next to the glue tube. Maybe she got in here with her suit on; then she took it off behind those life rings. I don't get the naked part?*" The officer shrugged his shoulders. "*Maybe she wanted to check out of this world naked, the same way she came in. It's hard to get into their heads when they go this far. They aren't nuts. They seem normal to everyone. They hide what they're really thinking. Most of them let themselves get emotionally stressed to the point where they can't take it anymore. They start hating themselves. Then they snap. They need help; but they won't tell anyone what they're thinking. Then they do something like this. It's their way of crying out. The naked part puzzles me though. That's weird. Maybe some guy wanted kicks? That's why I can't rule out murder. Poor girl. She's got a really cute face. Pretty girl. A little on the chunky side; but a damn fine, attractive, nice-looking girl. I can't imagine why anyone would want to hurt her. I just don't get it. Whenever I see one of these, it infuriates me. Kids are special. This should never have happened.*"

The cop shook his head. A grimace, set jaw, and a flash of anger-hate set his face; intimating if he ever fingered who caused this, they'd hang. "*Maybe some 'Shrinks and Winks' will tell you they can make sense of this. Therapy, my ass. It's all bull shit. There needs to be respon-sibility. Whoever fucked with this kid's head needs to swing from a rope. That's what's gotta happen. That stops the bull shit. Looks like she was maybe trying to send a message to somebody; maybe a boyfriend? I've seen some of those. Sad. Pathetic. Maybe no parental love? Lots of kids are fucked up with their parents these days. Who knows? She did what she did. The world is full of fucked up kids."*

"You're telling me?" agreed the custodian. *"I see it way too often. Lots of girls at this fancy school have neurotic fucked up parents. Mostly it's superiority complexes. Big houses, glitz, private jets; no time for their daughters; always pushing them to do more; be more perfect, like circus animals. Lots of girls can't take the pressure. Many have boyfriend issues on top of everything else. This place knows they can't cope. That's why they keep shrinks on the payroll."*

"Shrinks? This place has shrinks? No shit?" The officer pulled his head back in disbelief.

"Yeah, they keep them on retainer arrangements. It's like having a stable of horses. I don't understand their thinking. Maybe shrinks are cheaper than keeping horses. Horses would be better for the girls, if you ask me. But nobody asks me."

"Well, this one cracked. The paramedics should revive her. I think she'll come around. Hope so. Pretty face. Damn; really, pretty face; can't get over that beautiful face! Hopefully she'll talk; explain why she did it. I hate seeing a kid get this messed up. I feel for them, especially when it's a pretty girl like this one. Jesus Christ! I can't believe she did what she did. Listen, I gotta get going. When Admin opens, tell them she's being admitted to Community Hospital. Tell them no visitors allowed until after we talk to her. No shrinks, no parents, no friends, nobody talks to her until we finish talking to her. No exceptions. You got that?"

"Yeah, I got it."

"Good. We'll post an officer at her door and a nurse inside on suicide watch. Tell admin we'll want to talk to her teachers and the students who know her. Hell, this might have been an attempted murder. Who knows? Remember, we want everyone available. No exceptions. No one's allowed to skip town. Everyone stays available until we say our investigation is over. You got that?"

"Got it."

"Good. You can tell admin she looks like she'll live. Her vitals were stable, just way low. She got chilled and went unconscious. Her lips turned blue; but I think we got her in time. Probably she'll come around in the ambulance, before Community admits her. Give me your name for my report." The cop took the custodian's information. Then, shaking his head, he left.

"You cannot stay long. Do not get her excited," cautioned Maria's nurse to Marty. *"She may mumble a few words. She's still incoherent. She's sedated and restrained. Do not loosen her restraints. Don't try to make her relive what she did and don't ask her any 'why did you do it,' questions. Just be her friend and let her know you're here for her. I'll give you ten minutes. That's all, okay?"*

"Okay." Marty entered Maria's room and sat beside her. Maria had wide restraining straps across her stomach and legs. She wasn't going anywhere. She was in an elevated bed that could adjust to raise her upper body and head. Her face and hair were damp. The orderlies had just cleaned her up. A machine was monitoring her heart rate, blood pressure and oxygen level. It beeped every few seconds. Her right hand was bandaged where skin from her hand was removed. Her ten-pound weights had been taken from the room to make sure she couldn't conk her head with them. The only things in her room, besides her bed and machine that monitored her vitals, were a mobile tray table and a chair. The tray table held two plastic containers with flexible plastic straws in them.

The hospital wasn't taking any chances that Maria might try to hurt herself. Her room sign-posted: 'QUIET, SUICIDE WATCH, DO NOT DISTURB.' The patient in room 317 looked like a beached, strapped down fish. She recognized Marty; lifted her head, and smiled.

"Hi, how are you feeling?" asked Marty.

"Better, now. Sorry I made a problem for everyone. I didn't do it for attention, honest. I wanted to do it. I was going to."

"Nurse said you shouldn't talk about it. Don't get yourself excited. Stay relaxed. We can talk later."

"No, I want to talk about it now. I was going to show Mom and Mrs. Raybenald I could do a perfect butterfly; you know, prove it the only way I could. I wanted them to see that, even though I'm not a perfect person; you know, with my weight and all, I could finally do a perfect butterfly. Let them see that I was finally good enough for them. Let them find me naked at the bottom of the pool, my arms way out, legs and feet perfectly together, in back. You know: Butterfly Perfect."

"Maria, you don't need to do this now. I love you, Maria. I love you just the way you are. You're everything anybody could ever want. No butterfly is perfect, anyway. I'm so glad you're my friend. I just want to hold your hand, be your friend, and sit here with you." Marty's eyes watered. Tears flowed down her cheeks.

"Well, the hand you're sitting next to is all bandaged. They cut skin off to get the weight away from me. It hurts like hell, so you can't hold it. Just let me talk, okay?"

That was the Maria that Marty knew when they were younger. She still had that sassy, matter-of-fact way about her. Marty laughed, relieved to hear the old Maria's attitude. *"Okay. Talk,"* she said.

"Well, there I was all ready to do it. I ran through my final checks. I'd done my suicide notes. I'd finished taping my weights to myself. I sat at poolside thinking about going to the bottom of the pool, positioning my arms and legs, and then taking my deep breath of water. Then I asked myself: Is there anything else? That's when I thought about you."

"Me?"

"Yeah you, hot stuff. I thought if I went through with this you might feel guilty about necking with the twins at the beach, while

I sat there, stuck in the sand like a dufus. And then I thought you might start feeling guilty about what you were doing while you ignored me."

"Oh, Jesus, Maria, I'm sorry about that. Honest I am. I'll never do something like that again. I was just so totally into the moment. I could feel myself getting all stimulated. I had these overpowering urges. I was in another world. I wanted to do it."*

"You mean you wanted to fuck both of them, didn't you?"

"Maria!" Marty held her hand to her mouth. Maria hadn't used the 'F' word before.

"It's okay. We're big girls now. We can talk big girl talk, too. And Marty......" Maria's word hung in the air.

"What Maria, tell me. What?"

"I want you to do me a huge favor. It will really help me if you'll do what I ask of you. Okay? It would make me feel a whole lot better about myself."

"What, Maria? Tell me. I'll do it. Anything, Maria. I'll do it for you. Just ask. I love you. You know I love you."

"I know Marty. I know you love me. You're the only reason I'm still here. Okay?"

Marty nodded her head. Tears flowed down her cheeks. She laid her head on Maria's arm. *"Just tell me what I can do for you, Maria. Tell me."*

"Look at me, Marty," Maria commanded. Marty lifted her upper body a little higher and raised her head. Her watery eyes met Maria's. Maria smiled. *"Marty, I want you to call those twin boys up and go out on a date with them. And when you are out with them, I want you to fuck both of them. I want you to have the time of your life with them. I want to know you are cheerfully fucking your brains out! I want to know that Mother Nature took her natural course. I want you to be happy, Marty."* Maria smiled at her friend.

"What? Maria! Even Billy; your date, too? You're serious, aren't you?" Marty looked deeply into Maria's eyes; they were smiling back at her. Maria's whole face was smiling.

"Hell yes, I'm totally serious. If you'll promise me that you'll do that I'll be the happiest I've ever been; for myself and for you. So please do that for me. I was wrong to let myself use you to get me a date. And I was very wrong to get upset with you when you were simply feeling Mother Nature's urges. You are a stunningly beautiful woman, Marty. You draw boys to you like flowers draw bees. So, get free of all your hang-ups, including me. Go have yourself a ball. Literally! Ha!"

Maria laughed at her unintended homonym. *"Seriously, when I was feeling sorry for myself, I left a small box for you in my room, next to the suicide note I left for you. In it, you will find a year's supply of birth control pills and a dozen condoms for boys you suspect might have a disease or something. I mean this, you gorgeous boy bait, glamorous party slut in waiting. Go call those twins and date them; then fuck them every which way you can think of fucking them; even try doing both twins at once."*

"Maria! I can't believe I'm hearing this. And from you, of all people! You were always so reserved!" Marty was shocked. Here was prudish Maria having a full turnabout of mindset. Not only was Maria volunteering to be Marty's moral scape goat, giving her psychological comfort for slaking her sexual appetite; she was also complementing Marty with basic sex accessories, ensuring that her friend fully enjoy her dalliances without lingering concerns over consequential risks.

"Oh hell, Marty, that was just an act on my part, because I know I'm too fat. My face is okay; but I'm not a pretty body with a hot to fuck, juicy lady flower, like you. I've been laying here thinking these last few hours. My problem is my own problem; and I haven't done a damn thing about it. Yeah, I'm heavy, but I've let myself become gross. That stops now. I'm going to make big changes when I get out of here. I'll graduate from here, bandage and all. I'm dropping Swim. I don't care

who doesn't like it. I'm not even waiting for my graduation ceremonies. I'm leaving here. And I'm leaving West Virginia forever.

"I'm taking some money and I'm moving to Montana or Colorado. I want to be where there are open spaces. I want to start a new life from there. And I'm going to eat healthy and work out and exercise every damn day of my life, for the rest of my life. I'm going to work out my body until it hurts so much that I'll feel like it's killing me. I'm going to breathe fresh air and see blue skies and forget this fucked-up place and my fucked-up parents. And I'm going to forget all their neurotic bull shit.

"I don't care if I have to muck horse barns, or become a camp cook for some outfitters. I'll start at the bottom and work my way up from there. If I need extra money, I'll give hunters fantastic cum in my mouth blow jobs for tips. I don't care. That will be just fine with me. The old prude Maria, whom you once knew, is done and gone, forever. I want new. I will be the new, improved, kick-ass Maria. And I'm going to let some fella find me; and he'll be getting a good woman, because I'm smart. And most fellas need a smart woman, because most fellas are fucked up six ways from stupid. And most of them don't even know what's good for them. And when my good man finds me, I'm going to fuck that fella so beautifully, and so often, and so long; 'til he's damn near dead from exhaustion. He has no idea how good I'm going to be to him or how much loving he's going to get. I am letting the old Maria go! And.........."

"Your time's up, Marty," the nurse returned from outside the door. From the way she smiled, Marty surmised that the woman had heard the entire conversation, and that she was agreeing with Maria's advice. But Maria had gotten herself riled up and excited. That was a hospital no-no. It was time to leave.

As Marty got up to leave, Maria raised the free fingers of her good hand. Marty went to her side and held her hand. *"You make that phone call, girl. You promise me."* ordered Maria, smiling.

"I will, Maria, soon; but I want to get a tattoo first. It's important to me. But I promise you, as soon as my tattoo is healed, I'll make that call. And thank you for my naughty box of sex essentials. I promise I'll put them to good use. And Maria, I'll come by again tomorrow and visit some more. Okay?"

"Okay," Maria smiled. *"I'd like that."*

"I love you, Maria," smiled Marty to her from the door.

"I love you back, Marty," smiled Maria.

Marty's mind returned to her present day. She was home in Colorado again; still sitting on her sofa and sipping her tea; recalling her years at WEX, when the best friendship of her life first formed.

CHAPTER THIRTEEN

Passion, I see, is catching (Shakespeare: Julius Caesar)
Lesbia hath a beaming eye, but no one knows for whom it beameth
(Thomas Moore: Lesbia Hath)

TOGETHER

"What you're asking me to do will hurt a lot, young lady," said the tattoo artist during his consultation with Marty. *"I think you'd be able to bear the pain better if I put it on your back. Must it be between your legs, right up to and on your mons pubis, lightly against your vagina like that? I'm warning you; this will be extremely painful. There's less sensitive skin available. The skin on the small of your back, or the skin on your leg, lower down, closer to your ankle, would be less painful choices."*

Marty's tattoo artist tried to dissuade her from placing her tattoo on her uppermost inner thighs, but Marty wouldn't change her mind. Her eyes took him in. He was tall. His face was somewhat triangular and elongated, like his body. His eyes were a piercing shade of blue with pupils that came at her like his tattoo needles. She thought that his eyes were a nice complement to the work he did: pinpoint needling into skin. She wondered if anyone had ever mentioned that to him. His body grew black curly hair that showed out of the top of his shirt. His hair gave her thoughts:

'Funny that a man who does his kind of work has so much body hair? I would have thought he preferred smooth skin? Maybe just for

people he tattoos? Hard to figure him by just looking. He seems intense. Yes, very intense; very professional. All this equipment! I wonder how I'd feel if his big hairy hands were touching me everywhere, and tugging on my nipples? Will he want to fuck me? How would I feel lying naked under him; his big hairy chest rubbing me? He's very muscular. Must be he works out. I'd love to find out how he kisses. I want to rub my hands all over his back and sides while he fucks me; that's if he'll want me. I'll bet he's got great stamina. He has huge shoulders. I think he'd handle me like a man should handle a woman. I think I'd love fucking him, if he wants me.'

"*I don't care about pain.*" Marty got past her thoughts and addressed the artist's objections. She knew what she wanted. She wasn't about to be talked out of it. "*I'll get past the pain, all right. I want it exactly where told you I want it because I want it to send a message.*"

"*A message? To whom?*" The artist was skeptical about doing the procedure.

"*To men whom I allow to see it. I want them to get the right message. That's why I don't want it on my backside, or my ass, or on my leg above my ankle. Those would be okay places if I was a socializing high-falutin sorority girl; and if I was messaging that I'm trying to catch some loopy, lovey-dovey fellow to flutter through life with; a life partner and provider. That's not what I want to say. I'm trying to tell my sex partners that my affairs with them are based on freedom. Understand? The tattoo will tell them that I'm not about lifetime romance, chocolates, flowers, and kids. I want it to say I want sex-based intimate love, as long as it lasts. Can you get that?*"

"*Yeah, I guess I get it. But it seems off base for a woman to think that way, if you ask me.*"

"*Well, I didn't ask you. Okay?*" Marty lifted her chin, showing the artist she was a defiant, determined woman. "*I'm not like other women. I'm not trolling for a husband, okay? My friend, Maria, knows me well. She says I have a cold, calculating mind; and a hot, love-craving, must-have sex, penis garage for a pussy. And I keep thoughts about what's good for my life separate from what I need to satisfy my libido. And I don't intend to confuse the two. Okay?"* Marty's tone signaled that her personal preferences about how she wanted to live her life were not something she cared to dispute or discuss.

"Okay! Okay, I've got it." The tattooist shrugged his shoulders. Nevertheless, he shook his head to let Marty know that he still disagreed with her tattoo placement location. *"May I ask why you want a Monarch butterfly; and, why it must be so large?"*

"Yeah, I'll tell you." Marty smiled her sly fox smile and tilted her head. That was her way of giving a man a glimpse into her mind; drawing him into her world:

"When I was a little girl, Mom wouldn't let me in her kitchen when she was making something. That made me feel unwanted, so I went to a corner of our garden and made mud pies. I was mad at Mommy. I imagined Dad would love my mud pies more than Mommy's cooking. I made breakfast mud pies, lunch mud pies, dinner, and desert mud pies. That's when I started talking to my imaginary friends. I told them I was going to grow up and steal Daddy away from Mommy. Miss Shameless told me there was nothing wrong with doing that. Miss Iniquity told me that Mommy had it coming; and Miss Promiscuous told me that I should get Daddy alone, away from Mommy and that I should kiss him until he loved me more than Mommy. I hadn't given my friends their names yet. My voices got their names later. When I was a little girl, they were just voices. I knew them by their different ways of thinking about things and by what they told me.

"One day my voice friends and I were busy making mud pies when this kaleidoscope of Monarch butterflies came to our garden. One very big one sat on my finger. It opened and closed its wings. My eyes lit up with how beautiful it was. I believed it was telling me something. Miss Iniquity, my Decisions Voice, said the butterfly understood my feelings,

especially my desire to feel love. Miss Promiscuity, my Desire Voice, and Miss Shameless, my Devil May Care voice, said the butterfly was messaging me. It told me that I could take Daddy from Mommy; that I should be open and carefree about it, and never feel guilty about it. I never did steal Daddy from Mommy. She took him away from me, before I got the chance. She took him by the terrible way she treated him. Now he's gone."

The artist's eyebrows lifted and his eyes squinted as he tried to process what Marty was implying. He was concerned about doing tattoos for reasons clients might regret later. *"Hold on a minute, just so I understand your reason for wanting me to do this. Are you saying that the butterfly takes your guilt away? Is this some mentally symbolic thing? Are you saying that you are going to fuck your father so you can take him away from your mother?"*

Marty giggled. *"Now that's an interesting thought. I'll give you that. No, I was only four or five when I had thoughts about taking Daddy away from Mother. I was too young to even know what fucking was; otherwise, I might have tried it. Hah! Don't lose sleep over that. It's not going to happen. Daddy's dead. He died when I was five. You are not part of some scheme to commit incest. You're completely safe."*

The artist's head lifted. He exhaled a sigh of relief. *"Good you told me that. I was starting to believe we were enabling some bad thinking. So, perhaps this idea is some kind of a holdover from some little girl thoughts that you are now transferring to someone else. Is that it?"*

"No. You're close; but that's not quite it. It's not about transference of my quest to liberate Daddy to another man." Marty looked him in the eye and shook her head. It was her very serious, determined look. *"But I have decided the take away message that the butterfly gave me as a young girl perfectly expresses my current feelings about men in general. I now see all men as fair game for seduction, whether they are married or not. I now believe my butterfly messenger visited me for a reason. That butterfly told me to embrace life and pursue my special*

destiny. It told me to be free and to set others free. It gave me the right message for me! Now I know what I want to be."

"Okay, Ill bite. What do you want to be?"

"I've decided to become a highly promiscuous woman; possibly a prostitute or a porn star. And I want to feel free and shameless about my promiscuity. You see, when a butterfly flutters, it is free. It feels no guilt about anything it does. That's why I want my butterfly tattoo. And that's why I want you to put it where I told you to put it. I want it to constantly remind myself and others that I am a free woman; that no one controls me; that I make no permanent commitments, other than to myself and my happiness. I want the men I seduce to know that I've willed myself to be promiscuous; that they understand that is my choice. I want them to feel free about their relationships with me. They don't need to look out for me or take care of me. I want my butterfly to make them desire me sexually; remember me always; but also assure them that I make love of my own free will, and for joy and pleasure. But not because I'm trying to enslave them to care for me. Okay?"

The artist pulled in his lips to hold back a smile. He nodded. He leveled a serious gaze into Marty's eyes. *"You really want that sort of image, that sort of lifestyle, don't you?"*

"Yes. You bet I do. The world is changing. It's hard to depend on anyone or any institution or religion or government anymore. Nothing works like it did before. A woman needs to form new relationships to replace old ones. One man doing the husband thing doesn't cut it any-more. Now, can we stop talking about whether I'm thinking straight? Can we stop discussing philosophy and start working on my tattoo, please?" Marty's face was dead serious. Her eyes were commanding and penetrating. The artist knew she wasn't joking.

"Okay. You're the client." His lips assumed a closed smile as he nodded. He was ready to do what she wanted. *"Tell me what you want."*

"Well, I've looked through your sample book. I want it to be like a Monarch with its wings widespread. You have one in your book that's kind of like that, only I want my butterfly to be bigger. And I want its wings to be even brighter colors of oranges and yellows. I want the hood of my vagina to look like it's part of my butterfly's head; like my vagina is its butterfly body and its head extends up and above its 'where vagina loves doing her cock loving business' butterfly body. And I want my butterfly's front feelers to curl and form the outline of a heart above its head. That's to tell my lovers that making love with them is about intimate romantic love, not just sex. Can you do that? Can you make its head look like it's attached to and part of my vagina?"

The artist nodded and smiled. *"Yeah Babe, I can do that. I can do anything. If you can handle the pain, I can put your tattoo there. I must compliment you. This will be very creative; original. I've never seen one quite like that; never done one myself. You've thought about this, haven't you?"*

Now Marty smiled her winsome, come closer to me, smile. Hearing him call her 'Babe' relaxed her. She felt they were like partners now. *"Oh yeah. Lots of thought. You bet."*

"That's good. That makes it easier for me to work with you. Now, what about the butterfly's wings?"

"Well, here's where you'll need to do your best work. I want the colors extra bright orange and yellow; as bright as you can possibly make them. I came to you because your ad said you were the best tattoo colorist in the area."

His condescending smile assured Marty that the talent behind his smile was, indeed, the best. *"You see my shop? Let me assure you. I have the best hand made machines for performing intricate coloring. I have the right long and short needles that make the right skin spreads and deposit the exactly right colors, in the exactly right amount, at the exactly the right skin depths. I have the best ink colors that money can buy. I am experienced with different skin types, including soft, flexible skin, like yours. I can do perfect layering's within the skin to create the most vibrant, brilliant colors possible. I also give you a supply of products to keep your tattoo looking fresh and vibrant for years after you leave here. And I am careful and quick with my work so you will heal rapidly and safely. I am the best at what I do. And I do not work cheap. You tell me what effect you want this tattoo to have on the men who see it. We'll go from there."*

"Okay. You've sold me. It must express a woman's hunger for sex. When a man sees it, I want it to blast into his consciousness. He must instantly desire my butterfly vagina. Its image must sear into his mind; burn its brand image into his mind. And it must entice him; make him feel a lust surge; make him desire to fuck me; make him feel he absolutely must have me. I want him to salivate at the thought of putting his face into my loving vag; and then imagine touching his cock to my outer lips, signaling that he's dying to enter my slippery hot, anxious to fuck, honey pot. I want my butterfly to be so stunning that it makes men salivate and produces instant hard-ons. I want them to see it, then imagine having their cocks inside me; feeling my heat and slippery wetness. I want it to make them crave making their imaginations become reality, okay? I want it to make their cocks go instantly hard and anxious to be inside me, like their cocks have their own minds and won't be denied what they must have. Are you getting this? I want them, when they see it, to instantly think that I'm a shameless whore who has no morals or guilt complexes whatsoever, and who absolutely loves to fuck. Can you do that?"

"Yes, of course, I can. I get it. I can do it. I'm the best, remember? You've got the right man for this. We'll need layered coloring. I'll create a brilliant color scheme to first attract and hold men's eyes. The tattoo will have such brilliant coloration it will instantly stun men into a sharp concentrated focus on it. Believe me, they'll forget everything else. If they have other women, they'll be gone. Their minds will only think of getting their cocks inside your juice box. Your butterfly will instantly

capture their eyes. Their minds will forget everything else. Then, as I bring the coloration closer to your outer vag lips, I'll subtly increase the intensity of the coloration, making it progressively more mysterious and compelling. I'll create a smooth visual transition from the tattoo, channeling their eyes and mind to your beaver's pink outer lips. Psychologically, their minds will tell them that they need to go there; that they absolutely, positively, must get their cocks inside you. They won't even realize that it's happening. Your tattoo will cause an irresistible, natural movement of their eyes that will lead their thinking right into your love channel and hold their thoughts there; locked in. Their minds will obsess over getting their cocks into you. Their souls will forsake everything and everyone else to join your soul by going into your love channel. Your butterfly vagina will become their obsession.

"Yeah, Marty Babe, I'm totally into this now. I'll create a sensational effect. Your tattoo and pussy will be eye candy. Your tattoo will draw men's eyes to your pink outer lips and hold them there as if they are riveted in place. I'll bring your wings right up to and touching your outer vag lips so they will look like they are joined to your vagina's butterfly body; like they are part of it. I'll use butterfly feeler feet to border the wing edges and your outer lips. I'll create the visual effect that your feeler feet will hold a man's cock inside you while you love him out of his mind with the best sex he's ever known. I'll create a continuous, haunting, unforgettable effect. Men will never stop thinking of you after they see your butterfly. Your cunt will haunt them in their sleep. They won't be able to get you out of their minds. I'm really into thin now. I'll make your colorations gradually bleed into the subtle natural shades of purple on your vagina's outer lips boundary. That coloration will psychologically make men relate your psychedelic flower pot to heaven and royalty. It will convince their emotions, their limbic lusts, that you are a heaven-sent goddess and it make them want to be all the way into you; like wanting to surrender their entire lives and souls to you; hold

nothing back. They'll be willing to throw away all their past loves and all their money to have intimacy with you.

"Trust me. Your tattoo will make men psychologically believe that their penises belong inside your gorgeous juice box, just yours; always. And never anywhere else. If they're married men, their wives will become ancient history. I can promise you that. I hope you're ready for that. Ex-wives can be a pain in the ass. I hope you know that. Once a man has seen your tattoo and has had intimate sex with you, he will never get you out of his mind. He could have sex with his wife or girlfriend or with ten other women after he's been with you; but he will always want to come back to you. He'll find his way back. He'll come back. He won't be able to stay away from you. Are we good?"

"Yeah, we're good. That's what I want. You've sold me."

"Okay, then we'll do this. To create this mesmerizing effect will take me three, possibly four, sessions over a four-week period. Are you okay with my thinking?"

"Yes, very okay with it. I like that you'll bring my wings close, right up and touching against my vag lips. Inside my vagina is where I have my intense sexual urges. If I'm asked about my tattoo, I want to be able to honestly say that I feel free and unashamed about making love; and that I'm unconcerned about taking the man's love away from another woman; and that I'm proud to be immoral and promiscuous. The tattoo also needs to accent my credibility that way. It must match my thoughts and my words. Will it do that?"

"Oh yes, I'm confident that it will do exactly that. But I'm curious, may I ask you why it must be a Monarch butterfly? There are so many different butterflies. Some of the African varieties are brilliant in purples and reds and blacks. They scream passion to me. We could do one of those. Have you thought about that? Have you settled on the Monarch?"

"Yes, I have thought about it. It must be a Monarch butterfly because a Monarch has four life cycles to remind me and everyone who sees it that people can make terrible mistakes; but that there are always multiple chances for redemption. I seek to offer redemption to men who have made mistakes; especially the wrong wife or girlfriend. People need to feel confident to begin anew, with new relationships. My lovers can also think of their relationships with me as a chance for a renewed life with renewed happiness for them. I want those feelings I have for them to be communicated by my tattoo. The Monarch uniquely reinforces those feelings."

"Okay. Got it! And you want it to be extremely large, actually oversized for a Monarch?"

"Yes. I'm sure of that. When I flex my upper thigh muscles, I want my wings to ripple and shimmer with their brilliant colors, as if I'm a butterfly beginning to flutter; as if to message my partners that while I'm fucking them, I'll be fluttering with their cocks inside me, and they'll be fluttering along with me, like we are two butterflies mating. I want to be able to use the tattoo as body language to signal that I'm ready to flutter. It needs to be large, brilliant, and realistic that way. I need it to have some size to do that. I want all who see it to know that it is who and what I am. When I flex my thigh muscles, I will remove all doubt and show that I am boldly proud of who and what I am. I'm going to message my promiscuity unmistakably and honestly. I intend to be a shameless, iniquitous, immoral whore." Marty felt a little nervous. She rambled some while explaining her feelings to this new acquaintance, but she was determined to convince him to tattoo her perfectly.

"The tattoo will be my way of saying that I'm not ashamed or embarrassed about who or what I am. I'm proud to be a whore." Her artist was handsome, broad shouldered and muscular. She guessed he was about ten years older than she. She continued explaining herself, convincing herself as well as him. *"And I've decided it needs to be placed way high up, between my legs, because that's where life begins.*

I want to invite life and happiness into my vagina. I want my partners to understand that I want to give them my love. They must see and know me as a loving, unselfish woman. I want them to identify me as synonymous with love. I want them to give me their love by having their penises inside me and ejaculating their semen inside me. I want to be their antidote to stress, hatred, and meanness; their refuge from confusion, unfair demands, and bullying."

"You said your friend thought you had a cold, calculating mind." The artist frowned at the contradiction. *"But, to me, you sound like a very passionate, emotive, amorous, highly sexualized woman. Which woman are you?"*

"Yeah. Maria's got that right about me. We agree that a woman needs to look out for herself. But a woman can be both a sexpot lover and have a mind that looks out for her best interests at the same time. That's what enables a woman to change. Look, my dearest friend has changed. She's taken control of her life after years of getting beaten down. She suffered terribly from hatred and bullying because she was fat, which made her unattractive; but she couldn't help the way she was. She had emotional problems that she simply couldn't escape. She was trapped. She had no way out. So, she overate. But certain people were cruel to her because of the way she looked. That was nasty and wrong of them. She didn't deserve to be treated badly. But these people kept it up until they almost broke her.

"People can be mean, while they pretend that they are being cute or funny, or make believe they are trying to help; but I see that behavior for what it is. It's power over another person. It's bullying. It's hateful and terrible. It's mentally very destructive. Poor Maria; I'll always remember how they nearly destroyed her."

"Jesus, girl. You're on a mission, aren't you? That's what this is about, isn't it?"

"Yes. So? In my own way, in my own mind, I'm going to dedicate my life to bringing love into the world. I want men to know that they

can find love when they are inside me. Physical, erotic romantic love; and women too, for those who are so inclined. I want to be successful and all that. Sure, I do; but most of all, I want to be a lover. I want to make love! I want a circle of friends that love me and love themselves. That's how life should be."

The artist again checked to be sure he would be doing this for the right reasons and for a woman who possessed all her faculties. *"So, you're doing this because your friend was bullied? I'm asking because I don't want you coming back here in a few weeks and telling me to take it off. That would be much more painful than putting it on, and you'd be disfigured for life. I want to be sure you've thought this through, young lady."* His eyes signaled that he was skeptical.

Marty's face stiffened. *"I know what I'm doing. I have the money to pay you. Any other questions?"*

"Only this one, what about the women whose boy friends you'll seduce with your drop dead looks and this tattoo? Have you thought about how much love you'll be sending their way?"

"Yes, I'll be liberating them from their quaint possessive ideas about love and monogamy. They'll become more understanding of their part-ners and more committed to them because they'll appreciate their needs more and they will love them more. I think they'll come around to that; but it's everyone's choice, I understand that. I can't save the world from all its inhibitions."

"Are you seeing a shrink?" There, he finally asked her. He felt he had to. His skepticism was out in the open.

"Yes, I am." Marty beamed her confident smile, letting him know she had nothing to hide. *"I have seen shrinks most of my life. She's fine with my tattoo idea. She understands it's also my way of honoring my friend's wishes for me. It will remind me of my wonderful friend, every single day."*

"You're doing this to honor a friend?"

"Well, yes. But that's not all of it. I had issues about my relationship with my mother. My shrink, Mrs. O'Dell, thinks it will be helpful for my emotional well being to look beyond the relationship I couldn't have and look forward to the relationships I can have. She explained that relationships do not need to be permanent, like a marriage with all its restrictions and expectations. I may have something like that, someday; but until then, I should concentrate on acquiring relationships, many of them, that make me feel good and that give me a sense of accomplishment. New relationships help a person grow; she advised me.

"She asked me what I honestly thought I'd like doing more than anything else in the world. I told her I felt I needed to be loved. We talked about that. She helped me understand that I could help boys and men choose to give me their love if I fucked them and sucked their cocks. She explained limbic desires and how that led to intimacy and love. We decided that I should think of myself as a lowly caterpillar, eating milkweed leaves. And every time I seduced a new lover, I'd be taking another bite of milkweed and growing as a person who loves herself more. I see the wisdom in thinking about life that way. Every seduction, every lover, helps a woman, like me, grow my self-esteem and confidence."

"But why the butterfly tattoo?"

"Well, the ultimate goal of the caterpillar is to enter chrysalis and transform itself into a butterfly. And that's my goal, too. I'm hopeful that, by becoming expert enough and talented enough at sucking cocks and fucking my partners, that I'll eventually be able to change myself from being an ordinary, everyday, promiscuous girl into a professional prostitute or even a glamorous porn star. I've decided that I want to work myself into pornography and make erotic films. I want to become a porn star. And my tattoo will be my constant reminder that I have that goal and that I must honor my goal and try to be the very best seductress, the most sought-after whore I can possibly become. I hope

that I'll get the opportunity to create pornography. And when I do, I'll remind myself of my goal. I'll try to do things that set me apart from all other porn stars. I want to flutter above everyone else."

"But, Marty, you are so incredibly beautiful. You have a face that men dream about. Your smile is joyful and honest. It radiated happiness. It's glorious. Why wouldn't you want to become a regular actress and do Broadway or cinema films, or a television show? Why porn?"

"Because porn is not fake. It's real. The intimacy and emotive feelings a woman experiences, while she's fucking her partner or sucking his cock, is a real, honest feeling. There's love in those feelings. I wouldn't get those feelings if I was playing some role as an actress. I could never feel as good about myself as when I'm fucking a man I'm seducing."

"But there are thousands of porn stars. Why do you want to be just like the rest of them?"

"Don't be silly. Every porn star is different. Every film she makes has nuances that are different from any other film that any other porn star ever made. Do you watch football?"

"Yes."

"Well, is every football team the same? Is every player the same? Is every game the same as every other game?"

"No. So, what are you saying? I should watch ten different porn films from different porn stars to grasp all their subtleties?"

"Almost. Now you're getting it. I'm suggesting that you watch a hundred films from a thousand different porn stars; that's a hundred thousand films. And then you will have a better appreciation for how magnificent porn stars really are. But even then, you will not have captured even ten percent of their fascinating loveliness. Their films are as different as women are different. No two are alike. Some might say you would become addicted if you watched that much porn. But let them say what they want. I say, if you watch that much porn, you're making great progress in your understanding of women's feelings; and that's a good thing."

"Okay, I shouldn't feel guilty about watching porn. I get it. But what about the other women, the wives of the men you seduce? Don't you have feelings about them? Won't your whoring cause you some regrets?"

"No regrets. I don't have any feelings for them. And I can't hold myself responsible for any feelings that they may have. Why should I? They decided upon a path for their lives. They should know the men they married. If I take their men from them, that's their problem; not mine. That's life and all its vagaries. Life just didn't work out for them the way they believed it would. The spirits wanted to change things; the dice didn't roll their way; that's all. Why do you ask? Are you married?"

"Yes."

"Well, tell me the truth. Wouldn't you like to fuck me?"

"Yes. Hell yes, I would."

"And, do you care about your wife enough to say no to me? While you are holding me and kissing me, could you say to yourself: 'What we are doing is wrong. I must stop.' Could you say that? Could you stop?"

"No. I couldn't say no to you."

"Well, there you have it. You see, that desire for individual freedom is fundamental. It's the human spirit. It's wrong to stifle it and shut it down. It's beautiful to let it have its freedom."

"So, tell me, what are your shrink's thoughts about marriage?"

"Well, she believes marriage is a wonderful institution. It's a beautiful way for two people to express their love and commitment to each other. And, it's exciting and romantic. There's the honeymoon, the joys of togetherness and all the shared experiences and memories. But she also believes that the spirit which lives within each individual is the most important thing in every individual's life. And it is only natural for every human person to feel desire for someone at sometime who is not their spouse. It's a limbic thing. It arouses the libido. And it's perfectly natural. When the marriage acts as a constraint on that limbic desire, the marriage becomes problematic because it seeks to suppress the libido, which is wholly natural. It seeks to deny freedom; thus, it

causes frustration. The married partners must be honest with each other if they seek to preserve their bond of harmony. They must allow for the natural limbic desire to express itself; and they must set it free. A married woman must allow her husband to seek the company of another woman, or prostitute, or porn star, if that's what his libido is compelling him to do. A married husband must allow his wife to seek the company of another man, or become a prostitute, or porn star, if that is what her libido is compelling her to do. The married partners must have an agreement and an understanding that the needs of the individual cannot be controlled by a marriage contract. They must allow for natural changes."

"And you agree with your shrink about this freedom need, do you? You believe making love with you would give me freedom?"

"Yes, I completely agree with her thinking. And yes, I believe if we made love, you would experience a new sense of freedom. Love and intimacy creates a special, romantic connection. It would absolutely open your door to freedom. Love and intimacy respect your individual need to honor your natural limbic desires. Love and intimacy allows your libido to honestly express itself. Making love with me; having that intimate connection with me which that would create, would liberate the natural freedom need that resides within your soul. Don't you believe that making love with me would help you experience a refreshing sense of freedom?"

"Yes. I suppose it would. In fact, I'm certain it would. I've never looked at life that way before. You've helped me understand why I desire to make love with you. I feel good about that feeling now. Guilt free. Thank you. So, have we covered all the reasons for doing the tattoo?"

"Almost. The butterfly is also my way of greeting a new lover. Likely, he'll have seen it in one of my porn films. Then, when we're alone and having foreplay, while he holds me in his arms and kisses my neck and fondles my breasts and pinches and kisses my nipple buds, he'll have the sense that he's approaching his destiny."

"Which is?"

"My vagina, silly. When I take his hand; slide it into my panties and bring it over my mons pubis and gently press it against my vagina, he'll know I'm receptive to making love with him. He'll know he's finally touched his passport to freedom."

"Freedom?"

"Yes, freedom. Freedom from all the constraints in his life; freedom from whatever forces are oppressing him. His marriage. His work. Whatever it is that's bothering him. I'll be offering him a way to escape from any of it; and all of it. Freedom. Glorious, beautiful freedom. Then, when he performs cunnilingus with me; when I orgasm into his mouth, he'll understand that I'm accepting him into my world; that I am fine with him leaving whatever it was that troubled him; that I have no doubts that leaving whatever relationship he's in, so he can be with me, is the right thing for him and for me; that I'm happy to receive him into my world, as he is; without trying to change him or make him into someone he's not."

"So, when you orgasm into his mouth, that's your way of accepting him?"

"Oh yes, a thousand times yes! Absolutely it is! It's bringing my mind into intimate contact with his mind, through orgasm. It's letting him know that I'm ready; ready for him to enter me with his penis; connect his soul with mine; and experience fluttering pleasures with me; ready to help him become free, like me. And when he ejaculates his semen into me, he'll know that our souls have connected; that our intimacy is his new, real world. And he'll know that he's loved in his new world, as I will know that he loves me."

'New world? Love? Intimacy?"

"Yes, all of that. It's a spiritual thing, too; a joining of two souls; a coming together and an understanding that we are special for each other. I'll be welcoming him into my life and into my friend's life too. He'll surrender his life to our spirits' lives, come into our sweet and open *spirits; joining his soul to ours. He'll join my spirit of lust passions; open himself to my love. When he ejaculates inside me, our spirits' souls will become unified. My girlfriend and I are very giving and loving. We've discussed this. We want to offer our spirits to the world. My friend is correcting her weight problem. She'll be a gorgeous femme. I dream about her; that's how beautiful she is.*

"She has a stunning face and lovely eyes; a blue-eyed red head. She'll be more beautiful and promiscuous than me. She'll come to see you. She'll get an identical tattoo in the same identical place. It's our way of believing in each other; believing in our love and redemption. And believing in life's second chances. We can read each other's minds and feel each other's feelings. We're grateful for that. If she hadn't read my mind a few days back, she wouldn't be alive. If you knew her, you'd understand."

The artist set aside his skepticism. Marty's talk about her steadfast commitments to whoring, and her comments about Maria, caused his libido to triumph over his caution. "Could I meet her? I love meeting promiscuous chicks that can translate their limbic emoting into uninhibited sex. Please?"

"Later, sorry. She just finished her farewell visit to her mother and father. She stopped by WEX to pick up her course materials. She's going to finish school from long distance. She's flying to Colorado to start a new life. She'll be back to see me before I graduate next year. I'll introduce you. She's a hottie and a serious player. Handle with care. You'll be on your own."

"Okay, thanks. Well, let's see what we have here. Hop onto this table and put your legs in the clamps. I need to spread you wide and take a close look, all right?"

"Yes, let's start." Marty climbed up onto the tattoo table. It had a support that lifted her back and head. She lifted her legs into the clamps. The artist swung the clamps outward, giving him an unobstructed view.

"Wow, very smooth. Lasered or waxed?"

"Lasered, of course. Four treatments."

"Looks like they got all of them. I don't see a single hair. How long since your last treatment?"

"Almost four weeks now."

"How long since you last used creams?"

"Four days."

"Excellent." The artist touched, pulled, and pinched her mons skin around her outer vaginal lips and above her crown. *"Well, I can't find or feel any hair. I'm sure they got all of them. Your mons is pearly smooth and beautiful; just the right thickness; soft and plump to lay in my inks, too. Perfect! You're already breathtakingly beautiful from this end. You know, you don't have to do this."*

"We've covered that before. I want to do it. I'm sure. Okay?"

"Sure, okay." The artist lifted his head. Raised eyebrows and intrigued smile questioned Marty. *"I sense Gardenia and a touch of lilac? Am I getting that right? Do you buy it, or is it your home concoction?"*

Marty's face broke into a grin. *"I experiment. I blend oils with my scents. It's my own creation: gardenia, lilac, touches of jasmine, lavender, and sandalwood with a few drops of vanilla. Like it?"*

"Like it? Babe, I'm salivating. Love it! I want to put my face into you and kiss you there. It floats me over Elysium fields. You're heaven on Earth."

"I like that thought about where you want to place your face. Tell me. No fishy trace?"

"None, absolutely none. You have one hygienic, fuck-ready, delicious vagina. I'd love to do so much more than simply tattoo you."

"I'm getting that. That's possible."

"May I see you later then, after your tattoo heals? Could I experience that wonderful freedom you were talking about? Maybe you'd also give your friend a positive endorsement?"

"Maybe, everything is possible." Marty beamed her most seductive smile. *"Can I have a discount?"*

"Twenty-five percent off. Okay?"

"Fifty percent off and dinner first, at a five star, sounds better."

"You're going to love my tattoo. It will do wonders for your sex life."

"I promise, you'll never forget our night together." Marty smiled again and wetted her lips while batting her eyelashes, reinforcing her negotiating position. *"Well? What do you say? A long night with me? Fantastic love making which you'll never forget? A night that you'd gladly exchange your marriage for, if things came to that? But I'd never pressure you to leave your marriage for me, promise. I would just make love with you all night. We can do it two or three or four or five times, if you like. Will that work for you?"*

"Okay. Yes, that will work. Deal. You win, Gorgeous. I'll do your tattoo for you, half off and dinner at a five star. You've convinced me you're serious about this; and you're not crazy."

"I'm not crazy."

"Are you sure?"

"How can anyone ever be sure?"

"I don't know. Maybe I'm the one who's crazy. I've never met a woman who thinks like you or talks like you before. And I'm already crazy out of my mind thinking about you. You're remarkably beautiful. Do you know that? Here. Take this pill."

"Why? What is it?"

"It's a mild pain killer, like a doctor gives you after surgery. You won't feel pain if you take it."

"No, thank you. I'll handle the pain okay. And thank you for your compliments. I'm looking forward to our evening together. Just keep your mind on your work. Play time will come later, okay?" Marty cocked her head and smiled to let him know she was as enthused about their night together as he was.

"Okay, I understand. But don't you even want a topical for the pain?"

"Nope, just do it. And please keep your mind on your work and do the very best tattoo you've ever done. We'll have our fun time later, I promise. I very much want that evening with you. And don't stop working just because you hear me making mouth sounds; unless I tell you to stop, okay?"

"You're the customer, Gorgeous. Lay back, look at the ceiling while I keep your legs spread really wide. Just keep looking up while I work. Whenever you want to see how it's looking, we can take a break. I have a mirror you can use, okay?"

"Okay. Go ahead."

"Kiss your old legs good bye. You're about to become a butterfly."

Marty reclined on the table, with her legs spread widely apart. While the tattooist wiped her thighs with a preparatory solution, her thoughts turned to Maria:

'Maria, you will always be the butterfly I love. I'll honor you. And I'll hold you in my heart and my thoughts and my prayers every time I make love. I will never forget you. We will always be together.'

CHAPTER FOURTEEN

A friend may well be reckoned the masterpiece of nature (Ralph Waldo Emerson: Friendship)

You're my friend. What a thing friendship is, world without end! (Robert Browning: The Flight of the Duchess)

HER LETTER

Marty was in her own home this late summer afternoon, contemplating whether to see David. She put down her tea cup, laid her head back on the sofa and closed her eyes. Her mind returned to Maria:

'Maria, how happy I am for you. I wish you'd write more often, but I understand. You have a little girl now and another on the way. You must be busy, busy, busy. The last thing you sent was your post card from Paris, while you and Slim were at the Louvre. I can't stop thinking about you and how your life turned out. I wish you were with me. I need to make a huge decision for myself, like you did years ago when we talked in your hospital room. If you only knew how often I read your letters. They help me understand my own choices whenever I feel this way.'

Marty went to her spinet desk. She opened the top left drawer which contained Maria's letters. She took out the one from the top of the stack and returned to the sofa to reread it. Then she thought:

'Maybe I'm not being fair to my true self, sitting here reading this again, while keeping my voices in the closet. Mrs. O'Dell, my newest shrink, said I should always keep my voices in their closet, especially

when I'm trying to decide something; but if I follow her advice I'll be in uncharted waters. I'm afraid to change without first honestly knowing where I am. Miss Promiscuity helps me with that. I'll open my mental closet door. I'll let Miss Promiscuity out, without waking Miss Shameless or Miss Iniquity. I need Miss Promiscuity; only her. She's easy to talk to. I can bare my soul to her. I'll return Miss Promiscuity to them, after we finish talking. Then I'll decide whether to let all my voices out or keep them in the closet.'

With imaginary Miss Promiscuity sitting by her side, Marty reread Maria's letter from three years ago:

My dearest, sweetest friend, Marty,

I've been so happy since I married Slim Walker. It's wonderful hearing people call me Mrs. Walker. I cooked elk stew for him when we first met in elk camp. The hunters all called me 'Barn Girl' then. I saddled and mucked horses; cooked and gave blow jobs. I ran a great camp! I'll never forget when Slim asked my real name and told me Maria was a lovely name. That was the day he took me out behind the horse barn and started kissing me. I'll never forget that day. That's when 'Barn Girl' got her man.

Well, Slim hiked my skirt way up that very first time. It was a cool mountain afternoon. I was standing there, bare legged in my cowgirl boots; my skirt bunched up around my waist. Slim's big hand reached inside my panties. He didn't waste time. He never does. It felt so right when he first put his fingers inside me. I didn't protest one bit. I was totally ready for his huge cock to enter me.

When he did, it felt so right, Marty. It felt like we'd been together all our lives. I've been lifting my skirts for Big Slim ever since! After I first met him, wow! And Marty, he is really, really, big. You know what I mean. Well, since we met, my life has been going at blazing fast forward, non- stop fun; adventure and hard work, too. We have a three thousand acre working cattle ranch near Meeker. It loses money like crazy; but Slim figures it's a good tax write-off until we sell it. He likes seeing his cows. He knows a lot of them by name. Can you believe that? He shoots elk off our back porch. All winter we have an elk carcass hanging in one of our barns. We and the ranch hands cut our meat from it. Fresh elk is tasty! I have a totally different life now. And I love it. We have a new condo at the base of Ajax in Aspen; and we're keeping our condo in Beaver Creek. Mostly we summer at Slim's homestead ranch in Whitefish, Montana and fly to Colorado for our fun times; except when Pine Martin and Bobcat, that's our oil and gas company, drills a discovery. Then we take off for Europe for a week to celebrate. Slim has this fetish about me and Europe. He likes to take me to new cities and see the museums with me; then do fine dining. He says his goal is to fuck me in every city in Europe. I don't understand him that way. He's like a dog marking his territory. But I'm not complaining!

I've seen all the nice cities, London, Paris, Tenerife, Sintra, Porto, Lisbon, Barcelona, Vienna, Munich, Copenhagen, Oslo, really a neat clean place with great food; Florence, Geneva. Not been to Greece or Austria or Germany yet. Slim's a wildcatter. We've got royalties or working interests on over three hundred wells now. I never would have imagined I'd understand drill stem flow pressures and production decline curves. We just brought in a new discovery in Williston's Bakken, a really big one. Slim's excited about it. It's a fucking monster, top of a trap dome, high in the Bakken shale, ten thousand feet down. Slim's nose finds oil. We've leased a shit load of acres around it. Slim's land men were all over the area buying acres while he kept it tight holed before word got out. He's moved six of our deep rigs out of Colorado's DJ basin to North Dakota. I do all the books for Pine Martin and Bobcat. Its royalties and working interest revenues are running us two million a month now. Barn Girl is doing good! Slim says our new discovery should triple that. Can you believe that? Slim is my real gusher. You know what I mean! And the money keeps flowing in. I need to make calls for drivers, frack sand, and drill pipe; never can get enough drill pipe. We're paying premiums for drill bits and roughneck crews. I've come a long way from giving blow jobs in elk camp! My head spins sometimes. So much to keep track of. I need help! Come see me. I need a break!

Marty, never in a million years would my WEX body have gotten its fat ass on skis; but I'm down to 130 now; and I love skiing. I do blue intermediates at Beaver Creek. Slim wants me to do Aspen's Ajax this winter. That is a scary as hell steep mountain; but Slim says we'll handle it. He introduced me to a world I never dreamed existed.

And horses! I love them, love them, love them. I have my own, Beauty and Starlight, both mares. Sweetheart, gentle ladies. I love them. Absolutely love them. I can talk with them about anything. They understand me. I know how to bridle and saddle them, all by myself. Who would have thunk! It's fun to ride new trails. Slim has two geldings, Rusty, and Zeb; both strong, tireless horses. We trailer all four of them and ride in the Rattlesnakes and the Bitterroots; breaks up our day to day and clears our heads. We make wilderness love, of course. It's Slim's Barn Girl fetish. He can't get enough of me! I never thought I'd like camping out, and doing it under the stars, but I do. Absolutely, I do! I love it!

Here's my best news yet, ever! I'm pregnant! Yes! Slim and I are going to have a baby! I've told him if it's a girl I want to name her Marty, after you; and if it's a boy, Slim wants to name him Bill Jr. since Bill Walker is Slim's real name. I'm so happy, Marty. Slim's taking me to Paris, again, for our fourth time, to celebrate our baby as soon as he gets the six new Bakken wells spudded. Slim loves Paris; and I do, too. What's not to like! Every time we spend a week there, we think we want to stay another week, but Slim likes to be in the oil fields with his wells and drill logs. You know, geology stuff. You'd never know it to listen to him, Marty; but he also loves art. We buy tons of new artists' work. Slim will be a wonderful all-around father. He's a lot like Dad was, as far as attacking Mother Earth, but he's got a soft side that Dad never had; that side that Tommy, Dad's mine foreman had. Our child will be so blessed with love.

I know you're making terrific money, Marty, you hot stuff love bug. I see you are way up there in the porn world. I knew you'd make it big. I see your porn star ranking keeps rising. But, really, Marty, how much do you need? You're going to inherit a boat load from Susan, the richest woman in Colorado. So, what is it with you? It's people that matter most, you know. Are you still doing your frenzied pace of sales? Would you please break away from the grind and come up to Montana; spend some time with me and Slim? Give your busy butterfly a rest, please.

If it's a man you're hankering for, we've got plenty of them; just keep your pretty paws off Slim. We don't do that sharing stuff. Well, maybe we would with you. You're special. But seriously, we'd love to have you. I miss your sweet face and I'll never forget how you saved my life from Mrs. Raybenald. Oh! That reminds me. WEX fired her after they checked out my story about her, but I guess you already knew that. She was a total nut job. If they gave out Olympic medals for BITCH, she'd win the gold. Ha!

Please, please, come to Montana and visit; or meet us when we're in Meeker. The art on our walls will blow your mind. Slim goes for abstracts and explicit erotica. He's not your typical stereotype cowboy! We could have you pose for some erotica with a local artist. Would you? Maybe both of us, together? How about it?

Bring handsome Bob along, that man you write about. I want to see his wild blond hair that gets you hot all over. I want a good look at him. Tear him away from that Indian Princess who wiggles her ass at him. I know you can. I'll help you. Or bring your favorite porn partner, Josh, the guy with the body you rave about. You can have the guest suite with the California King bed. It has erotica art on all four walls. You'll love it. You'll get hot looking at the art! We'll all go camping. Give your man some unforgettable nights under the stars. He'll never look elsewhere afterwards.

Not suggesting that you need our help, sexpot; but Slim and I would give you lots of romantic privacy so you can feel your moods. There are waterfalls, overlooks and animals; tons and tons of animals. Come watch the horses play. We have music like crazy and a pool and hot tub. And we have me! Please, come. I want to see you and relive our good times at WEX. Whoa! Gotta go! Getting called about drill pipe. Gotta get it! Can't let this guy get away. Bye.

See ya. Hope real soon,

Love ya. Will always love ya,

Maria

CHAPTER FIFTEEN

Oh, make this heart rejoice or ache; decide this doubt for me; and if it be not broken, break and heal it, if it be (William Cowper: Olney hymns)

If you don't know where you're going, no matter which road you take you're going to get there. (Rosemary Ness Bitner, Author)

FEELINGS AND CHOICES

Marty allowed imaginary Miss Promiscuity out of Marty's imaginary closet. Marty seated her in a chair directly across from her. Mrs. O' Dell had advised Marty not to share her thoughts with her voices, but Marty felt she could not exclude Miss Promiscuity tonight. She was the voice that best understood Marty's nymphomania disease. Mrs. O'Dell, Marty's newest shrink, had explained her latest theories about nymphomania to Marty. She was certain her theories explained Marty's condition. She declared that aliens had visited Earth long ago. They bred with the animals that were already evolving here, including the monkeys, apes, and chimpanzees.

These aliens were extremely promiscuous. Their goal was to breed their DNA into Earth's creatures. Over millions of years, the aliens' DNA combined with the DNA of human earthlings. Mrs. O'Dell opined that between one out of every hundred women caries this mutated, promiscuous alien DNA in their bodies. By about twenty thousand years ago, Mrs. O'Dell believed, based upon her research into ancient civilizations, Paganism, with its emphasis on prostitution worship, was firmly established and widely practiced. Then, around five or six thousand years ago, male hierarchical ordered religions gradually displaced those Pagan religions. She opines that humanity is now reverting to its natural pagan tendencies. Modern prostitution worship, expressed as pornography, is naturally displacing misogynistic hierarchical religion.

Mrs. O'Dell adored Marty. She recognized the young, nubile porn star as living proof of her theories. She believed that Marty was a change agent, reshaping world opinion. Her special psychology patient-client, would, with her guidance, convince the world's peoples that all religious teachings; Hebrew Torah scriptures, Christian Gospels, and Islamic Quran were all misguided male misogyny; and erroneous reverences. These mistaken foundational beliefs of male dominance were, in Mrs. O'Dell's view, being swept away and cleansed from human morality by Marty's glorious pornography. Mrs. O'Dell championed Marty's licentious whore-lust; guiding her philosophical protégé toward greater name recognition and moral authority.

"So, you see, Marty," had explained Mrs. O'Dell during their recent sessions, *"between one percent and ten percent of all women are nymphomaniacs, just like you. The condition is nothing to be ashamed of. It's perfectly normal for your population subset. You should never suppress your nympho tendencies. If you do, you could do your psychic wellness terrible harm. My professional advice is that you should embrace your nymphomania to the best of your abilities. You expressed an interest in becoming a porn star. That's excellent. I highly recommend that you pursue your interest. Pornography is an outstanding career choice for you. It is your natural calling. You should discover career satisfaction and immense personal fulfillment."*

Marty took her psychologists' advice seriously. When their advices conflicted, she took the advice of the psychologist who appealed to her feelings. For this afternoon's session of reflective thinking, Marty selected the advice of her most trusted shrink, Mrs. O'Dell. Marty knew Mrs. O'Dell predicably defaulted to her advocacy. She consistently advised Marty to seduce males who interested her; upend other women's marriages; ignore divorce's collaterally damaged children; and use media to trumpet her lascivious peccadillos. Now, harkening back to Mrs. O'Dell's advice sessions, Marty considered David's offer to return to the Firm. Should she simply quit? She was ahead. She didn't need to go back. She had money, prostitution clients and her porn career. Should she return to the Firm with its many benefits? Dilemma! Marty did not feel mentally strong enough to resolve this issue by herself. She needed the help of one or more of her voices. But which one(s)? She considered this matter seriously. Then, she had invited Miss Promiscuity to discuss her decision with her. In Miss Promiscuity, Marty had her most trusted sounding board.

"*Let's start by telling me what you've already learned about men, Marty,*" spoke the voice of Promiscuity.

"*Well,*" said Marty, "*starting with Mr. Blanton, whom I observed as a young girl, men can be useful in helping women get ahead in life. Mother flaunted her sex appeal to Mr. Blanton to get a nice piece of business from the WEX School. That made Mother about two hundred thousand dollars a year, after Mother's lover, Marvin, tripled the investment money. Maria's dad was useful to her, too, in a different sort of way. He was a workaholic. He was the kind of man that worked to stay away from his wife. Her mother's misery about the loss of their son drove Maria's father crazy. But he made enough money to get Maria a good education at WEX. He was an exception from most male types. Many men, like Ed Blanton did with Mother, and like Carl, Darren, Mr. Sorber, Fred, and many other men do with me, escape from their miserable relationships by having sex with prostitutes. We've previously discussed in detail how I can spot men that want to have affairs with me.*"

"*Yes, I know the things we do to turn men on. What else have you learned about men?*"

"Well, most of them aren't very smart. They don't look for opportunities. They're kind of dull and unimaginative, like those men on the WEX board, or like many of my regular clients. They expect someone else to figure things out for them, like Mother did for Ed Blanton. Most men want to not think. Thinking is harder than work for them. They'd rather watch football. They take the easiest path they can to get through life. By the time they die, most men will have watched over a thousand football games. And they won't remember any of them. They believe someone else will always be there to take care of them."

"Anything else?"

"Oh yes. They love to make love, especially with a beautiful woman, unless they are gay; but even lots of gay men are bi-sexual, and they will have a woman when she presents him with the opportunity. Except, possibly David, I don't know what to make of David."

"Let's save our thoughts about David for later. We'll get to your choice issues last. Okay?"

"Okay."

"Now, what have you learned about women?"

"Oh, they are all over the place. Some, like Barbara, that fucking skinny Indian bitch, are as smart as whips, like Mother. Those types are fiercely independent. They man hunt differently than me. Instead of fucking their man at the get-go, they lay in wait and kind of channel their intended man into a position where he turns to her and wants to partner with her, not to use her; but to partner with her and love her through and through as her friend and her equal partner. Mother and Barbara understand corporations, business law, board room politics, regulations, and how to use rules and tactics to their advantage, like Mother did when she got the WEX account. These types succeed by knowing every conceivable detail that must be considered for them to succeed. They are diligent and dangerous to their enemies, like Mother was to Mrs. Blanton and like Barbara might be to me."

"But your mother and Barbara are unusual; how about most other women?"

"Many of those are completely dependent on a man, like Marge Blanton was on Ed, or Carl's wife was on Carl, or how Carol was with Darren. They want to have kids with the man, like Carol hoped with Darren; but they live at the whims of their man. They can be jealous, possessive, and unpredictable; even self- destructive.

"When something in their relationship goes off track, they can become unhinged. Then they react in unpredictable ways, like when Mom was doing Ed Blanton. Somehow Mrs. Blanton found out. I think Trudy snitched on her dad. Marge caught Ed standing in their driveway one morning. The garage door was open. Ed didn't notice that Marge had started their Benz. Well, Marge floored the car while it was in reverse. She ran right over Ed and killed him. She was so consumed with jealousy that she killed her meal ticket, unless Ed had lots of insurance.

"Then there's Carl's wife. I knew she was totally dependent on Carl, so I taunted her for years. I took away her money, bit by bit. I reduced her to rags and near starvation. I pauperized her. Then, that day at the cabin, I got into her head. I used sex to murder her. You voices are the only ones that know how I did it. Now David wants me to see him tomorrow. He's asked me twice to tell him how I committed that murder. My murders fascinate David, especially that one.

"He wants me to take him through that entire day, explaining every minute detail. He wants to hear every little tidbit I said to Carl's wife; everything she said to me; and everything I sensed she was feeling; and every thought that was going through my mind as I took control of her. He wants me to tell him what I did with Carl before, during, and after she died; and Carl's reaction to the whole thing; and how I handled his reaction and ended up with all his money. If I decide to go over to David's tomorrow, I'll need to tell David the entire story. I'll need to relive it so his mind can savor it. He's ghoulish that way. That's okay. I'm a little ghoulish myself. I want to share what happened that day with

him. After all, he is my friend. Besides, reliving that day helps me feel all my emotions. Everything pours out of me: My wickedness; hatred; love; passions; contempt; lust; joy. I sometimes think about that night to relive my beautiful orgasms. After I got rid of Carl's wife, they were incredibly sweet; best flows ever."

"Well, let's save the decision about going to see David for last. Okay?"

"Okay. Do you want to know about Carol?"

"Sure."

"I shocked her. She became hysterical, bawled her eyes out; and eventually she had to be institutionalized. She never got over what I did with her precious Darren."

"You want to talk about your feelings, don't you?"

"Yes, I do. Mrs. O'Dell believes talking them out helps me focus on my needs. She says I must know my needs to improve my well-being."

"Okay, then let's go through your feelings first. Then we'll discuss your choice issues. Fair enough?"

"Yes. Wonderful. Can I lay my head back and close my eyes?"

"Of course."

Marty took off her shorts and wrapped a light cotton throw cover over her bare legs. She moved to her sofa, laid her head back and closed her eyes. She recalled her favorite seductions. Carl came to mind.

"I need Carl," began Marty. *"I remember the weekend when I destroyed his wife. Our fun started the day before we made those unforgettable photos. Carl surprised me in the cabin's kitchen. He came up behind me, locked his huge arm around my waist and pulled down my panties. He entered me from behind while he kissed my neck. I felt fire rush through my blood. I instantly wanted him. It was spontaneous. I love reliving it:*

"Oh, Carl, hold me tightly. Keep Big Dog all the way in while I twerk against you. That's it, Carl! You've got it. OHHH, wonderful! I

feel you. Yes, Carl. Yes! He's hitting my clit perfectly now. Carl, oh, baby. You couldn't wait. I couldn't either. I've wanted Big Dog so much! I'm coming, Carl! Yes, I'm coming now! Already. Oh, baby, you are so good to me. I'm so spoiled. You fuck me beautifully. We are good together. Are you going to come? I feel you. You're going fast. Yes, Carl, come inside me. I want you to. Yes, please, please, I want to feel it. It feels so good! Oh, so quickly, Carl! You're coming already! OHHH, baby. I feel you shooting inside me. Big Dog always comes when I push down on him like that. I knew he'd come for me! Tee hee. Your cum is sooo hot! Yes, Carl, I love it! YES, PUSH! Keep shooting darling. YES! YES! You feel SO wonderful! Hold me close, Carl. Keep me tight against you. Keep Big Dog hard for me, please. I'm, YES! I am! I'm starting again. I'm going to come again. Yes, yes! Can you feel me? There it is! OHHH, YESSS! baby. That is soooo sweet. Take me to the bedroom. I can't wait. Carry me there. I'll hold you and kiss you and play with your marvelous balls. I want to kiss your fabulous cock. I love Mister Big Dog. I want him to stay hard. I want to fuck some more. I'll get him hard. I need to fuck more. Let's fuck all night. I want to. I feel into it. I'll make you come again; okay, baby? Wow, Carl! Is this a preview of our photo shoot?"

"Tell me how you felt while you were doing it with Carl," asked Miss Promiscuity.

"Okay. It's much like the feeling I get when Bob is making love with me," replied Marty to her imaginary friend. *"I feel totally loved by a man who gives me all his love, who wants to give up his wife to be with me. He often **tells** me he'd do just that, and I have considered it. But Carl loves me for how Carl feels loved when he's with me. Bob loves me for how I feel when he's with me. There's a difference. It wouldn't work being with Carl all the time, so I always remind him he already has a wife. That excuse died when I murdered her. He still loves me, like before. But marriage isn't in my future with Carl. I want him for erotic sex and his marvelous cock; but I won't marry him."*

"How are your feelings for Carl different than Darren?"

"Well, I felt powerful when I first made love with Darren. I remember it well. I started by whispering a little tune I made up for him: 'I'm all alone. Tonight, is our night. Come closer. Come kiss me. Yes, kiss me just once.' Then, it suddenly happened. There we were, soul kissing in front of Carol. She screamed and cried and called me a whore. But Darren didn't want me to stop. So, I didn't. While I seduced him, she became a hysterical slobbering mess. Darren came inside me while Carol cried and begged him to stop. He repeatedly told me that he loved me. He knew I was an incorrigible whore; and that I'd already fucked another man earlier that day; and that I'd likely make love with another man the next day. But Darren didn't care that I had no morals; and didn't believe in religion; or that marriage was the furthest thing from my mind; or that I loved feeling a penis inside me. He loved me for the whore that I was! He needed a contrast from Carol.

"After Darren finished coming, he continued lying on top of me. He ran his hands through my hair, petting me. And he kneaded my scalp with his fingers while he kissed me all over my face. He kissed my forehead, my cheeks, my temples, my lips, my eyes; my entire face with the sweetest, most loving kisses I've ever gotten from any man. And all the while he was kissing me, he kept repeating that he loved me and that I was adorable; and that he wanted to be with me whenever I could see him. He looked into my eyes as he tenderly kissed my lips. I think his kisses twisted knives in Carol's heart.

"I did not understand the importance of what was happening with Darren that day; but I do now. When a man releases his semen into a woman's womb, he experiences more than just getting off. Darren's limbic mind expressed, through his tender eyes and kisses, that he gave me his life's essence. He told me, without words, and without his conscious mind's understanding, that he was imparting his soul and hopes of eternal life to me; shooting that into me; trusting me and my womb with his soul. I became Darren's soul mate that day. Now I can look back on that

profound, shared moment. I realize that neither Carol, nor any other woman, will ever take Darren away from me.

"Hearing him confess his love to me, over and over the way he did, blew my mind. I became his world. I laid there, face up on the bed. I was unable to see Carol, but I heard her sobbing. I knew she was devastated, realizing that Darren had left her and would never marry her. I remember feeling a momentary twinge of compassion for her; but it passed. After all, she caused that afternoon's happening. I imagined she felt like her guts were being shredded. I feared she might heave up vomit or throw things; but she didn't. She just slobbered and cried. My thoughts didn't stay with Carol. They came back to Darren. He said such sweet things while he kissed me.

"He continued his sweet kisses; but moved them lower between my breasts. He didn't kiss my breasts or my nipples; rather he directed them between my breasts. He seemed to be blessing my heart with his kisses. He kept kissing me; but still lower to my stomach. He kissed it at least a dozen times. Then his kisses moved even lower, until they reached the crown of my vagina. As he kissed my crown, he gripped my tush with both hands; then he laid his head upon my stomach. I had never had a man nuzzle up to me in this way before. He was like a baby. I didn't know what to make of it at first; so, I simply placed my hands upon his head and stroked his hair to assure him that I appreciated his affection. Then he lowered his head to my vagina. He began kissing my outer vaginal lips. These were not the types of kisses that a man gives when he's initiating cunnilingus. They were sweet bud kisses. He lovingly touched his lips to my outer vaginal lips and continuously delivered these kisses in this way for the longest time.

"My vagina still throbbed from his thrusts and his semen was still flowing out of me. I was highly sensitized. I felt emotive; blessed; honored for what I did with him. Darren praised and adored me. He then lifted his head up and stared into my face; not my eyes, my entire face. He was beholding me. I saw love and commitment in his eyes. He hadn't

lifted his head to talk. That wasn't it. I struggled to understand before I appreciated what was happening. He was capturing my porcelain white doll-face, my blue eyes, red lips, and my halo of dark hair with its reddish streak. He was digitizing my face into his memory, pixel by pixel. He framed my face and committed it to his memory. He was saving that mental screen shot for nights and years to come. Darren adored me! He wanted my eternal love! That's when I had this sudden bolt from the blue. It was my realization! And it explained everything. I was living a flashback to something that took place twenty thousand years ago! That's when Darren's soul and my soul fused together and became one soul, unified by our undying love and our pagan beliefs.

"I, Darren, and Carol reappeared in my vivid recollection. I was a pagan temple prostitute at Baalbek Temple. Carol was Darren's woman; and Carol had objected to the tribute gifts that Darren had given me. She screamed that he gave too much. She offended me and Baal, our God of Fertility and Fornication. As retribution for her offense, I ordered her execution. While Darren made love with me; ejaculating his semen into me, two temple assistants restrained Carol. They held her back by her outstretched arms. She was forced to watch Darren make love with me and pass his semen seed into me. I Tortured her mind with a glimpse of procreation while she was murdered. She could see she would never conceive a child by Darren. His seed was inside me. It was a sadistic ritual. While dying, she would know that I was fertile with her man's seed. I would produce life and she would die. As I ordered the sun to arise from its southern slumber and return to us; and bring us new warmth and life, a third assistant dismembered Carol's body with a huge obsidian blade. She screamed her agonized death screams while watching Darren drive his thrusts deeply into my vagina. Darren called out to the Sun, declaring that Carol was his past and I, his most desired glorious temple prostitute, was his future. He held me tightly; whispering that he loved me and worshipped me; while we heard Carol gurgle her final sounds. He requested my forgiveness

for his wife's transgressions against me, his most adorable temple goddess, and Baal, our Pagan God. While Darren clung tightly to me, my assistants eviscerated Carol and rendered her flesh from her bones. Her flesh was fed to the camp dogs. Her bones were thrown into the raging fire pit. After she had ceased to exist, Darren kissed me between my breasts; then moved his kisses lower and lower until he was kissing my vaginal lips with the same reverence then that he had now, twenty thousand years later. Darren was again honoring me; uniting his soul to mine; paying homage to my shameless immorality; worshipping my vagina's creation powers and my glorious fornication. Like before, our souls had once again fused together and become one soul, committed to our eternal love."

"Eternal love? I thought that was Bob?"

"It is Bob. It's him and Darren, along with many others. A soul gathers many soulmates over time. Darren left this life in a car accident."

"I see. But this is when Darren's soul bonded with yours for a second time, right?"

"Yes. When I knew that was happening, my priorities became clear. I confirmed my loyalty to Darren. I placed my hand on his cock and gently stroked it while assuring him that I'd always be there for him, whenever he wanted me. I knew that I had control of both him and Carol. Over the millennia, I reaffirmed how easy it is to steal another woman's man. Millions of men silently pray for another woman to steal them away from their situation. I understood that I didn't need to pretend that I was something I wasn't. I only needed to let Darren know that I was devoted to pleasuring him; that I loved our intimacy; that I could shut the world out of my mind while concentrating on our lovemaking. My power of sexual seduction arises from my immortal soul.

"But you sought to understand the differences in my feelings by asking me to compare Darren and Carl. Carl is, without doubt, my most accomplished lover. He excels at lovemaking. But Carl is just one

lover in a long string of confirmations that I know how to take another woman's man. Darren was my real eye opener. That seduction lifted me to a higher plateau. I, an immoral whore, had displaced society's queen bee! I demolished her life and her dreams! Imagine how Carol felt after hearing Darren tell me that he loved me those many times, while kissing me tenderly like he did; after he fucked me so sweetly.

"Her experience had to be surreal. I can only imagine what she went through. Darren's two friends forced her to face her new reality. They lifted her chair, with her in it, and placed it before the foot of the bed. They held her head in place and forced her to watch. There was my tush, propped upon two pillows, right before her face. Carol must have felt seated in the front row of a wide screen theater. Before her eyes, my colorful butterfly wings were openly splayed, completely filling her vision field, as if my vagina commanded her entire theater screen. The soft track lighting of the hotel room was focused on my vaginal lips. It captured the soft flesh-white patina of my vagina's creamy smooth surrounding flesh mounds and its perfectly shaped crown. Being so close to my incorrigible vagina must have horrified Carol. But Darren's friends told me that I was positively glorious.

"She had to notice that my blood-filled vaginal lips pulsed and quivered from sex with Darren. The cup of my womb overflowed with his semen. It gushed out from my vagina's inner lips and continued coming and coming. It was an enormous flow! I miss that about Darren."

"What's that?"

"Oh, his fabulous semen flows. He always filled me completely. Most men produce only a thimble full or two. But Darren produced a whole cupful, time after time. I don't know how he did it. Such strength! Such manliness! He used to call me his adorable creampuff and then he'd tickle me and tell me he wanted to eat his creampuff. And then he'd perform fabulous oral sex with me. I loved him and the way he loved sex like he did."

"What else do you miss about him?"

"Oh, his mannerisms, his sense of humor. Most of all, I miss his tenderness. I miss the way he would say: 'I love you.' A lot of men say that to me; but I knew by the way Darren said it, he meant it with all his heart. And when we made love while watching my porn films, he would hold me in his strong arms and kiss me. Then he would tell me that he adored me for being an unrepentant whore and a porn star; and that he loved me for being so immoral; and that I was the most wonderful woman in the entire world and the only woman for him; forever. And his cock stayed hard inside me while he said those things. I remember feeling how it throbbed while it pressed against my clitoris and gave me so many sensational orgasms. That's how I knew Darren deeply cared about me and loved me. I knew that he meant every word he said. I knew I could trust the sincerity of his love. I knew I was loved. That's everything to me."

"And you think it was your casual immorality that attracted Darren to you? You think that's what took him away from Carol, don't you?"

"Definitely. Carol let out a shriek when she saw Darren's semen gushing like it was spilling over a waterfall. That freaked her out. Her horrified shriek clued me that she couldn't process my casual immorality. It revealed that she was an ignorant prude; one of these women who lives in storybook fantasylands, who doesn't understand what men love or how to deliver it. She masqueraded as a sophisticated femme fatale. But she was an ignorant dummy with a doll face, fancy clothes, and a fancy car.

"I didn't destroy her psyche. Darren did. He delivered the coup de grace. He rubbed his still hard penis inside my inner lips, bathed its head in my semen flow. It was Darren's way of proclaiming loyalty to shamelessly profligate me; honoring my nympho psyche, my immoral whoring, and my glorious, iniquitous, cock-craving nymphomaniac vagina. He, symbolically, gave himself a ritual immersion bath, baptizing himself into my immorality; adopting immorality as his way

also. He thereby renounced his soul's loyalties to Carol and joined his soul and its loyalties to me and my pagan ways. By tenderly kissing my vaginal lips and telling me that he loved me those many times, he had professed his sincere belief in me, and my pagan ways and beliefs. He was paying homage to my timeless life-affirming sacraments; my glorious, immoral fornications. With me, he celebrated nature's intended freedom. He turned his back on Carol's hidebound prejudices, religious entanglements, and fairy tales.

"She knew that he heard her call me a whore when he and I began kissing. She must have known of my reputation. I can only imagine what horrifying imaginings went through her prudish bigoted mind while she watched my glistening, cock craving vagina eagerly receive Darren's cock and meet his thrusts with my own. She saw that I joyfully participated in our sex act, shamelessly, wantonly, and cavalierly. She saw I was supremely confident; that I had not one scintilla of doubt about what would happen between Darren and me. She had to see, from the outset, that I knew she wanted him to spurn me. She had to know I was confident that she never had the slightest chance against my seductive playfulness and my sexuality. And she had to be especially horrified, knowing I had already enjoyed sex with dozens of other cocks before I did Darren. The notion that 'her man' would prefer me, a known profligate whore, to her pristine, virginal chastity, must have shaken her beliefs to her core. I believe the stark realization that I had outplayed her and done it so quickly and easily was the real mental knock out from which she never recovered. Those crushing blows to her psyche and self-esteem, are what sent her into emotive shock.

"Put yourself in her position, Miss Promiscuity. How could she sit there, traumatized, watching with her close-up full-screen view, as Darren ardently kissed my profligate, whoring vagina; observing that tenderness between us; hearing him saying his heartfelt, sweet 'I love you's;' knowing he was affirming, adoring, my immoral whoring with his sweet, tender kisses, and declaring that he wanted more of me, after

she had already just seen us making passionate love? How could she stomach seeing him kissing me everywhere, especially watching him deliver those sweet, tender blessing kisses on my vagina? She had to notice that Darren had become obsessed with me. How could she stomach hearing him telling me that he loved me at least twenty times; and how could she sit there watching me stroking his cock, like I had taken possession of it and now owned it; knowing that she would never touch it, suck it, or make love with him; realizing that Darren and I would make love again, many times? And knowing that my ravaging, insatiably cock thirsty vagina would be fucking him night after night; knowing that he would be repeatedly ejaculating inside my vagina, filling me with semen, and it would be spilling from me, night after night, like it had that afternoon in the hotel room; while the two of us laughed in our enjoyment of each other. How could she stay home alone for long, in her state of shock, crying her eyes out?

"She must have known she was going insane. I suppose she did. I heard later that our bedroom scene depressed her so much that she tried to harm herself. She needed to be institutionalized. In the mental hospital she spent days sitting in a chair, staring out of a window, mumbling my name, and telling everyone that I was the living Satan. Sometimes she screamed incoherently. She stopped taking care of herself. She could no longer string together coherent thoughts. I tried to make amends. I called the sanitarium and offered to come visit her. They replied that she didn't wish to see me; not that day, and not ever. Some people cannot accept change. Oh well.

"Carol's situation was unfortunate. But love's real tragedy was mine and Darren's. He died in an auto accident less than a year after that day. I tried my best to transfer my passions for Darren into my work. I missed him terribly. I made more porn films, imagining that my partners were Darren. I made some of my best porn films that year. Many men wrote me fan letters saying they were the most exquisite erotica films ever created. That's when my directors began showing those wide

angle, full screen shots of my vagina, pulsing and throbbing with semen gushing out of me after my partners came inside me. I'm just sorry that Darren didn't live to perform porn with me or watch those scenes with me. I've never stopped missing him. I would have loved to have been sucking him and fucking him while we watched my films together, like I do with Carl; and like I hope to do with Bob. I totally fall in love with men who can love me for being a deliciously immoral porn star and unapologetic whore. I love them; love them; love them; and can never get enough of men who can feel heartfelt love and adoration for me while I'm performing porn. It's the exhibitionist in me. I can't contain it; and I don't want to.

"Mrs. O'Dell says I should never try to contain that expressive part of myself. I should always be proud of it. I must let it out; let it flow naturally from my persona; even put it on magazine covers for the entire world to see me. And she tells me that I should encourage all my lovers to comment about my insatiable love of sex, right along with me. She says that, by releasing my expressiveness, especially when I scream out loud while having my orgasms, I make incredible progress with my mental health. She's told me that shameless expressiveness is essential. It's what makes me a wildly successful porn star. She believes my expressiveness helps change the world's morality. I'm sure she's right. She's right about everything. I love being filmed and watched while I make love."

"Well," Promiscuity asked, "You had love with Darren and you had power over Carol. Which feeling do you like more, love, or power?"

"That's a hard question, Promiscuity. More than anything, I love feeling love and being loved while making love. That feeling is strongest while I'm being filmed. I know I'm loved by my fans, who love seeing me making love. Many fans tell me they watch my films dozens of times. Essentially, they memorize them, especially my expressions while I have orgasms. They fantasize that they are my sex partners in my films.

"That's why the cameras are my secret aphrodisiac. They make me feel like I'm making love with every man on the planet. It's my

performance high. My porn downloads confirm my feeling. Millions of men love watching me making love. They love me for the uninhibited, incorrigible whore that I am. I love that feeling; knowing that many men love me as my immoral, promiscuous self. I especially love my feelings while I'm the main attraction of an orgy. It's shamelessly slutty. It erotically stimulates me into another world. I become lust-crazed for endless sex. I don't know the word for it."

"It's called nymphomania, Marty. You're a nymphomaniac."

"Yes. I know. Every shrink I've ever had has told me that."

"Don't you want to break free of your addiction to sex; heal your condition?"

"Never, Miss Promiscuity, never! Mrs. O'Dell told me that my condition is perfectly normal. Denying that truth would cause me tremendous anxiety. I could become mentally unstable. I might try to hurt myself. Rather than trying to suppress my eroticism, she says I must enhance my mental health by embracing my addiction. Whenever I sense anxiety, I am to comfort myself by giving succor to my need for eros. She says sex is my most basic need. She's right. I crave sex far more than I crave food."

"Then, can you describe how you feel while you slake your sex craving?"

"I'll try. It's this sensation I experience while I'm seducing a new Premium Member; or when I'm meeting a favorite lover for our first time after being apart for a while; or when I'm doing the initial seduction scene on a porn set. I think of it as my 'Darren Moment.' That's the feeling I enjoyed while I seduced Darren in front of Carol. I feel like my soul is shedding its virginity; like it's becoming predatory and taking charge of my partner's soul."

"Even though you are not a virgin?"

"Yes. It begins with the excitement of our foreplay; that sensation of knowing that I am desired. My craving for intimacy builds while I'm kissed, fondled, touched, and fingered. I love foreplay. I love guiding my

partner's lips to my nipples. I love helping my partner's fingers find my vagina and my clitoris. I become anxious to be deflowered. My mind makes a transition. My bra and panties become my morality. I cannot stand having them on me. They confine me. If my partner won't unsnap my bra and pull my panties down, I will. I must free myself from them! My soul must toss off its modesty and innocence. It must feel no inhibition to enjoy the iniquities of natural animal lust. I feel like I must lose my virginity; and enjoy losing it, like I first did that afternoon with the twins.

"My mind throws open widely a magical door to beautiful erotic love. I love gently biting my partner's lips and digging my nails into his back while he penetrates me and begins thrusting into me. My heat, my wetness, my craving for close touchings of his body flesh to mine, all explode into glorious intimate wonder. I take his soul into mine and make him part of me; make him become someone who will always want me and love me; who will forsake all others for me; who adores what we are doing together; who treasures me and this natural gift of our magical experience. I love that feeling. I crave it. Even if my partner is my fourth or sixth partner of that day, I will experience those same feelings. I must have them. I live for those feelings. That's how much I need to fuck. I love to fuck. I am a total, uninhibited woman. I need those feelings."

"Okay, well is nymphomania the feeling you crave most?"

"No. There is another feeling that I crave even more. It's a similar feeling to making a porn film, but with a more ethereal, nirvana feeling. It comes over me while I'm having a threesome orgy with my two assistants after I murder of one of David's designated victims. That's the most wonderfully erotic feeling of all. It's when my rampaging lust combines with my belief in my superiority. I call it my nirvana feeling. It's vivid. It's alive inside me. It's completely unrestricted and unchained. I feel I've been released to run wild, like a freed animal. I feel the intense love of my helpers by their passion for intimacy with me while they thrust into

me and by how they hug and kiss me, cherishing their eternal closeness with me; partners in the glory of our murder. Their enthusiasm for me and the murder I committed comes strongly through. I feel their unbridled, devoted love; at the same time, I have this incredible sensation of being the conqueror and destroyer of life. I am a holy, power lusting, blood thirsting, pagan goddess.

"I'm victorious over the man I've murdered. I feel my life is superior to his; triumphant over his; more worthy of life than him. Making love in his blood is my disdain. I mock his insignificant life. Its purpose was to offer itself up to me, so I could ceremoniously end it. It's my goddess feeling. It elevates me to divinity. When I lay on the red vinyl table top and roll in his blood, while my helpers and I have our threesome, I know I am adored. I reaffirm my goddess status. Unconditionally, they love me and my execution performance. I'm sure David pays them well; but that's not why they are there. They love me and what I did. I know by the way their love making ravishes me. I experience an intensely private, wholly immoral, inner feeling. My blood lust is venerated and glorified. It's an ethereal, trusting, erotic feeling.

"The assistants stay on the other side of the room watching my performances until after I've murdered the victim. They come to me. They hold me and kiss my neck. They French kiss me and rub my nipples between their thumbs and index fingers, I get this hot surge-like feeling while they praise me; telling me my murder was beautiful; breathtaking; fabulous. I have the most wonderous feeling of all. I bask in their approval. I love how they begin touching my vagina; massaging it; fingering me. I become hot and wet in my loins. I want to make love with them in every way and every possible position. A beautiful urge to be explicitly shameless overcomes me. I'm a wild animal then; proud of my kill and my horrific sin of murder. My paganism blossoms. I feel like I'm reliving a human sacrifice from ages past. My assistants accept and understand me. They worship my need to sin. They unleash my nymphomania. They love their inclusion in my immoral deed. My

urge waves come. They swallow me; bind the three of us together; consummate my unconscionable sin. Passion overwhelms me. I'm deliriously euphoric, sublime, breathtakingly wonderful. I know what I did is understood, sanctified, and glorified by the Spirit. I must feel this feeling. I want it to last forever. I only stop when I'm too exhausted to continue. It's my ultimate pleasure.

"David tells me my performance was fantastic; he is proud of me and pleased. I know I elicit eroticism from deep within him. When he praises me, I feel we're close to intimacy. David's intimacy will be my ultimate seduction. He is strong willed, Promiscuity. A challenge. That's why he is my goal. After every murder, he places a huge bonus payment in my pay check. He's very supportive. Before the others, he calls me his model employee. But I want him more than the money. I crave his positive reinforcement and moral support. He helped me understand that murder is a healthy outlet for me; that I must continue them. That's why it would be hard to leave David."

"Do you ever dream about your victims?"

"Maybe. I'm not sure. Butterflies are flying in many of my dreams. big, beautiful Monarch butterflies. I fly with them. We're going to a jungle to copulate and lay our eggs. I remember my dreams. We butterflies are in our life cycle's third iteration. We talk. We laugh. I talk to other girl butterflies; never to boy butterflies. Possibly the boy butterflies are reincarnations of men I've murdered. Maybe they don't talk because they are unhappy."

"Boy butterflies don't have names?"

"No. I'm never told the names of the men I murder, even after I've murdered them. Maybe David is safer if he keeps their names a secret. That must be why I don't know who they are."

"But you talk to the girl butterflies?"

"Oh yes. We have great conversations. It helps us pass the time. We forget we're tired."

"Do your girl butterflies have names?"

"Yes; and I remember them. We have many conversations as we flutter south; but my conversations are always with the same girl butterflies."

"Please relate them to me. You've never told me about these butterflies before, Marty. And I'm your favorite voice!"

"I know. But you've never asked me. And you're only a voice. So, I can only hear you in the daytime, while I'm awake, like now. I flutter with my butterfly friends at night, while I dream. That's why you voices have never heard me talking to my butterfly friends. I'll tell you about each of them in the future. They are all fascinating women. And they all have fascinating stories and romances and love scenes with handsome, wonderful men, that we all love to talk about.

"Please tell me a little about them now; and tell me what you butterflies talk about while you dream you are a butterfly, Marty."

"Sure. My favorite butterfly friends are Sheila and Cecilia, or CC. Sheila thinks butterflies are reincarnations of real people. She was a brilliant mathematician in her previous life; and in her life before that, she was me."

"You mean she was once really you, Marty?"

"Yes, she was. I believe her. She's a very smart butterfly. She knows everything about where we're going while we're fluttering and where we must put down to rest and eat. Sheila knows everything. She's the smartest butterfly, like she was the smartest human during her human life."

"What did she do, Marty?"

"She worked on top secret government projects, like missile interceptor software programs and ways to defeat drone attacks on football stadiums."

"And she and you and CC are pretty close?"

"Oh, yes! We are extremely close. We even share our sex lives. Sheila and CC are lesbians who both loved Hud. They had many threesomes with him. Sheila also had a bizarre tryst with two professors

from Braindead University, and another tryst with Pasqual. He was an artist who wanted Sheila to show him how to make love the way dragonflies make love. Sheila showed him. It's kinky; but lots of fun. I'll explain it to you when we talk about Sheil's story. Sheila went crazy over Pasqual. She wanted to marry him. But he loved her too much to marry her. I know that sounds weird. But when you understand how Pasqual's mind worked, it makes perfect sense. Sheila also fell in love with Danny, a red-headed farm boy. She was deeply in love with Danny, twice! She didn't understand that her nymphomania pulled her away from him. They rode horses together and had a special intimate relationship with an Asian girl named Lotus. Sheila managed her affairs while maintaining her love triangle relationship with Hud and CC. She's an incredible woman.

'Imagine someone who has all the love emotions and erotic desires of a nymphomaniac, like me; but who doesn't have the mental problems that I have. That's Sheila. Sheila was so gifted that U, the universal spirit of all living things, wanted her help with some things here on earth. Sheila loved butterflies when she wasn't being one herself. She especially loved Monarchs. She was able to communicate with us, human to butterfly. Sometimes, she'd kiss us between our wings. We love when she kisses us like that.

"When I listen to Sheila's Monarch tell about her previous life, I'm certain that Sheila and I share the same soul. Mrs. O'Dell explained our spirit soul lives to Sheila when she went to Mrs. O'Dell's cabin. Sheila learned how our souls work with our spirits; how we pop up in new lives, like the way Aspen trees sprout up in Aspen groves. The world finally makes sense to me. I'm not confused or afraid of death anymore. There's nothing to fear."

"What about the other butterflies? Do you know them?"

"Pretty well. We all have something in common. We often talk about it. Remember how Mrs. O'Dell believes a few women out of every hundred are nymphomaniacs?

"Yes?"

"Well, we've figured out that in our previous human lives we were all nymphomaniacs. That includes Connie, who was a spoiled rotten rich kid. And Jo Anne, who was a beautiful waitress in a bar, living with this guy named Gibby. He was the meanest, nastiest man in the world. Jo Anne was the only person in the entire world who could handle him. There's Linda, who worked with Carlos to overthrow the government of Venezuela; Sandra, who was Walter's mistress. Walter ran the world's most powerful bank. There's Patty, the meanest butterfly of all. She shouldn't even be a butterfly. She was cruel. She felt the need to dominate men; but Patty really is a butterfly. In her former life she was a prison warden, a total control freak. She whipped and tortured her inmates and had kinky sex with two different prisoners, every single day. Seeing men in pain helped Patty have her orgasms. And Patty needed her daily orgasms. So, Patty gave men pain to make herself feel like a total woman."

"You haven't said a whole lot about CC."

"Oh, CC! Such beauty you'd never believe could be in a woman! If you saw CC, you'd never forget her. In her real life she was so stunning, so incredibly beautiful that every man and woman who met her wanted to have sex with her; all the time. In an earlier life she was the prized wife of an Aztec king, Then a conquistador fell in love with her and murdered the king and hundreds of others, just so he could have her. She worked as a night club dancer before Sheila met her. When she talks about the kinky sex stuff she did at an exclusive men's club, she makes my blood sizzle. After CC met Sheila, they had amazing lesbian love. We girls can't stop talking about them while we flutter along. CC is the most beautiful butterfly of all. She makes all our mouths water, if you know what I mean; except we can't do anything but look at her while we're butterflies. When we get into our new human lives, we'll all go find her."

"So, you are all nymphomaniacs. And you've all found each other as reincarnated butterflies, somehow?"

"Yes. It's true. My dreams are so real! I know they are true. I know I'll die and become Sheila and that Sheila will die and become a butterfly. This will go on for eternity because of this weird DNA strand that we have."

"Do all people become butterflies when they die?"

"Yes; but not all people can be Monarchs. Most people will need to be reincarnated ten times or more before they can become Monarchs. Only nymphomaniacs can be Monarchs. U makes most people become Pieridea, or common, butterflies. These are the butterflies that come around when there are special things happening in our lives. They came around when I was making love with Carl at our mountain lake. One of them even fluttered onto my head and kissed my strand of red hair while I was having the spectacular orgasm that Carl captured on film. That's Carl's perfect photo. The Pierideas also showed up for Barbara, the Indian woman who outwitted David and discovered how he got rid of all the dead bodies. I have issues about Barbara. She was a thorn in my side, you know. When she had her first orgasm with Bob, the Pierideas showed up. Whenever I see a Pieridea, I get upset. I never used to feel that way about them. I'll never understand what Bob sees in Barbara."

"Well, Marty, you can't have every man in the world."

"I know," Marty pouted, "but I wish I could. I want all of them to love only me; especially Bob."

"Have you talked with Mrs. O'Dell about the butterflies in your dreams?"

"Yes, a little. She wants me to take notes about my dream butterflies right away in the mornings when I wake up; and then give my notes to her. She's trying to get me to focus on David. She thinks David causes many of my problems. She thinks he gets my mind mixed up;

and when I get mixed up, I engage in high-risk behaviors and do crazy things. I don't know whether I do crazy things, Miss Promiscuity. I just know I'm facing some serious choices. And I've got to make them soon. I let you out of the closet so you would help me. I can't think well when I try to think by myself. Will you please help me?"

"Yes, okay. Let's talk about your choices now. You know Mrs. O'Dell, Miss Carboy, Mrs. Schnell, and Mrs. Martinson all agreed you should separate your choice issues and never conflate them, so let's do as your shrinks recommended and take them one by one. Let's save David for last, since your choice about whether you go to David's tomorrow must be made before tomorrow afternoon. That way, your choice about David will be fresh in your mind, okay?"

"Okay."

"All right. Let's take Bob first. What are your thoughts about marriage? You've told him you'll marry him. You're starting your third month carrying his child. Are you going to marry him and have your baby, or not?"

"I can't make up my mind about keeping the baby until Bob and I have a serious talk. Since I told him I'd marry him, my porn career has skyrocketed. The film I did about the Immaculate Conception moved my nationwide ranking from below a thousand into the top twenty. My rankings and download sales continue climbing steadily. I think I'm number five already. Whenever my porn rank rises, my film demands go up exponentially. When people see one of my films, they tend to buy all of them; even hundreds of them. My new Erotica Coach assures me that this is a unique, once in a lifetime, phenomenon. She's urging me to capitalize on it. She and my principal promotor, Dominick, have scheduled me to star in ten full length motion picture films.

"Each film will feature me performing exquisite, explicit erotica in five exotic, romantic locations with the most handsome porn partners; men who have the most fabulous cocks, stamina, and ejaculation *volumes in the entire world. And, I've been assured that they all crave performing oral sex with women. Hearing Dominick describe the project makes my libido throb. I can't wait to start filming. Dom has hired the best writers and film crews. I'm excited about doing these performances. I've seen the first three scripts. I voice lots of seductive dialog, perform in highly emotive scenes, and make love in the most erotic ways imaginable. It's the chance of a lifetime to show off my acting skills. I know I'll love every minute I'm on set."*

"But remember those films that Mrs. Schnell made you watch? I'm talking about those ultrasound movies where you could see the little baby in the womb getting its arms and legs ripped off by the suction tube; and the anguish on the baby's face when the tube sucked its guts out. Wouldn't you feel terrible if an abortion doctor did that to your baby?"

"Well, yes, I'd feel a momentary sorrow for it. But empathy for my fetus cannot be the deciding factor here. What's important is the progressive march of civilization; and my pornography is leading that advance. Besides, you know the Great Spirit made humans different from all other living things. Uniquely, we all have a soul. Our souls live in perpetuity; and are reincarnated endlessly into infinite numbers of new lives. So, by killing my fetus, I am not killing its soul. Its soul will go on to its next life. It's present life is cut short, that's all. Look, Promiscuity, when I was a pagan temple goddess, we thought nothing of impaling unwanted babies and children with our swords; then throwing them into the fire. We did that when we decided the tribe couldn't take care of them or didn't want to be troubled by them. We didn't have long discussions or guilt trips over doing what was necessary. We simply resumed our fornication rituals. Nothing has changed, Promiscuity. We are, today, just as pagan as we were twenty thousand years ago. And humanity continues its advance. Mrs. O'Dell says we cannot stop the forward march of humanizing porn for a fetus, now, can we?"

"I suppose not. You're right. I'm okay with the abortion idea. So, what about Bob?"

"What about him? Bob will simply need to understand how much being the star in ten feature length porn films will mean. Those films will help humanity move forward and they will do wonders for my career. It's my opportunity of a lifetime. As my partner, Bob needs to appreciate that a successful career requires the ordering of priorities. Getting an abortion will be much easier for Bob to accept after he sees how my new films will put me on top of the porn world for years to come.

"My Ultra-Premium Club membership is soaring too, thanks to my 'Conception' film. My appointment service tells me I must raise my prices because of the high demand for my premium time. I must price some men out of the market. If there were forty-eight hours in a day; and if I could have sex every hour, it would still be impossible to do all the men that want private appointments with me. Last week a famous movie star and a famous athlete called for me. They both want me for a full week. They're willing to pay crazy money for me. It's totally crazy! So many men suddenly want to fuck me! That's a huge new development since I told Bob we'd get married.

"We'll also need to discuss how he'll feel about being married to me, knowing that I'll be very busy. I'll need to go away for entire weeks to fuck other men; and I'll frequently need to stay out late for my orgy parties. Bob indicated that he'd be okay with me having other lovers. I think he knows I might need some sexual freedom; but I don't think Bob has any idea how involved some of my other relationships are, or how much my private appointment demand has exploded."

"Couldn't you simply say no to a lot of your appointment requests?"

"I could, but I have my fan base to consider. I don't want to displease any of my fans, especially my Premium Members. They are my lifeblood as a porn star. They are my influencers; and they are

intensely loyal to me. They love me as a person. They're interested in my career and my life. They help me all they possibly can. And I have sincere, honest relationships with many of them. It's difficult to decline them after they've given up so much of their personal lives to have their relationships with me. I'd need to think hard about saying no to any of them."

"Marty, have you even told Bob that you make porn films?"

"No, I haven't exactly told him that; not yet. How can I when he's being so sweet to me? Just yesterday, I awoke before he did. I freshened myself and lubed with my special scented oil, my gardenia and lilac blend with a few drops of vanilla, jasmine, and sandalwood. I teased him awake by licking him erect. I was so ready! So, I straddled him. I had just begun rubbing the head of his cock against my lady lips. That's when he showed me how much he loves me. He wouldn't let himself have first pleasures. He clasped my hips with his big paws and lifted my mons over his face.

"I remember how thrilled I felt. I knew what he wanted. He began by kissing my mons softly, everywhere; all around my vagina. These were very tender kisses; like he was being reverential to something holy. I felt chills run through my body at the same time I felt the heat and wetness come into my vagina. I started saying: 'Yes, Bob, oh yes. You know I love this, don't you? You've come so far, baby. You want to show me how much you love it too, don't you?' Then, after his tongue caressed my inner lips and found my clitoris, he showed me how wonderful his tongue craft was; how far he'd come since I first told him to try it; how he'd perfected it; how he delighted in pleasing me. I swear, Promiscuity, my orgasm that morning was the sweetest, most meaningful orgasm I've ever had with any man.

"And after I came, when it was his turn, he lifted my hips over his penis. I've never had any man look at me that way. His eyes were teared up and his lips formed the beginning of a kiss. His face told me that he

loved me more than anything in the world; that I was his whole world. And when I settled my vagina over his shaft, he sat himself upright and held me in his huge arms and kissed me. It was so wonderful, tasting my woman self on his lips while my clitoris was getting thrills from his penis strokes. I told myself this was one of those special moments in life; realizing that I was Bob's entire world; that his love had no limits; that he loved me for me; just me."

"Then why do you continue to trouble your mind about Barbara? She probably doesn't even shave or wax herself. I mean, after kissing your mons like he did; tasting your clean enticing scents, do you realistically believe she has a chance with him? Marty, wake up! He rarely even sees her in the office anymore. David has them on separate floors. He sees you. He wants you. He loves you. What more do you want, girl?"

"I know, Promiscuity. But she has that lovely olive-toned skin and those beautiful almond eyes. And the way she flashes those eyes snags men and reels them into her. And her slender body, and the way she bounces it when she walks……. I don't know. She has that way about her that drives men crazy. I'd feel so much better if she was out of the way; if only David would let me murder her. Maybe I'll just murder her anyway. I can't let David rule me when it comes to something concerning the man I love. You know how important Bob's love is to me." Marty pouted. Even when she was by herself, talking with one of her voices, she could not refrain from facially expressing her frustration over Barbara.

"Marty, you need to remember who you are. Your soul is in a modern woman's body now. You are no longer a pagan temple prostitute who lived twenty thousand years ago. You are not the high priestess of life and death. You cannot order people to be executed or thrown into the fire because they displease you. You cannot simply murder another woman because your favorite man looked at her. And David has repeatedly told you that he's not going to let you murder Barbara.

Besides, you're not even sure you want to marry Bob. Do you want him or don't you?" Miss Promiscuity wished Miss Iniquity were here to reason with Marty. Logical choices were not Promiscuity's strong suite; but she was trying her best to reason with Marty in the same ways that Miss Iniquity would.

"Yes, I do want him. I love Bob very much. I need him with me at night. I don't feel right unless he's here with me. He calls me his butterfly. He says I'm the butterfly he loves. I know it's true love that I have with him. And I'm certain my baby is Bob's. I imagine it will look just like him, with that same mop of blond hair, and button blue eyes, and Bob's handsome, broad shoulders. I keep thinking I'm carrying a beautiful boy. That's what makes my decision to abort him so difficult. But Mrs. O'Dell, whose judgement I trust completely, reminded me that, even though the baby might look like Bob, he still would not be Bob. I can't have another Bob. And, even after I abort my baby, I'll still have Bob. Mrs. O'Dell insists that I need to stop thinking about my baby, get my abortion, and concentrate on making more porn; staying on top of the porn world for as long as I possibly can. It's very confusing."

"Yeah, Marty, it's confusing to me, too. You know we don't need the money."

"I know that. Mrs. O'Dell says it's my ego and my pride. I've come so far, thanks to her. Through pornography, I almost have the same status I had when I was a pagan temple goddess. I'm revered and adored in much the same way; and my following goes way beyond my ancient tribe. The whole world idolizes me now. My Private Member Services says demand for my time has exploded. I'm getting unbelievable offers from top porn film producers; half the revenues! I have come very far. Promiscuity, I honestly don't know what to do. You know how much we both love to fuck. You know how much we adore the cock. I can't imagine stopping now. Mrs. O'Dell says I can always have another baby, later; after another five years of performing fabulous porn. And then there's David. I feel I am very close to breaking through. I'm certain

he wants intimacy with me. You know how badly I want him to share control of the businesses with me. If he really wants me back, if this is not one of his games, I'd have the cover of the companies for my prostitution services; and I'd have all my sales income; and I could continue doing my murders with David. And, I'll only need to wait until Mother retires. I'd have everything then."

"Marty, we both know how hard it is for you to make decisions. So, let's talk through it. If Bob were sitting here with us right now and you could say anything to him; anything at all; and if you knew that he'd understand you and accept whatever it is that you told him; and that he'd still love you, what would you tell him?"

"Oh, wow, lots of things."

"Well, then let's hear you say them. Make believe you are now sitting in Bob's lap, hugging him, and you are speaking honestly and freely. Make believe I'm Bob."

"Okay. Bob, the butterfly you love, loves you back. She loves you more than everything and everyone else in the world. She can relate her thoughts and feelings to you like she could relate her thoughts and feelings to her daddy when she was a little girl.

"Bob, there are so many things I need to share with you. I know when I share them, you will love me even more than you love me now. I need to reveal to you my innermost me. I'm an internationally famous porn star. I want you to know what I think and feel while I'm making porn with my partners; and how I think and dream about you while I perform salacious, explicit erotica with many of the biggest cocks; especially with the hardest and blackest of cocks, in the world; even performing BDSM in my different film scenes. I love the thrill of penetration by a huge cock. They stretch my vagina and drive millions of nerve endings into this indescribable lust frenzy. I love that feeling.

"I'm notorious for some recent scenes where my lips and tongue licked and savored the eighteen inch long, very thick shaft of an erect

black cock while I stroked it. I kissed its head while I alternately coaxed it with my adoring, twisting hand strokes; and I licked it, shamelessly, like it was my favorite flavor of ice cream. I praised its beauty and continued my stimulations until it ejaculated its explosive volumes of cum into my open, adoring mouth. I proudly beamed my smile of accomplishment to the cameras while I exhibited my tongue basked in cum. I burbled the cock's cum on my lips while I winked to the cameras, inviting viewers to join my Premium Member Service so they, too, can join me in erotic sex. I'm world famous for my fellatio, Bob. And I love performing all my scenes. My gleeful smiles in my porn videos radiate my shameless joy at being a world class, thoroughly immoral, porn star. My nymphomania and my films have made me world famous, Bob. Billionaires, sports, and movie stars call my Premium Service, requesting personal time with me.

"I have become the world's most notorious, adorable, fun loving, immoral whore. It's the image that fits me, Bob. It's all true. I am a profligate sinner. I accept that about myself. I welcome it. I even crave it. I don't have any morality hang ups about it. I'm very proud of who I am. And that's a huge positive for our relationship, Bob, because the more famous I've become, and the more men that I rescue from relationships that no longer satisfy them, the more intensely become my feelings of love for you.

"We porn stars have the same insecurities as all women, Bob. We need to be loved. We must have a man who loves us; a man whom we can trust and count on; one whom we know is our man; all of him, all our own. You are that man for me, Bob. You are my sanctuary, my rock, and my true love. Come share my full actualization as a woman, Bob. What I do and who I am is nothing to be ashamed of. Be proud of my pornography and my fame. Find it in your heart to love me. I'm a working girl, Bob. I won't deny or hide it. Understand my dedication to perfecting my work; becoming the best I can be. Let my porn make you proud of me. Then, love me more intensely, as I love you.

"The world is changing, Bob. Nothing stands still. Porn stars are celebrities; highly desired, sought after by wealthy and powerful men; and by free spirited women. We glorious femmes are loved by millions. Once considered fallen women; once shunned, we are now exalted; lifted high upon society's highest pedestals; honored, revered, praised; adored for our erotic performances; applauded and glorified for the marriage breakups we cause; accepted and revered for our titillating works. We release people from bondage to outmoded ways, and from institutions and moralities that failed them. We are the Avant Guard of society's new, refreshing immorality. We are returning humanity to its natural, pagan roots; fulfilling a deeply seated human need for freedom, immoral carnal honesty, and love.

"I'm not an ordinary woman, Bob. My pornographic films have become a worldwide phenomenon. Last week, I was invited to escort an older Chinese man to an awards ceremony. I was the person they honored! What a surprise! I was shocked. They gave me a framed plaque of pure gold with the inscription of a torch in a circle. My name is engraved with the words: 'World's most progressive humanitarian.' The whole audience applauded me, Bob.

"Finally! I realized my years of studying porn technique and my tedious hours of working with sound mixing were recognized. Those countless hours memorizing the subtleties of other porn stars; the hours perfecting my films' musical scores' to 440 hertz tuning; dissembling normal human emotions with my erotically induced adrenalin rushes; causing viewers' addiction to my explicit scenes; rhyming my intimate expressive thrusts, licks, explicit tongue stimulations, and partners' ejaculations into my mouth and vagina with my music's measured kick beats and my welcoming smiles, my full screen, freeze-frame shots of my flared tongue while I licked cocks, my opened vagina and mouth while I received ejaculations: all those years of dedicated work and hours of sound mixing and editing has paid off! I succeeded! I created addictive, unstoppable, adrenalin rushes that dissembled viewers' minds. My

explicit scenes captured my viewers' hearts! I now hold their hearts and souls in my hands! Millions of film viewers have become bonded to me, Bob! They have forsaken their other loves; even all other porn stars! They are passionately addicted to my eroticism more strongly than other's addictions to nicotine, alcohol, or drugs.

"Day after day; night after night, these men lust after me, Bob. During every moment of their lives, they imagine thrusting their tongues and penises into my insatiable, semen flowing vagina; tasting it; exploring it with their tongues; feeling the sensational eroticism of their penises inside me, savoring the wonder of fucking me. They slake their unquenchable lust thirsts by drinking endless rivers of my porn! They are powerless to stop their cravings, Bob. The ways my porn controls their thoughts is addictive and cruel. That's the artistry of it. That's my talent. I don't care. I believe it is less cruel than taking infants and young children, who have no choice in the matter, and force feeding them religious indoctrination. My addicts are men who want something different from what they already know. They seek out my immoral messaging and my pornography of their own volition.

"That evening's emcee declared that the assembled audience had voted me the one who has done the most to deconstruct America's outdated morals and set people on humanity's progressive path forward. He said that I and my enlightened pornographic films had unraveled the moral fabric of America and rewoven it into a refreshing, humanistic mosaic. He thanked me for my spectacular film work on behalf of all struggling peoples throughout the world. He praised me for being the enlightened American icon of Beauty, Goodness, and Truth! Wow! He said my pornography was the most breathtaking and wonderous embodiment of humanity's timeless, universal, and heavenly moral principles. He praised my explicit scenes which emphasized close ups of my vagina. He declared that my vagina was humanity's Mandate of Heaven! Can you imagine that? He then added a personal note, telling the audience that he adored my work

and felt overcome with awe by being on the same stage with me. When he finished, he walked across the stage, kissed my hand and both my cheeks, hugged me softly, and gave me my award. The people in the audience rose and applauded. Their applause went on for at least ten minutes, Bob. Imagine that! My social progress award has framed pictures of Vladimir Lenin on one side of my gold plaque, and Mao Zedong on the other side. It's a beautiful award, Bob. I'll mount it on the wall in my bedroom.

"The emcee then pronounced that my films made me an honorary member of the Worldwide Globalist Communist Party. Later that same night, another Chinese man made a deal with my film distributing agent to license five of my films for the Asian market. They paid me five hundred thousand ounces of gold for perpetual licensing rights, Bob. Imagine! My erotic screams and seductive persuasions will be translated into every Asian language! Isn't that exciting? An additional billion men will soon be able to experience my films! My films will be in all major markets. I'll be the world's most famous porn star!

"Aren't you proud of me, Bob? I hope so. Honestly, I never sought or expected their award. I'm not a political person. I'm not power crazy, either. Mrs. O'Dell assures me that I'm a normal, healthy, emotionally well-balanced woman. This award and the licensing deal just happened unexpectedly. My licensing agent said my films are experiencing something called 'demand pull.'

"I draw my inspiration from Mrs. O'Dell, Bob. She is a genius psychologist. She guides me on the most fulfilling path for my life. She describes conception, creation and consecration, and sacrifice as the foundational cornerstones of all life. I embody them in my erotic works. My emotional imagery communicates these core religious principles. Through my films, they are offered up to be accepted, embraced, and revered. Surely, you can see how seduction, copulation orgasms, and obsession afterwards lay the first three cornerstones in the human psyche? The last cornerstone is laid by family breakups. My prostitution

displaces wives, and children are forsaken. Do not pity them, Bob. When a cat tortures, dismembers, and eats the breast of a hapless sparrow, the cat is perpetuating natural order. Feel joy that the cat played its role; that nature goes forward. There are endless supplies of sparrows. Feel nothing for the victim bird. Likewise, when I, as prostitute, torture, dismember, and devour a marriage, a child may suffer. In reality, it may not, because some marriages are terrible for the children trapped within them. Regardless, Bob, rejoice that I helped perpetuate life's natural order. Like so many sparrows, there will always be endless supplies of unfortunate children. The strong find their way; even thrive. The weak simply encounter their misfortunes sooner than otherwise. It's also their opportunity to address their shortcomings sooner rather than later.

"Bob, I need you to romantically love me. I'm like all other women that way. I need to know I'm loved. But the love I seek with you is not the same kind of erotic, explicit love that a porn star has with one of her stage partners. Yes, I want our love to be erotic and explicit; but it needs to be so much more than that. You see, Bob, I'm not even an ordinary porn star. I want us to make love in a way that causes you to experience my true essence. I want to join your soul to mine while I sit naked on your lap, with your penis inside me, while we watch my 'CONCEPTION' film.

"In that film you will observe my vagina as I deflower twelve penises in harmony with musical tones from the ancient Solfeggio scale. I created the film as my immoral sacrilegious retort to a fourth century Gregorian homily chant which praises the fictional story of John the Baptist. Your spiritual consciousness will lift as I ascend the scale with my first six penises and descend the scale on my second six penises. It's my personalized meditative creation. It will enthrall you with the glorious spiritual splendor of the female vagina receiving and giving life's creation. It contradicts scripture by bringing into focus humanity's creative and spirituality reality.

"You'll love the film, Bob. Between each penis deflowering, you will observe me shaking my bootie. My partners' semen overflows my vagina, oozing freely while I'm performing my salaciously erotic scenes. While you watch me performing on screen, I'll need you to hold me, kiss me, and fondle me. That, I believe, will enlighten your understanding of me and my need for your love. I am an uninhibited, incorrigible, unapologetic, insatiable pagan goddess. I have come to you from across the millennia, from before man created religions, to claim your soul and forever bind it to mine.

"Bob, we first became soul lovers twenty thousand years ago, when I was a pagan temple goddess. Can you remember? It was a time when homosexual men, who did not want to worship female temple prostitutes, were relegated to herding the tribe's goats. Those outcast homosexual goat herders often wandered for days with their goats, unable to find another male sex partner. In order to become more compatible with their goats, they even grew beards that helped them look more like their goats. Those ancient goat herders often hallucinated through food depravation and by using psychedelic drugs. They made-up simple homilies to amuse themselves.

"Over many centuries, these bearded goat fuckers met and shared their imaginary fairy tales. These tales became religions' oral traditions. These foundational homilies found their way into written tribal scrolls. Eventually, these recorded scrolls became foundational scripture for male ordered religions that deemphasized prostitution worship. These new, unnatural, religions elevated their story telling goat fuckers to their leadership. The newly empowered bearded goat herders abused non-homosexuals for thousands of years. They especially targeted women. They marginalized us in their theological hierarchies. They created an imaginary God. They made women worship this God apart from men, stigmatizing us as lower humans; less worthy than males. Women were often treated as chattel animals. Some tribes traded us for goats, camels, and horses. When one woman, Mary Magdalene, became a disciple

and the wife of the Rabbi Jesus, she was harshly marginalized. The new Christian religion labeled her as a camp follower whore, rather than accepting her with equal status of the religion's male disciples. Yes, Bob, those bearded homosexual goat fuckers have retarded human enlightenment for many millennia. But over the last century their power has waned considerably. The days of the power crazed bearded homosexual goat fuckers are receding into our past. The male ordered religions have shed or masked many of their earlier identifying characteristics; except one. Many of religious types still regard us women as an inferior sex. They pay lip service to our equality; but they do not practice it.

"Thank goodness, everything is changing back to normal. But the Chinese communists appear to be frightened by this new wave of human enlightenment. Unfortunately, and insanely, there is not one woman in their politburo. Perhaps she refused to have her feet bound? Regardless, sanity in freedom loving countries is being restored. We are returning to the way things were, Bob. Over five thousand years have passed since the bearded goat fuckers took control of religious thought and worship. The world's peoples are regaining their senses. Through pornography, people are returning to natural heterosexual-based worship of female prostitution. What Mrs. O'Dell calls the New Morality Order is really the twenty-thousand-year-old pagan religious practices reclaiming society's morals. Pornography is humanity's moral high ground. It leads the world religious and moral thought.

"And, Bob, ever since I did my 'PORN'S WEDDING DAY' film, I am suddenly at the forefront of this universal movement. The film is a direct attack on traditional religious values. I play the role of bride with my lovely white dress and white gloves and panties. Before the altar, I take the gloves off on religion, figuratively and literally. Then, my panties come off and my tush is placed upon a large purple pillow. The top of my wedding gown is pulled down by the groomsmen and the celebration of my wedding day begins! I simultaneously suck the cocks of three of the groomsmen, who lick and suck my nipple buds and squeeze my

boobs; while my future husband groom, the preacher, and the best man take turns fucking me. It's my coming out announcement film as a porn star, Bob. It's filled with symbolic imagery that connects with human psychology. There I was, a bride's innocence and purity, represented by my white wedding gown, all crumpled up between my vagina and my boobs. The gown symbolized the Church. Its image of innocence and purity are bracketed by the sinful things my mouth and vagina are doing. I conceptualized the film as religion's losing battle in its two-front war. It preaches salvation and mercy, but throughout its history it condoned the genocides of Native Americans, Spanish Muslims, and European Jews. So, it has a credibility issue. It also takes in money; has vast riches. Did it use its power to attack evil Naziism? No. Does it use its power to attack evil communism? No. While its parishioners feel put upon by a failing social order and governments that betray them, the Church stands by like it's observing spectator sport; but it keeps raking in money. On a local level, it preached good will and kindness, while it hid its pedophile members from prosecution. So, is the Church a moral institution? Is it a credible institution; or is it a sham? My film brackets the Church's lack of morality with my honest immorality, my insatiable vagina, on one side; and it's bold, insensitive hypocrisy with my shameless love of pleasure, my sensuous mouth, and nipple buds on the other side.

"The film was wildly successful. My downloads skyrocketed. My porn ranking soared. The film struck a nerve in the public psyche. My fan mail was telling. For every piece of hate mail, I received twenty-three letters and emails that praised the film. Fans raved about how it moved them spiritually and boosted their confidence in their own belief in porn; and how it removed their shame about watching porn. And, the fans adored my performance. Many said it lightened their burdens and relieved their stresses. Some said it made them cry for joy. Some said the film mocked the bridal industry's extravagance. Opinions came out of the woodwork! My Premium membership skyrocketed. Hundreds of

men joined my service. Many said they, too, wanted to fuck the bride. 'Wonderful World of Porn' magazine noticed the sudden uptick in my rankings. I was called by Consuelo Lovely to do an interview on her 'Porn Beat' television show.

"I knew I was on to something. I realized the public was disillusioned with religion and traditional institutions. They felt let down by religion, government, and in many cases, family. So, I decided to launch a series of films that question the basic tenants of religion and government. I, Marty Mallory, porn star, would lead the entire world back to its pagan roots; back to honest, basic immorality and the beauty of tribalism. I would help the world turn its back on big thinking and return it to small thinking. I would lead the crusade against globalism and its illogical buffoonery, hideous hypocrisy, and ridiculous silliness. I would reclaim the souls of humankind and return appreciation for the things that matter most: intimacy, love, pleasure, and adoration of the human vagina. I'll reclaim your soul too, Bob, while we make love and watch my latest films. My spiritual powers will reacquaint you with our souls' timeless love for each other. I'll also microwave two bags of popcorn. We'll have a fabulous time. And we'll make love!

"Bob, know this, it's important. After death, our souls will be together again, for eternity. My spirit soul will be reborn in a Monarch Butterfly. That butterfly will seek out your headstone, visiting it day after day, night after night, calling your soul to arise and join my butterfly soul. Your soul will arise and flutter away with mine; until the Great Spirit joins our souls to our next lives. We will live in this cycle of life, death, and rebirth until the end of time. While watching my film, you will remember the times our lives and loves came together before. You will remember when my pagan temple goddess soul and your soul became true lovers. Our rejoining of souls has occurred endlessly ever since. We are each other's destinies. This is why, for as long as I live in this life, you'll find your soul entwined in my love. The spirits gave your soul to me, Bob. And that is why Barbara may not have you.

"Bob, are you in my life this time to confuse me? This uncertainty about marriage makes my head spin. Sometimes it makes me feel nauseous. Do my emotions bounce back and forth like a ping pong ball about this marriage idea; or is it because I'm pregnant? Why does this marriage decision and my condition make me question my assumptions about my career? Am I not to become the world's most notorious porn star? Understand, I'm not angry about this. I'm also not trying to chase you away; not ever! Please, never leave me. I need you. I'll tell you a secret I've never told anyone. I make my best porn when I'm thinking of you. It's true, Bob. When one of my partners is kissing me, or biting my nipple buds; or while I'm smiling into the cameras while I'm twerking my vagina over a cock, I often imagine it's you I'm fucking. That somehow enables me to become hotter and wetter; and I just go crazy for that scene. Most of my fan mail talks about those scenes where I was imagining you were my partner. They feel awed; as in spiritually lifted. See, Bob? What we have together is magical. Our feelings uplift souls! And while I'm doing those scenes or reading my fan mail, I start wondering: why I don't just give up porn and be with you all the time? I love you so much, I think I could do that and be happy. I can't think straight when I get like this, Bob. Are we fated to stay apart? Has the Spirit condemned me create porn for all of my lifetimes? Am I never to have children and family? Why is life so confusing, Bob? Will you help me? I need you. I want to slow things down and make love, so I don't have to think about such huge decisions.

"Is it odd, Bob, that a porn scene is where I feel I must go to affirm my self-respect; while most women feel they gain that respect from marriage? And Bob, I often ask myself: am I, a notorious porn star, afraid to commit to a life with just one man? I wonder: am I crazy? Am I incapable of love to the exclusion of all others? That's a hard question. I can't answer it. Why does that thought make me feel like running away; only to feel relieved that I'll soon perform in another film? Why do I sometimes seek refuge in your big strong arms; and other times seek refuge by performing porn? Why do I want your loving warmth and

tenderness one moment; and in another moment want to fuck other men with wild, animal passion? And pretend you are them? Can you accept me in your life this way? Can you love a woman who does not know herself?

"And Bob, please do not disparage or think less of me for performing porn. Society is disordered; and it is reordering itself. And I'm leading this great reordering. Feel proud of me. Not very long ago, men were reluctant to perform in a porn film with a porn star. They feared people might discover their identity. Now, many famous movie stars, corporate executives, and sports stars pay money to perform porn scenes with top porn stars. It confirms their own high status and proves their liberation from morality and religion. Many wealthy, famous men love fucking me, Bob. They tell me that their intimate time with me is their most special time. And I love fucking them, too! This is how natural morality should be, Bob. It is nothing to be ashamed of; or to feel repulsed over. I'm simply living out my destiny.

"I'm enjoying my role in this great disorder and reordering. I'm delighted at the social upheaval my films cause. I love hearing men tell me how much they love what I'm doing, while I take their balls into my mouth; lick their scrotums and suck their cocks; how much they love the taste of my vagina while I sit on their faces, and while they perform cunnilingus with me; how much they love ejaculating their semen deeply inside my vagina. I feel liberation and joy! I feel myself reliving my past lives as a pagan temple prostitute. And I take pride in helping the world revert to its natural immoral order. I'm liberating so many people, Bob! I can't explain what draws men to me, Bob. It's eerily similar to the compulsions men had when I was a temple prostitute. They queued up to worship me and consort with me, then; and they're doing it now. Only now it's my Premium Member Service bookings and producers bringing me film scripts. In past millenniums, men brought me tithes of cattle, foodstuffs, and jewels. Now, I'm paid electronically. I guess that's progress.

"But human nature has not changed, Bob. Males' prurient desires to make love with a vagina that previously received ejaculations from hundreds of other men appears to be our species' natural obsession. Must be! What else explains their compulsion? Is it as simple as the way I French kiss men while stroking their cocks? I don't know why they love me? But I'm pleased that they do. I love their desire to fill my vagina with their cum. I love the sensations of their cocks pulsing within my vagina while they are coming inside me; and feeling my clitoris basking in their hot cum. I don't think I'll ever tire of that, Bob; or ever stop enjoying the orgasms that I have. I'll never say I've had enough. My natural nympho obsession mirrors theirs. We fit together! Ha! Seriously, Bob, I truly love intimacy with other men. I'm being totally honest. I can't change that about myself. My sex addiction disease destines me to play this role. But please know that you are the only man who has my true love.

"My love for you is the deepest, truest love that any woman could ever have for any man. I want to share my soul with yours for this beautiful lifetime. I want to be there for you, to love you when you need me. And, Bob, I adore you. I know I'll never be able to get enough of you. I love how you entwine me in your arms and squeeze me until I can hardly breathe; how you pull my naked body onto yours and how you greet my anxious kissing mouth with yours. I live for those moments, Bob. You are precious to me. I love when we make love; when I pull you deeply inside me. I love the beautiful orgasms we share; and I'm thrilled by how loving and sensitive you've become while performing cunnilingus. I'm so proud of you. I love surrendering myself to you; flowing freely, cherishing the tender touch-taps of your tongue. I feel more loved than I ever have before. It's wonderful! And I love lying beside you; being held in your strong arms while my head rests on your big chest; running my fingers through your crazy-wild, thick hair. I just love being next to you, talking with you; kissing you.

"And, Bob, the butterfly soul that is inside me, the butterfly you love, has feelings and emotions that go flying all over the place. I

don't understand these feelings, and I often can't control them. It's an aspect of my nymphomania disease. I hear voices which often cause my emotions and behaviors to run wild. Sometimes they speak to me from my past lives, like when I was a pagan temple goddess performing ritual fornications, ensuring my tribe's fertility; or when I was a biblical seductress; or a medieval courtesan whose romances changed the course of history.

"I'm a thoroughly liberated woman, Bob. My soul shamelessly takes what it pleases from the world. I am natural and unapologetic. I experience uninhibited shamelessness while performing in lengthy, sex-crazed orgies, especially with black men's spectacular penises. Yes Bob, black cocks are a whole new experience for me; and I love it! It's true, Bob, they fascinate me. Many black cocks are my intimate, personal friends; each with their special, individual personalities. The physicality and sexual fulfillment of black cocks; how huge and hard they are; how they stretch my vagina and arouse every sensation; I've never known before. They are my wonderland!

"I love the thrills of seducing new and interesting men; learning everything about their cocks and how they use them while making love. Seductions intrigue me, Bob. While making love with you, Bob, I often think about seducing other men; romancing, exploring, and loving their cocks; even about having foursomes. I can't help myself. It's how I am. I often feel consumed by my nymphomania. I am hopelessly addicted to sex. I do not care what others say or think about me. I am who I am. I am an enthusiastic, hopelessly sex-addicted, loving nymphomaniac. But honestly and sincerely, I truly love you, Bob. You are my one and only true love, best friend, and soulmate.

"I would love to marry you, Bob. I think about that a lot. I imagine we could find a little cottage on the beach or by a lake somewhere. We could have a garden where I could grow fresh vegetables for our dinners. I could have a rabbit hutch and a chicken coup. I could raise cute floppy eared rabbits and little baby peeps. They are so cute! And

we could have our baby, Bob. We could play with our baby on the beach and build sand castles with him. I think I'm having a boy, Bob. We could push our son around the neighborhood in his stroller; and swing him on his backyard swing set. And we would watch him eat and grow to become a strong, healthy boy.

"I often think about married life, Bob. I try to visualize myself as a wife and mother. I wonder how could I suppress my nymphomania? How long could I restrain myself? How long before I seduced men in our neighborhood? How long before I was doing delivery men, and workmen? How would the neighborhood women react when they discovered I seduced their husbands? How would you feel coming home to a line of men outside our door, waiting for their turn with me? How long could I last between orgies? How long before I sneaked away to make a porn film? Could I bring my porn partners into our home and film porn inside our house? How would you feel about turning our home into a porn studio? Who would watch our baby while I make orgy films in our bed, Bob? When I think things through, Bob, I realize that it's one thing to remove this porn star from doing porn films; but it's likely impossible to take my porn compulsion out of me. I love the seductions and the eroticism of porn, Bob. It's natural and it's beautiful, Bob. And I love doing it. Being honest with myself, I must admit: porn is my first love. It's the nymphomania gene that I carry within my DNA, Bob. I can't stop myself; and I don't want to. I'm a sex addict.

"So, Bob, the butterfly you love is, deep-down in her gut, afraid to get married and terrified of having babies. Perhaps we'll have our babies in another life, Bob; but I do not want babies in this life. I'm being totally honest with you. I'm afraid of monogamy and the responsibilities of being a mother. Those limitations would drive me out of my mind. So, if we do get married, will you please understand me? Will you please accept me as I am, and continue loving me; even if this butterfly you love decides I'm simply not ready for babies and family? Will you completely and honestly love me, even though I continue to

perform in pornographic films and continue my nympho ways? I know I'm asking for a great deal of understanding, Bob; but I, very much and honestly, love only you in my very special way.

"Sometimes, Bob, I have this weird premonition that your soul was selected by the butterfly spirits to love both me and Barbara. None of us can help what the butterfly spirits do. But if my premonition instinct is true, it means you will have babies; but not with me; with Barbara. And that would be beautiful for you; and my soul will be happy for you and for Barbara. But it may also mean that my lifetime is short. I do not pretend to understand these things. They are in the hands of the spirits.

"Finally, Bob, the butterfly you love also has a secret life. I am a cold-blooded murderess. My crazy relationship with David got me started with murder; and now I enjoy it. While I commit murder, a raging torrent of passion lust is unleashed within me. I am transformed into a glorious goddess while I murder. I'm taken to another world where I'm with the spirit of my dead father. When I complete a murder, I get this sublime inner feeling. It's the emotional feeling I crave most, Bob. I live for it. It gives me serenity and peace. I become a little girl again. I recapture the warmth and security I knew in Daddy's arms. I murder to recreate those feelings, Bob. It's a deeply rooted psychological thing.

"I'm confiding in you. My shrinks don't know about this. Only David knows. He understands my compulsive need to murder. He arranges my murders so I can connect to Daddy's soul. I need that connection David gives me, Bob. I must have it. Does this sound crazy, Bob? It isn't. It's real. Please understand and accept it. It's an incomparable feeling. It draws me to it; like an iron filing drawn to a magnet. I can't resist it.

"So, please, Bob, this butterfly you love, who truly and deeply loves you back, and who wants you to be with her always, needs you to understand her; really understand everything about her. Please under-stand my different needs, desires, and complications. I may have some

minor psychological issues; but I have expert help. My shrink assures me I'm emerging from my cocoon and becoming a typical, emotionally healthy American woman. I need you, Bob. I need you to take me in your big strong arms, hold me tightly to you; kiss me; place your huge hands on my hopeful breasts; kiss my nipples and my hot to trot, juicy honey pot; and stir my blood. Make me believe that you crave intimacy with me; that you'll desire me forever. Your passions make me feel alive and wanted; and I need that now. I need you to love me; really, truly love me. Love me now; right now; and keep loving me, forever."

"Is that everything? Have you gotten all your thoughts and feelings out? Is there anything else?" Miss Promiscuity's head was spinning.

"I don't know. I think I should also tell him about Mother's diamonds and rubies. I love him. I should be totally honest. I shouldn't hold anything back."

"But you promised your mother that you would never tell a soul about the jewels."

"I know I promised her. But Mother never loved me like Bob does; never loved me for me; never loved me as a person. Do you remember when we were alone in Mother's house and we went through her drawers? That's when I found that envelope of her photos. She was lying naked on white satin with the jewels surrounding her and on top of her. She was swimming so deeply in jewels that they partially submerged her. She was stunningly beautiful. Marvin took those photos. He obsessed over Mother. Those photos made a statement back to him. They assured him that Mother was his most exquisite jewel of all; that she was worth more than all the other jewels combined. I believe Marvin looked at those photos many times. I think he told himself that the risks he took to get her those jewels were worth it. Even the slimy arrangement he had with Colonel Peron. Those photos were Marvin's way of telling Mother that he loved her more than he loved his wife, or David, or his religion. Mom and Marvin were crazy over each other.

When I saw those photos, I knew that Mother and Marvin discovered true love. That meant everything to them. They held onto that love for all Marvin's life. They excluded every one and everything from their love, even me. That's the kind of love I want with Bob."

"But if you tell Bob, you'll be breaking your sworn secret. You don't know whether you can trust him. There were thousands of Jewish families that paid Marvin those jewels to get people out of Germany between Kristal Nacht and the time deportations began. The world still has Nazis. They are on the rise again. Marvin played the Nazi's for over half those jewels. If word gets out how Marvin set up Nazi rat lines for jewels, Nazi's will come for Susan. If the Mossad figures out what Susan has, they'll also be after her. If Bob mentioned one word of that fabulous wealth to anyone, people would surely come for those jewels. They'll claim they were stolen, just like all the art, gold, and silver that Hitler, Goehring, Himmler and the other Nazis' stole. Besides, Marvin never paid a dime of taxes on those jewels. It was brilliant money laundering. Those jewels are easily worth a hundred billion dollars or more. At the least, someone would likely turn in Susan and David for the tax bounty. Let sleeping dogs lie. Stay silent."

"But, don't you see, Promiscuity? Those photos tell me something very important."

"What? That Marvin obsessed over Susan's lady parts?"

"Yes, of course he did. He adored Mother. He obsessed over Mother's breasts and vagina. That's obvious from the photos. But the photos also speak to Marvin's heart. When I look at them, I realize that Marvin looked at them, too. I then put myself into Marvin's mind. Marvin was already beyond filthy rich. I can imagine him staring countless times at Mother's delicious foo foo before he put those photos away; before he crawled into bed with repulsive Eloweiss. His heart must have cried to be with Mother instead of her. That's why Mother and Marvin spent so much time at the office; why they stayed late so many nights. It's why

they so often escaped on investment junkets and research seminars. They loved being alone with each other. They fought and scratched for every moment of time they had.

"That made me realize that love is so much more important than money and wealth. Marvin placed his love of Mother above all the jewels that thousands of Jewish families paid to save their few precious loved ones from the holocaust. Many sacrificed everything to rescue one family member from Nazi Germany. Marvin never gave those jewels back to the families of the holocaust; not one single stone. That's profound. I wonder, did Marvin secretly hate his own religion? He must have figured that, by dealing in live and death, he earned those jewels fair and square. He treated life and death like any other business; then he gave all those jewels away.......to Mother! That's a profound form of love, Miss Promiscuity. Realize that when you think of Mother and Marvin."

"And you think you can have that same love with Bob that Susan had with Marvin? You think revealing the stones to Bob will get you that same devoted love?"

"Maybe. Mother was dirt poor when she got involved with Marvin; but love overcame that difference. Mother gave Marvin all her love. And Marvin gave Mother all his. Don't you see? When Bob came to the Firm, he was also dirt poor. But Bob gives me something no one else does. He gives me all his love. He loves me for me. I feel Bob's love in my heart, not just in my muff. Bob is the only man who loves me, for me, in this sincere way. I feel I belong to him; like the two of us belong together, forever; like I should share everything about myself with him. I've never felt Mother's love this way. She doesn't love me, for me. She never did." Marty's tears flowed down her cheeks. She became overcome with self-pity like this whenever she realized how little love she received from her mother.

"And you think by telling Bob the secrets about the diamonds and how Marvin got them while he was part of the Roosevelt administration; and by revealing the chain of bribes he paid; and by disclosing

how they are now secretly hidden under Susan's mineral rights hold-ings; and by how she uses her power over the jewels to torment David; and that by revealing all these things to Bob, that Bob will love you more? Do you honestly believe those revelations would keep him closely bonded to you; and loving you? Is that it? What are you thinking?" Miss Promiscuity sensed Marty was becoming illogical. She wished Marty would awaken Miss Iniquity and allow her to join their discussion.

"Well, yes. It's the right and honest thing to do. When two people love each other, they should share everything equally. No secrets."

"But, one hundred billion dollars? Marty, you're a whore, remember?"

"I know; but this is not about money, Promiscuity. This is about love. People have gone to war over love. Empires have been destroyed over love."

"Wars are fought over money, too."

"I know. But when you have true love, like Bob and I have, that's everything. At least, to me it is. I've never had that before. It's rare and special. It's worth more than all the wealth in the world. You cannot place a price tag on that feeling."

"But, are you sure Bob loves you as much as you love him? What about Barbara?"

"I don't know. Honestly, I'm not completely sure. That's why I need to murder her. I need to stick a knife in her like I stuck a pencil into Kenny's toad. Once I'm rid of her, I could be certain that Bob doesn't love her."

"Well, since David won't let you murder her, I think you need to hold off telling Bob about the jewels."

"For how long?"

"It's not a matter of time, Marty. You will know when your heart tells you that you can be sure of him; that you can be sure his love is only for you."

"You mean by how he performs oral sex on me? By how his tongue makes my clit feel?"

"No, no, no, Marty! This is 'not' about 'how' he makes love. It's about 'who' he loves. You say Bob is very honest, right?"

"Yes, he is always honest about everything. I can not imagine Bob telling me a lie. He's an unusual man that way. He's special."

"Then, that's your key to when you can safely tell him about the hidden jewels."

"When?"

"When he looks you honestly in the eye and swears to you that he loves only you; and that he does not love Barbara. It's hard for an honest man to swear he does not love someone when he loves that someone. Bob won't swear you are his only love, unless it's true. When he bears his heart to you like that; when he pours out his soul to you; then you can trust him. That's when you can reveal the secrets of the jewels."

"Okay. I won't say a word about the jewels or where Susan buried them until Bob swears to me that he loves only me; and not Barbara. I promise."

"Good. It's important that you wait until you hear those words from him. Absolutely, do not mention the jewels as an enticement to make Bob love you. That would be a terrible mistake. You'd never know if you could trust his love for the right reason after that. His love must only be about love; not money. I'm glad we got that straightened out. So, the next time you're with Bob you should begin explaining your feelings to him. Let him know how deeply you love him; but do not, under any circumstances, mention the jewels. Also, do not reveal how you feel while you are committing murder. Keep your feelings about murder to yourself, until after you are married with legal spousal privileges. And that's only if you decide to get married. Okay?"

"Yes, Promiscuity. Thanks. That makes sense."

"Good, now let's look at your situation with Carl. Will you continue seeing him now that your films are in high demand and your porn star ranking has shot up?"

"Yes, of course I will. We've loved each other for years. And since I got rid of his wife, our affair is much more manageable. Remember, porn rankings change. Young, hot girls constantly enter the business. If my career turned down, I'd need Carl and our fabulous sex more than ever.

"I see. What about Maria? She wants you visit her in Montana. Will you go?"

"I don't know. I'm afraid to go. I might make love with her husband, and that might ruin our friendship. My nymphomania often overrides my self-control. In one letter Maria said she doesn't doesn't share; but that she would share with me, because of our special friendship."

"Well, why not take Bob with you? Wouldn't that be easier?"

"Maybe, but there's another reason why I'm afraid to go."

"What's that?"

"Well, Maria and Slim have a successful monogamous marriage. I'm afraid to see how comfortable that is. I might want that with Bob."

"What's wrong with that?"

"Well, I might try to resist my nymphomania. That would seriously conflict with my psyche. It wouldn't be natural. Mrs. O'Dell diagnosed me. She says I'm a natural nympho. I'm one in a hundred; possibly one in ten women that must seduce new men. She says my wanton lifestyle is good for my mental health. For example, she assures me that Aaliyah's genital mutilation is not my concern; that her condition is the reason why I should feel guiltless about my love affair with Marshawn. I'm supposed to ignore the fact that a man is married; whether the wife is a sex pot like Maria, or a sexual cripple like Aaliyah. I must focus on the male libido and block out the wife's feelings while I seduce her husband. I must become even more promiscuous when a wife blocks my advances to her husband."

"Ratchet things up?"

"Yes. She assures me that predatory behavior is natural and healthy. She observes that every man is already attached to some woman, some way; even if the woman is his mother. It's normal and necessary, when

I want a particular man, to break the attachment he has with that woman. I did not let my prince's mother stop me, did I?"

"No, you didn't. You snipped his Mommy strings. Your seduction was a sensational success. Many others tried and failed."

"That's why I follow Mrs. O'Dell's advice. It works. She is highly encouraged by my latest seductions and the CONCEPTION film. Innovation like that comes from dedication, she says. She believes my goal of becoming the world's favorite porn star is admirable and achievable. She pushes me to work hard on that goal.

"She enthusiastically tracks my progress. Seeing me on porn magazine covers and in tabloids about causing marriage break-ups confirms that her advice is producing tangible results. My therapy sessions are helpful. I'm becoming the most notorious, best immoral whore in the world. Mrs. O'Dell says I'm almost perfect. She says I'll never be a well-adjusted, satisfied woman if I settled down with one man. I'll become a neurotic nut case. She says I'm unsuited to cook and clean; or to pick up messes after a man. I'd also have no patience for his obsession with football. I'd tire of reminding him of things he forgets to do. And I wouldn't appreciate him coming home late or inebriated. She warned me that he'd want kids to play with; but I'd be stuck with the housework.

"She's warned me to not have babies. They would pull me in a thousand different directions. I'd need to feed them and clean up their messes; pick up their toys; drive them to their activities and doctor appointments; kiss and bandage their boo-boos; read to them; put them to bed for naps and bedtime; be their patient, understanding, nurturing mommy. She said I'm unsuited for family life. That's the life Barbara wants. Having a baby would switch my life off. Nursing a baby would ruin my boobs. They would sag, instead of the way they are now; perky and up-lilted.

"Promiscuity, you know my breasts are a hugely positive attraction in the porn world. My boobs and nipple buds are world famous! Also, babies would make my tush would sag and spread out. That's

unacceptable. You know how my fans drool while I twerk with a cock inside me. My firm tush tone; my tight ass; my 'I love to fuck' look, that makes men salivate, would disappear. I can't let that happen. Having babies would destroy my porn career! I'd be living a lie; being dishonest with myself. The entire time I was with my husband and our babies, what I'd really want was to be in bed with a handsome man; making passionate love with him; sucking him; fondling his balls; feeling his lips stimulating my buds and his tongue inside my honey pot; experiencing those breathtaking thrills when his cock first opens and enters me."

"But Bob, as your husband, could do all those things. He does now! You've told me many times that Bob is a fabulous lover." This was one of those rare times when Miss Promiscuity second guessed herself.

"Yes, he is. But the stress and responsibility of domestic life would overwhelm me. Mrs. O'Dell told me that I'd feel like I was in a straightjacket. I'd go out of my mind. I'd surely get depressed; possibly even become dangerous to myself. No, Miss Promiscuity, Mrs. O'Dell showed me how dismal married life would be. Monogamy is monotonous drudgery. It frightens me. I'd be living in a trap. That scares me. I can't do it; not unless Bob agrees to let me have my life as a porn star and a whore; and we can agree to not have babies."

"Well, why wouldn't Bob let you live your life as a porn star?"

"I don't know, Promiscuity. I think Bob is smart. And that makes me wonder if he thinks I'm a shallow thinker. Maybe he would think my talents as a porn star aren't that interesting? That's when I worry, he'll take up with Barbara. She's smart, like he is; maybe she's even smarter."

"Never sell yourself short, Marty. Show Bob that your porn films have redeeming social value. They create fabulous artful messages. After all, you've said your goal is to change the way the world sees morality. Remember?"

"Yes, Promiscuity. I remember."

"Well?"

"Oh, I see! I could make love with Bob while we watch my 'DAY-NIGHT' and my 'CONCEPTION' films.

"Okay. Now we're getting somewhere!"

"Yes, I can visualize it. I could sit on Bob's lap with his penis inside me while we watched 'DAYNIGHT.' I could French kiss him while explaining how the film breaks down racial barriers and how semen from black men and white men looks and tastes the same; that there's no difference. I could describe the joys I feel while I suck a cock, regardless of whether it's a black cock or a white cock!"

"Now you're making progress. Bertie would be proud of you for thinking that way."

"Yes, she would be. My scenes with Marshawn and my orgies with black men fascinated her. She was a wonderful Porn Coach."

"Bertie also conceived of 'CONSECRATION,' didn't she?"

"Yes. She was so intelligent. She understood the public's mood for morality. She knew how to whet the public's appetite for sin. She conceived of all those salacious scenes in 'CONSECRATION.' She had a genius for packaging imagery into a scene. It was her idea to position my vagina on that altar in that special evocative way. Using holograms to show my vagina devouring those religious men and their icons was Bertie's concept. And then, the way she used holograms to show what I did once those men entered me was incredible. So original! Our messaging worked wonders! Many people pledged to the New Morality Standard after that film's release. Bertie knew the public was ripe for our freedom message. They were ready to leave their straight jacketed thinking."

"You miss her, don't you?"

"Yes, of course I do. But David said we needed to tie up loose ends; so, I did."

"That's okay, Marty. It's done. And how do you think Bob will respond to your messaging?"

"I'm not sure. He's already told me that he loves me with his whole heart."

"Yes. A lot of men will say that to a woman. But think. What is it that you wish to accomplish by revealing your messaging to Bob?"

"Well, I want all of him. I mean, while we're watching 'CONCEPTION,' while he's visualizing me on the path of twelve cocks, I want his cock inside me. I can imagine how wonderful that will be; how it will open his mind to adore the porn I create in my professional life. I want his cock to become his path to my essential soul. Then, he'll love and understand me. Through his cock's unity with my clitoris, he will feel my passion for the profound, social changing message that I deliver in that film."

"So, say what you want to tell him. Tell me. That makes it easier to get."

"Oh, okay. Yes. I see what you mean. All right. Bob, I want more than your heart. I want more than your cock inside me at night. I want all of you. Remember the way we were, Bob, when I was the high priestess of Baalbek? Remember how we enslaved the Gobekli Tepe tribes to build my altar atop the eight-hundred-ton stones? Remember how splendidly I fornicated; how our tribe praised me when I impaled the children of the non-believers and threw them into the fire? And then, after my days of exertion, I came to you in our bed and we made sweet love all night through? Humanity has not changed, Bob. I have not changed. I need you now as I needed you then. Allow me to recapture your soul, Bob. Kiss me and fondle me and make love with me while we watch my films together. Hold me close while we make intimate love. I love the feeling of your hot cum inside me. I always want you to come inside me. I can't get enough of that feeling. It's so wonderful and special with you, Bob.

"Know me as the unholy sinner and incorrigibly naughty temptress that I am. I want you to know how wonderfully naughty I am and how much I love sucking and fucking cocks. I want you to love

and appreciate me for how nonchalant I am and how oblivious I am to the ghastly, horrified dismay that my exquisite pornography inflicts upon the religious faithful. I want you read their letters and emails to me. They express how apoplectic and disturbed my performances have made them; how I've unsettled their sensibilities with my cavalier disregard for decency and proper decorum. Their letters are hilarious, Bob. My shrink, Mrs. O'Dell opines that they prove I am successfully opening their limbic minds to freedom, and causing their conscious minds to react; hoping to retain behavioral control. She tells me their letters prove that their religious indoctrinations were not voluntary; rather, forced upon them. I want you to love me for loosening religionists' grips on peoples' rigid minds, Bob. That's important to me. I want you to know that I love performing pornography and the effect my pornography is having on the peoples of the world; so much so, that if I wasn't paid, I'd gladly perform my porn for free! Yes, I would, Bob. I'm a naughty, sacrilegious girl. Then, Bob, after you appreciate how incorrigible I am, I want you to accept and love me as the immoral goddess Queen of whoredom. I want you to join your soul with mine; lose your soul in my immoral abyss and love everything about me. Tell me you appreciate my wonderfully immoral world.

"Open your soul to me, Bob. Immerse it in my world; in me. Revel with me in my immoral world. Unite your soul with my pagan soul. Let us become one; dedicated to honest, righteous immorality. Love me for my dedication to my creative work; appreciate the majesty of my artistry. Understand me; appreciate my creativity; my eroticism. See me and honor me as an exceptional artisan and creator of spellbinding erotica. Stand with me, Bob. Stand by my side, always and forever. Tell me you love how my mind works, Bob. I need you to understand how hard I've worked to create my exquisite films; how far I've advanced my porn career; how I've trained myself to feel free of inhibition; how I've conditioned myself to love performing. Performing is what I live for, Bob. Appreciate and feel the same freedom

that I feel while I create beautiful intimate artistry. Feel my same releases, Bob. Feel the freedom from distraught wives and religious naysayers that I feel. Feel my disdain and contempt for them. I'm opening the eyes of the world to the glory of freedom and uninhibited immorality, Bob. I'm showing everyone that a pagan lifestyle is beautiful, free, and glorious. Be with me, Bob. Tell the world my conduct and immoral lifestyle pleases you; tell everyone that you are happy that I am conscience free; happy about the lives I've changed; that you love me for my work; for how I am reintroducing humanistic paganism to the world; helping others to embrace love and worship the female vagina. Proclaim that you have no regrets or misgivings about loving me. Be unwavering in your support. Honestly love me while I create more morality changing films like 'CONCEPTION,' 'DAYNIGHT,' and 'CONSECRATION.' Make romantic love with me while we watch my films. Appreciate each film's creative message. Above all, Bob, love me. I need you to love me.'

"Bob, you don't know how anxious and terrified I become when I'm not scheduled to perform in a film; how much I wonder if I'm needed and wanted. Sometimes I sit awake nights and cry; waiting and hoping I'll get that important call. Then, when that call comes, asking me if I'm available for a seduction scene or an orgy, you can't imagine how elated I become. I then know my life has meaning. I love meeting the film's porn partners and discussing the scenes and my lines with my director. That's my life's purpose, Bob. I must make many more films. It's my calling. I love the attention and the lights; knowing I'm the female star; the girl people pay to see. I love how special I feel while performing; the warmth and acceptance as my partners hug and kiss me; the sublime sensation when their cocks become erect from my licks and kisses; the elation while their hardened cocks explore my hot slippery wet vagina; the ecstasy of magnificent cocks thrusting and erupting with hot cum in my vagina. There's no life more wonderful than this one I have. So, please, Bob, encourage me and believe in me.

"Do not let the lives I corrupt or the marriages I crush dissuade you. They are inconsequential to my goal of changing the world's morals. You can't expect me to feel responsible for men who fall in love with me, or the relationships my love displaces. That's a natural feature of my world. It's my business model. But those loves are not the same as my love for you, Bob. Hold me, kiss me, and adore me for my debaucheries. Love me for the ways I open the floodgates of men's passion lusts. Appreciate how my films make immorality the new cultural norm. Please join your life to mine, Bob. Assure me that you love me and all that I do; everything about me. That will bring me happiness."

"Very good, Marty." Miss Promiscuity felt certain that Marty would win Bob's heart with her heartfelt plea for his understanding and love. *"That was beautifully spoken and from your heart. Now, if Bob does commit himself to you and your lifestyle; and if you feel secure in that connection with Bob, will you still need to fear that Barbara could steal him away from you?"*

"No, I guess I wouldn't need to fear her anymore."

"Good. Then you wouldn't need to murder her, would you?"

"No. But I've decided I'll murder her anyway, as soon as I get the chance. By murdering her, I could stop thinking about her. Making me think about her is her way of tormenting me. I don't like those thoughts. I'm sick and tired of them. I want them to stop. I just dislike her. I can't stand her and I want to be rid of her. Besides, I can't have a loose end lying around. David has often said that when your enemy is defeated that is not enough. Your enemy must also be destroyed. He often quotes Cato, that Roman Senator who ended his speeches by saying: 'Carthage must be destroyed!' Cato didn't want Rome to have any competition from Carthage, even though Rome had already defeated Carthage in the first two Punic Wars. I will not tolerate competition from Barbara. She is Carthage. I am Rome. I defeated her by taking Bob from her. Now I must destroy her. Like Rome obliterated Carthage in the third Punic War, I must obliterate Barbara. Like Rome erased the existence

of Carthage from the world, I must erase Barbara's existence from the world. I must do as David says."

"All right. I give up. So, we are going to murder Barbara?"

"Yes. I told you we will. Nothing will change my mind. It's settled."

"Okay. Now, what about David? What are the pros and cons of staying away from him, versus going back to the Firm?"

"That's touchy. It makes sense to stay away. My house is paid off. My porn films make millions. I don't need to work for him. I have plenty of savings and even a little gold. Eventually, I'll also inherit Mother's fabulous wealth; so, I'm financially secure. But, like I've asked you before: If my porn ranking drops, what else could I do? I need my steady supply of sales leads. I love my professional executive woman image. It's a perfect disguise for doing prostitution, which I thoroughly enjoy doing. Besides, if I stay with the Firm, I will eventually take over the servicing of Mother's large accounts. Her clientele is older. They would be easy on my body and my time; and the compensation is outstanding. Also, I'll inherit the service company which controls the mineral rights where the billions in diamonds are buried. I'd only need to be patient.

"Then, too, consider the murders. They are the only way I can connect with my father. And I love performing them. They give me deep, rewarding emotional satisfaction. Plus, David gives me huge bonus payments for doing them. David will open seven to ten more houses over the next two years. Demand for my executions should grow, just to keep pace with David's illicit businesses. The murders thrill me. I must continue doing them. Life isn't only about money. It's also about living a satisfying life. There, I gave you several well thought out reasons for going back to the Firm."

"Listen to yourself. You are not willing to give up anything. You're running yourself into the ground. How long will you keep going at this pace?

"I don't know. Lately my appointment service has taken calls from some well-known billionaires, top sports athletes, and movie

stars. I might have new venues for my promiscuity. You should like that."

"Yes, of course I do. I love when we perform our initial seductions. We're good at doing them. They are thrilling and titillating. I love welcoming a new cock to our lady lips as much as you do. It's always exciting. But we're doing this exercise to assess where your life is going. So, we're dissecting your feelings and choices; making sure you think things through, like your shrinks said you should. We should cut back somewhere. How about your Premium Member services? You could get more selective, and much pricier."

"I know I could do that. But, tell me your thoughts about David. Do you think I should go see him?"

"I don't know. You should be asking Miss Iniquity that question. You should let her out of the closet."

"I know, but I don't want to let her out. She second guesses every-thing I want to do. So, tell me, if I go to David's, do you think he'll want to make love with me?"

"I don't know, Marty. I've told you; he is very complicated. You know Miss Iniquity understands these things better than I do."

"I know, but I've left her in the closet. Well, let's say I decided to go. Do you think I should wear a pair of shorts or a skirt? David has never seen me in pair of shorts."

"Well, what does it matter?"

"I thought if I wore a skirt, he might think I expected him to have sex with me. But if I wear a pair of shorts, he likely would think I'm just there for a casual business discussion."

"Well, what if you wore shorts and he wanted to have sex with you?"

"Oh, that would be easy. I've thought about that. I won't wear pant-ies. I'll just slip my shorts off."

"Are you sure you want to keep Miss Iniquity in the closet?"

"I don't know. I'll sleep on that and decide about listening to her in the morning. I always think better in the morning."

"Well then, are we going to go to bed now? Just you and me? Are you going to leave Miss Shameless and Miss Iniquity in the closet tonight? Will you let them out in the morning?"

"I don't know! You always want answers. You know it takes me time to think. If I let them out, you'll start laughing and playing with them. Then I won't be able to talk with you. Look. Let's the two of us go to bed and leave them in the closet until morning. When we wake up, we'll talk some more about David. If we can't make up my mind about seeing him then, we'll ask the others for their thoughts. But before we fall asleep, I need your opinion about one more thing.

"What's that?"

"Well, if I go to David's, and if I decide to wear shorts, should I wear red shorts or blue shorts?"

"Oh, blue. Definitely, blue. I love your new baby blue ones. You look stunningly beautiful in blue."

More to come.

Well, dear readers and listeners, our Marty seems to have trouble making up her mind about seeing David. Why do you think she locked the voices of Miss Shameless and Miss Iniquity in her closet and only listened to the voice of Miss Promiscuity? Perhaps that's because of her nymphomania disease; or perhaps it's some inexplicable fascination that she has about David. We can't know just yet. In the meantime, let's flutter on like little butterflies to a cabin in the mountains. There we'll discover how Marty was able to separate Carl's wife from her husband; expose her secret truth; and use her butterfly imagery to create Carl's wife's spectacular destruction.

We'll explore how Marty's evil thoughts helped her accomplish her fateful interaction with Carl's wife. Her unapologetic promiscuity will dramatically explode into our story series and startle our consciousness. We'll receive our first flavorful hints of an incredibly talented woman's conflicted search for true love in 'A WOMAN'S VOICES,' the second book of our Series. How can Marty reconcile her need for love with her insatiable appetite for immoral lust, wealth, power, and murder? Where and when might she discover a man who will understand her conflicts; and accept and love her for the woman she is? Come flutter along with me, Melanie Monarch, your audio book narrator, as I narrate 'A WOMAN'S VOICES™,' our second book of THE SECRET BUTTERFLY SERIES™.